Praise

Bro… …ngs

"Jessica Cale's mastery of capturing the human spirit, dark and unsavory as often as it is resilient and hopeful, is magnificent. If you love historical fiction, this series will feel like the freshest of air and if you are anything like me you will inhale it. If you are ambivalent toward historical fiction, this is not your granny's historical romance." *Smexy Books*

"If you like romance in which the history is as rich and deep as it is accurate, and if you like well rounded deeply imagined, realistic characters with genuine issues that come to a believable and satisfying conclusion, you will love her entire Southwark Saga. This book is no exception. I can't praise it highly enough. Nobody but nobody writes about redemption as well as Jessica Cale." *Caroline Warfield*

"Ms. Cale writes historical romance the way it should be written: with grit and fire and passion. She gives us real people. Her characters don't simply talk the talk. They inhabit this world. In them, you can see it, taste it and smell it. Hers is a world peopled with prostitutes, innkeepers, highwaymen and fighters...and those are just some of her heroes and heroines. Finishing a Jessica Cale book is always bittersweet because as much as I relish the stories she provides, I become immediately homesick for Southwark." *Rosanna Leo*

Broken Things

Thanks for reading!
With love,
[illegible]

Other books by Jessica Cale

The Southwark Saga

Tyburn
Virtue's Lady
The Long Way Home
Broken Things

Anthologies

Holly and Hopeful Hearts: Artemis

2017 Corbeau Media LLC Edition

www.authorjessicacale.com

First paperback printing: May 1st, 2017

To my family: my grandmother, my real-life Ruta, for the Yiddish and the obsession with baked goods that makes it into all of my books; my mother, for being a fantastic parent in spite of every single thing going wrong; and my grandfather, for being a real hero and encouraging me to be my own.

Acknowledgements

Although parts of this book are light-hearted or even slapstick, a great deal of work went into its research. I would like to acknowledge the work of Rabbi Mark Golub, Achsah Guibbory, Cecil Roth, and Stephen M. Wylen for helping me to better understand (and totally fall in love with) my hero, Jake. Any errors are mine alone.

Being an author isn't easy or glamorous, but I am very fortunate to have the support of some truly amazing people who make the whole experience a little less daunting. First and foremost is my editor, Dr. John Polsom-Jenkins, who continues to be an invaluable resource for 17th century history and dialect (as well as the world's greatest husband). I would like to thank my all-star beta readers, Matt Harper, Angela Mizell, Amy Quinton, Jack Smith, and Caroline Warfield, for their patience and enthusiasm, and PJ le Sauvage for teaching me to swear in Dutch. I would also like to thank my friends and readers for keeping me (relatively) sane, in particular Jennifer Johnson, Courtney Butler, and The Bluestocking Belles.

Broken Things

THE SOUTHWARK SAGA, BOOK 4

♥

Jessica Cale

Chapter 1

1678

Backstage at Bear Gardens, Jake Cohen was washing the blood out of his hair when Larry Throckmorton appeared.

He felt the man's chubby fingers on the still-tense muscles of his bare back before he heard his high-pitched whine of a voice. "Good fight."

Jake nodded and ran his wet hands over his face, his short hair dripping red water into the basin. It had been a hell of a fight. He'd won, but only just.

Larry handed him his shirt. Jake took it and pulled it over his head, wondering at the man's attendance. After the bets were paid out, he customarily shut himself in his office with the profits for hours.

Not tonight. He stood awkwardly to the side as Jake slipped into his coat, his eyes darting this way and that. He twisted his hat in his hands. "Come have a drink in my office, hey?"

Jake frowned. He'd known Larry for years and had only been offered a drink once. If he didn't know better, he'd think he was about to get jumped. He re-wrapped his knuckles as they walked around the pit to the office at the other side. One could never be too careful. He looked around to see if anyone was lurking, but the only other person there besides them was the boy they paid to sweep up the bloody sand.

He ducked under the doorway as they reached the office, taking a seat in the battered chair facing Larry's desk. Larry's plush leather cushion wheezed as he sunk into it and reached under the desk to retrieve the decanter and glasses he kept there.

On the wall behind him was a portrait of a woman. Though it had been rendered skillfully in muted colors, there was nothing subtle about it. Too beautiful to be real, she could have been Venus herself, with outrageous curves cinched into a green dress that left nothing to the imagination. Her hair was pure gold, undiluted with amber or flax, and it framed her face in errant wisps that had escaped her high chignon. It was her face that drew his attention every time he saw it. Her emerald eyes tilted up at the corners, cat-like, while her rose red lips curved into a smile that hinted at laughter, saucy as it was charming.

Larry caught him looking as he set the decanter on the desk. "Like that, do ya?" He gave a raunchy laugh. "Meg Henshawe. God bless those tits! Glorious!"

Jake eyed him suspiciously. "You ever…?"

"Me?" His eyes looked as though they might pop out of his flabby face. "God, no. She was so in demand it was like trying to get an audience with the Queen."

Jake smiled at the image. It was all too easy to picture a crown on her head. "Why keep a portrait of her, then?"

"Why wouldn't I? Just looking at her has kept me warm over many a long, cold night, I can tell you!" He laughed at his own shameful confession.

Was that why he spent so much time alone in here? Jake cringed.

Larry kept right on talking. "That Townsend boy sold it me years ago. Gives the boys something to fight for. I told them, I says, you could have that woman right there, you've just got to fight Tom Callaghan for her first." He cackled.

"Reckon that's why he gave up fighting?"

Larry frowned. He clearly hadn't thought of that before. "Tom? Nah, he just got hit in the head too many times, is all."

Jake nodded. "That's what I said."

Larry pointed a finger and Jake and grinned, revealing a row of grayish teeth. "You're a right joker, you are. I'll miss having you around."

Jake raised his eyebrows. "Am I going somewhere, Larry?"

Larry cleared his throat and poured two glasses of what looked like brandy. "About that. Listen, tonight was rough. You're not going to last much longer out there. It's time you thought of settling down. Go back to your trade, stay out of the pit."

Jake leaned back into his chair and flexed his raw knuckles beneath the linen. "This *is* my trade. I'm thirty-eight, you want me to train as an apprentice?"

Larry raised his hands in defense. "I'm telling you, you won't make it 'til Christmas. Your leg's going again, ain't it?"

Jake looked away.

"If I noticed, other blokes are gonna notice, and they'll knacker you. Won't be able to do anything with one leg, will you? Better to leave while you can still walk." Larry set a pouch of coins in front him. "I'm doing you a favor."

Jake emptied the pouch into his hand and counted the coins. "Larry, this is ten guineas. You only owe me three."

"Take it," he insisted. "Least I can do. You made me enough over the years, God knows!"

Jake slipped three guineas into his coat and handed the pouch back to Larry. He'd never been overfond of the man and didn't want to owe him anything. "I'll make my own way," he said, standing.

"Don't be a fool!" Larry protested even as he locked it back in his drawer.

"Keep it," Jake said as he pulled the portrait off the wall. "I'm taking this."

"Be reasonable!" Larry stood to stop him, but Jake shot him a look and he seemed to think better of it. The physical disparity between them was all the more obvious in the cramped room. Larry could protest all he wanted to, but they both knew he wouldn't try to stop him.

Jake paused at the doorway with Meg tucked under his arm. "You pay the Townsend boy seven guineas for it?"

Larry snorted. "Of course not."

"Then you just made a profit. You'll have to find something else to keep you warm this winter."

Jake left the office to the sound of Larry's disappointed sputter.

He didn't look back as he reached the exit, too angry to spare even a moment of sentiment for the closest thing he'd had to a home in twelve years. He'd fought there, trained there, and very nearly died there once or twice. To be paid off and sent away was a fine thank you for all the blood he'd spilled for it.

He was leaving for good this time, and there was no one left to see him off but the bears. Half a dozen of them watched him with sorrowful dark eyes from their pens. Some of them had been there longer than he had. Sampson, the biggest, had always seemed more human than most of the miscreants Jake had to deal with on a daily basis. Scarred, weary, and mistreated, he would know that long-suffering ache in Jake's bones better than anyone.

Jake paused in front of him, pressing his hand to the bars. "*Yasher koach*, Sampson."

The old bear watched him go.

The only way out of Bear Gardens was through the gateway of the enormous triple brothel, The Bell, The Barge, and The Cock. From the cacophony of cackles and melodramatic moans spilling out into the street, he'd filled a good few purses this evening. The Cock's only Dutch girl loitered in the doorway with a pipe, her lank ginger hair gleaming copper in the light of the dozens of tallow candles in the windows above. "*Goedenavond*,

Anneke," he greeted her.

She looked past him as if he wasn't there. It must have been a profitable night. She only ever responded when she was in need of money, and then she was difficult to shake.

He took a deep breath once he reached Bear Gardens Alley on the other side of the brothels. The crisp night air was tainted with the tang of cheap beer, so sour he could taste it. Mingled with the meaty smell of the burning tallow, it was enough to turn a man's stomach.

Though his left thigh screamed in pain with every step, he charged down the lane as quickly as he could manage it. He was ready to put as much distance between himself and the pits as possible. The sign above The Beerhouse creaked mournfully in the wind, its faded bear little more than a darkish smudge in the dark, fading into inevitable obscurity along with the brothel's original name.

He turned the corner in front of the theater and followed Rose Alley to Maiden Lane beyond. There was music at the Unicorne tonight, lazy loops punctured with notes struck too hard lending a sinister quality to the merry refrain. Two young girls giggled together outside, clearly shivering at twenty paces. "Oi, mister!" One of them shouted in an accent broad as the filthy river. "Give you a ride for a penny."

Her friend smacked her arm. "Shut it, Sandy! That's the scary one."

The girls eyed him with something between fright and interest. He nodded to them courteously as he passed.

He'd gone no more than a few yards before they resumed their conversation.

"He doesn't look so scary to me."

"Suit yourself, but he's not pretty like Tom Callaghan, is he?"

Jake rolled his eyes so hard his head hurt. Would he ever be rid of Tom Callaghan? His greatest rival had quit all of three years before and still he plagued him. Jake had beat him more than once, but Tom was the one they remembered because he had the charm of the devil himself. Never mind he was something of an imbecile and named after one of the Garden's bears, the Tom Hunckes of legend. Who would name a child after a *bear*?

It took everything in him to pass The Shipp without stopping inside for a glass of wine. He rarely drank and never to excess, but tonight he was sorely tempted.

When at last he reached his apartment, he trudged up the stairs with the weariness of a man twice his age. He had only been in this one for a few months. There was little to recommend it except that it was quiet and cheap. Although the three guineas in his pocket could last him a good long while, there would be no more where that came from when it ran out. He'd have to find a job.

Leaning the portrait against the wall above his hearth, he lit a candle and looked at it again. He couldn't say what had so compelled him to take it except that the idea of Larry amusing himself with it disgusted him. Poor Meg Henshawe probably didn't know the thing existed, let alone where it had been hanging and for what purpose. He shuddered.

"*Verdomme!*" he muttered under his breath, kicking the wall with his good leg. Between the fight and his visit with Larry, he was wound tight as a spring. It would be hours before he could sleep. Resolved to burn off some of his agitation, he extinguished the candle and left again, locking the door behind him before he hobbled down the stairs. A good long walk would help him sleep, and then he'd look for a job in the morning.

Southwark was dark as pitch at night. It was dangerous for any one, not least a man with a limp and three guineas in his pocket. Thieves tended to go for easier targets, but he was on his guard. If anyone had thought to go for his bad leg, he'd drop like a bag of bricks. Though the pain had come and gone over time, he always did what he could to compensate for his injury. Weakness was preyed upon inside and outside the pit.

Jake had not survived as long as he had by being weak.

As he turned on to Love Lane, he heard the crash of broken glass followed by a pained grunt. The noises grew louder the closer he got to the river until he saw a man get thrown out of a broken window at The Rose and Crown. Another chased him into the street and throttled him in the gutter.

The inn looked like Jake's vision of Bedlam. Dozens of drunks fought each other in the largest and bloodiest brawl he had seen in years. He sidestepped another pair of combatants as they stumbled into the street. Looking up at the sound of a shriek, he saw Meg Henshawe, of all people, standing on the bar holding a pot over her head. She was shouting, but he couldn't hear a word over the noise.

As far as he could tell, she was the only person working or trying to keep the peace. They were ignoring her, for now, but he didn't like to think of her chances against a few dozen drunken fools, should they turn their attention to her. Just as the thought crossed his mind, a pair of dirty hands reached up to pull her down from the bar.

Without a second thought, Jake ran inside.

Chapter 2

Meg stood on the bar, her hair brushing the beam in the ceiling above. The hanging lantern swung inches away from her ear, and her cheek burned from the heat. Clutching an iron pot in her hand, she inched a little further away from it, stepping carefully around sticky puddles of spilled beer and shards of broken glass.

The noise of the fight was deafening. Shouts and crashes echoed off of the walls, making it sound ten times worse than it probably was. She attempted to count the heads bobbing back and forth in the melee and came up with thirty-six. That couldn't be right. She counted again and came up with forty-one and those were just the ones she could see.

One man threw another over the bar and almost knocked her on her arse. The man being thrown flew straight into a new cask of wine and they both crashed onto the floor. Half-conscious, he twitched in the river of cheap red that gushed from a crack in the side of the cask.

Meg gritted her teeth. She had a hard enough time keeping the bar stocked without her punters bathing in it. She raised the pot high and banged on it with a spoon as hard as she could. "Oi! Stop that, all of you! Stop!"

Not a single man gave any indication they had heard her. She hammered on the pot with the spoon, shouting, "Stop it this instant! You! I see you, Jeffrey Blackstock! You drop that boy now or I'll straighten you out myself, make no mistake!"

Meg felt a tug on her skirt and turned to see her ten-year-old son, Tommy standing at her feet behind the bar. "Mum, can I help?"

Meg shook her head. "Go upstairs."

Tommy frowned, glancing toward the door. "What if I run and get Mark?"

A stray punch almost caught his ear over the bar. Meg's heart sped up to see him so close to harm. Truth be told, he'd be safer at Mark's house, but Meg would be damned if she asked that man for help. "Absolutely not. Wait upstairs with your Aunt Judith and the baby until I tell you to come out. Keep the door locked, you hear me?"

Tommy nodded and ran for the stairs.

He would be safer in their rooms above the bar. Besides, if she got hurt, she didn't want him seeing it. Meg took a deep breath and kept shouting. "Stop this nonsense this instant! Stop!"

At last, a man near her feet noticed that she was standing on the bar. He looked up at her with a stunned expression, his eyes glassy with drink. They focused on her breasts and he licked his lips as he reached for her skirt. Disgusted, she kicked him in the face. He pulled himself up again, clearly enraged, and reached out to pull her from the bar. Meg clutched the pot, ready to take his head off on the way down.

Big hands clamped around the man's waist and he disappeared. Meg looked for him, tightening her hold on the pot, but she couldn't see him anywhere. He hadn't been dragged into another fight, he was just *gone.*

Now that she looked again, the crowd did seem to be thinning out. She counted heads and only came up with thirty-two this time.

The front door slammed. Thirty-one.

Slam. Twenty-nine.

Slam. Twenty-eight.

Every time she heard the door, she counted fewer people in the fight, as though they had tired following their two-hour brawl and were slowly leaving.

Slam. Twenty-six.

Now there were fewer of them to count, she spotted a dark-haired man weaving in and out of the fights with rapid, precise movements. He didn't seem to be involved with any one foe, but dodged punches and seized men, dragging them to the door.

Slam. Twenty-five.

He was throwing them out into the street.

He grabbed another by the collar of his coat and tossed him out the door, locking it again behind him. That man's pursuer noticed and charged him, but he knocked him out with one of the finest hooks Meg had ever had the pleasure of seeing.

A rather familiar hook, come to think of it. Her heart began to pound and she tried to get a good look at his face.

As he unlocked the door and hefted the man's unconscious body into the street, she smiled and began to count aloud. "Twenty-four."

She lowered the pot and tucked her hair behind her ear, standing useless as the man single-handedly cleaned the filth out of her bar. He took a few punches himself, but they didn't seem to slow him down as he threw them out one or two at a time. He even managed three as he threw weedy Jeffrey Blackstock over his shoulder and grabbed two of his nasty little friends by their ears. She laughed aloud as he locked them out, leaving them pounding furiously on the door.

He took a breath and headed for the remaining sixteen. Seeing him coming, eight of them left on their own. Only two of the others needed persuading. He ducked as one leapt at him with a bottle, catching the man on his broad back and rolling him onto another clumsy assailant. Striking the second in the face with a well-placed elbow, he fought off a fourth with a pair of neat jabs and had the lot of them out the door within moments, the last four running from him in terror.

Locking the door behind them, he sighed and ran a hand through his short black hair. By the time he turned to her, she knew exactly who he was.

Jake Cohen. She would have known him anywhere.

He was a fighter she had seen many times, and she was amazed she had not recognized him sooner. He was a rather remarkable looking man. A good two yards tall, he was even taller than she was, and built like a carriage and four. He was swarthier than any Englishman Meg had known--and she had known plenty--with eyes dark as his expression. While his nose had been broken so many times it was nearly flat, his jaw was so strong it was boastful, daring anyone to get try to get close enough to take a swing.

It had been a few years since Meg had been to the fights. She lost her taste for them after Tommy's father had taken to using her for practice. Jake was certainly older than she remembered. That long grey coat of his had seen better days. Perhaps his face looked a bit more worn-in, but if anything, the man was just getting more handsome.

Meg, on the other hand, felt like an old boot.

He sauntered up to her and lifted his arms to help her down from the bar. Her heart flipped and she caught herself before she lost her balance.

She couldn't have resisted the invitation if she wanted to. He caught her waist as she stepped into his arms and slid down the length of his body to the floor, her breasts pressed against his chest.

Good lord, he was even prettier up close. Eye-level with his lips, she let her gaze travel over stubble-shadowed cheeks to meet his. He regarded her with unflinching heat, irises deep and brown as burnt coffee.

Her heart kicked against her ribs and she realized she was

holding her breath as though time itself had stopped. She exhaled with a shudder, giddy as a maiden with her first man. He wasn't, but he was certainly the first to make her lose her wits.

His hands were still around her waist and he didn't seem to be in any particular hurry to remove them. Meg smiled. With any luck, she was about to get a chance at living out an old fantasy of hers. The door was locked, and there was no one left in the bar except her and Jake.

Joe Ledford's snore invaded her reverie from the table by the fire. *Them and Joe.*

A trickle came from behind the bar. The wine. That bloke was probably still passed out back there. *Them and Joe and the bloke passed out behind the bar.*

Meg cringed as she remembered her sister and their children hiding upstairs.

Jake raised his dark eyebrows at her expression, the heat in his cooling.

Don't be stupid, she told herself. *What would he want with a thirty-five year old mother of three?*

She sighed, bringing herself back to earth. She poked his chest with an accusatory finger. "You want to tell me why you chased all the punters out of my bar?"

He blinked, taken aback. "You could say thank you." He replied in a voice that was all grit and smoke with the hint of an accent.

Meg had never heard him speak before. She could have purred at the pleasure of it. Still, she had never given a man the upper hand, and she wasn't about to start. "You want me to thank you?" She pushed away from him and walked around to the other side of the bar, needing to put something physical between them before she embarrassed herself.

The local boys liked her well enough, but she didn't kid herself that she was still pretty enough for a man like Jake. The last thing she needed was another rejection to remind her she wasn't twenty anymore. She waded through the wine, kicking the unconscious man in the leg as she passed. He didn't flinch. A whole new cask of wine, gone. She'd be lucky if she could keep this place open another year.

She grudgingly poured two glasses from the more expensive cask beside it. Jake had probably saved her, if she was honest, and he deserved it. She passed him a glass. "Here."

He took it with a quirk of those eyebrows of his and sipped it like a gentleman.

Meg downed half of hers in one good gulp. "What's Jake Cohen doing in my bar?" she asked, genuinely curious. She'd seen him around often enough, but he'd never come in before. She would have remembered that.

"You want me to go?" he asked, bristling.

Meg shook her head. If he went, she wouldn't get to look at him anymore. "May as well stay. Curious, is all. Haven't seen you around in years."

He pulled up a stool and sat across from her at the sticky bar. "Passing through," he said. "I don't think we were ever introduced, were we?"

Not exactly. Back in those days, Meg had gone to every fight she could. She liked watching them all, but Jake's had always been her favorite. Nothing ever seemed to get to him. He fought his opponents with patience and precision, conserving his energy and disabling the competition with a few efficient hits, never pandering to the crowd. As for the way he looked half-dressed, *well.*

That was not something Meg was likely to forget.

She finished her wine. "Meg Henshawe," she introduced herself with a half-arsed curtsy.

His lips twitched into a smile. "I know who you are."

Meg raised an eyebrow. "Do you, now?" Over the months she had watched him fight, had he noticed her?

"Everyone knows who you are."

Meg crossed her arms defensively. She had always been

popular and had her fair share of lovers--more than her fair share, perhaps--but she'd have to be deaf not to realize she'd gained something of a reputation. People could say what they wanted to, she didn't need to please anyone, but for some reason the idea that Jake Cohen might have the wrong idea about her made her uncomfortable. "What have you heard?"

He sat back and let his gaze drift over her slowly. Unlike every other man she had come across, his eyes didn't stop at her breasts but carried on and only paused at her lips. While more and more men were making her feel cheap these days, his eyes on her body made her more excited than she cared to admit. "You run this inn on your own. You fight like a man, and you're the most beautiful woman in England."

Meg rolled her eyes and poured herself another glass of wine. She topped his up without asking. "Ten years ago, perhaps. Much good it's done me." She set the glass in front of him. "Someone once told me my tits could cure the King's Evil. What do you reckon?"

The inn owed much of its continued success to her low necklines, and few men could drag their eyes away from her assets. To his credit, he didn't even look. "Can they?" he asked, deadpan.

Meg shrugged. "Never cared to find out. Enough people try to touch them as it is."

Jake frowned. "Do you really run this place alone?"

Meg straightened her spine. She didn't need his pity. "I do all right. They were right about the fighting. I can hold my own."

"I've seen you. You're good." He regarded her with appreciation. "Does anyone else work here?"

"My sisters. When they have time. Well, two of them. Alice fucked off to France last year and no one else is half as fast. My boy helps, here and there. Why?"

He lifted his chin and looked her in the eye. Even sitting on the stool, he was as tall as she was, and that was saying something. She had heard he wasn't English by birth. He couldn't be. They didn't make men like him around these parts. "I thought you might give me a job."

Meg raised her eyebrows, taken aback. The only people who still worked at The Rose were women, and much as she'd like to watch him bending over tables, he'd look ridiculous in an apron. The only other kind of job she'd like to give him was not something she'd ever had to pay for, and she didn't mean to start now. "What sort of a job?"

He shrugged. "Keep the peace. Keep hands away from your tits, that sort of thing."

Meg blinked. Although he'd said *away*, some part of her lust-addled brain had rearranged the words so she was treated to an image of his hands there instead. *His* hands might even be big enough to handle them properly. She swallowed. "You want me to pay you to be *the man* in my bar? You've got a gorgeous hook, Jake, but I can handle myself."

He narrowed his eyes, not put off by her refusal. "You need the help. I just threw thirty men out of here on my own. They could have brought this whole place down, and you with it."

She looked away. "Forty-one."

He sat back, clearly surprised. "You...counted?"

She leaned back on her heel. "You *didn't*?"

Jake spread his hands and again Meg's eyes were drawn to the size of them. They would definitely be big enough. "Caught up in the moment, I suppose. I didn't want you getting hurt."

"Truly?" Meg blurted in her surprise. She could count on one hand the people who'd be upset if something happened to her, and all of them were locked in a room upstairs. Her sometimes abrasive honesty hadn't won her many friends over the years, and she wasn't the kind of distressed damsel men felt inspired to save. At best, she had been an amusement to them. At worst, a vice. "You don't know me. Why would you care?"

"You don't know me, but you assume that I wouldn't?" Even confusion looked good on him. It wasn't fair. "Your ferocity is not in question, but it's getting rougher around here. It might not hurt to have somebody around to get between you and them."

"You could be useful, I'll give you that," she admitted grudgingly, "But I'll not pay you to sit on your arse drinking my beer all day. You can help out around here or you'll be out on your ear. I can't pay you much. What are you asking?"

He shrugged and Meg thought he almost seemed bashful. *Preposterous.*

"Got any spare rooms?"

Meg's shoulders dropped. A man his age ought to have a place of his own. Children, even. "You married, Jake?"

"I am not. You asking?"

If she was another sort of girl, Meg might have blushed. "Don't need more people living here, is all." she dismissed, embarrassed that she was relieved to hear it. She met his eyes, defying him to notice her discomfort. "Room and board and ten shillings a week. You can have your meals here if you help out in the kitchen. Keep your hands off of my sisters."

Jake raised an eyebrow. "Your sisters?"

"Hands. Off." She wouldn't be despairing in her mirror over her few grey hairs while Jake had his way with eighteen-year-old Judith down the hall.

"I promise I won't touch your sisters." he pledged, clearly amused.

"Don't be so cocky. You haven't seen them yet." She stepped over the man on the floor as she went back around the bar. "Come on, I'll show you your room."

♥

Jake let out a long breath as he followed the sway of Meg's hips up the stairs. This was quickly becoming one of the strangest nights of his life. He won a fight, broke up a brawl, got sacked, and re-hired within an hour by the subject of the painting in

Larry's office. He ran a hand over his eyes, exhaustion catching up with him.

The hall at the top of the first flight of stairs was short but contained several doors, presumably for guests of the inn. Darkness swaddled everything in sight, relieved only intermittently from the poor light from three tallow candles mounted on the walls. "We haven't been taking so many guests of late, so it'll be quiet."

"Any reason?"

"The inn needs repair and some of the rooms are falling to pieces. This one's all right."

Meg turned and opened the door to the immediate right of the staircase. She took a candle off of the wall and carried it into the room. He followed her inside hesitantly, not wanting to crowd her in the narrow space. He knew he could be imposing at times, and he didn't want her to feel threatened.

Nonplussed, she popped the candle into an empty candlestick on the dresser and turned.

He had only ever seen her from a distance before tonight, and he was amazed she was even more beautiful up close. Her skin was alabaster in the candlelight, unlined and warm, and her lush figure was like something out of his dreams. Her eyes were even greener than they were in the painting. The Townsend boy hadn't done her justice. In fairness, one could hardly hope to capture her spark with something as mundane as paint.

She narrowed those eyes at him as though she was rethinking her decision to hire him. He caught himself holding his breath as she examined him. "This is it," she said at last. "The bed's there."

Jake threw a glance in the direction she indicated. Apart from the dresser she was leaning against, he hadn't noticed there was furniture in the room. As his eyes adjusted to the darkness, he saw a narrow bed against the wall beside his bad leg. It was almost certainly too short for him, but it had been made up as if for a guest and the turned down blanket looked inviting. It was nicer than what he had in his apartment, but they'd never *both* fit into it.

Jake almost smiled. Wishful thinking, perhaps.

Meg eyed him up, appearing to consider the same thing.

Jake took a step backward. Meg was his boss now, and his future depended on keeping her happy. He didn't need to get off on the wrong foot by treating her like strumpet. He cleared his throat. "A dressing table." He nodded toward the table and mirror beside the door. "Can't say I've had one of those before."

Meg shrugged one creamy white shoulder and her smile was even more beguiling than the smile in her portrait. "Man like you ought to have a mirror."

Having been hit in the face as many times as he had, Jake knew he wasn't much to look at. Was she teasing him? "So I can curl my hair?"

She laughed and her gaze settled on a spot just above his left eye. She stretched out her hand to touch it, but stopped short. "You'll want to see to that. It'll be green by morning."

He lifted his hand to his face and winced as he touched a sore place beside his eye. He checked his reflection and saw a red patch that was already beginning to swell. The linen from the match still bound his knuckles, but now it was covered in spots of red and brown. His blood, theirs, it didn't matter. Over his shoulder, he saw Meg watching him with a curiously soft expression. It was almost wistful. He hadn't expected her to be kind, and he certainly hadn't expected her to be witty. She looked startled as her eyes met his in the dim reflection of the mirror, and he wondered about the woman behind the legend.

Jake tensed as the door opened a crack behind him. "Mum? Is it safe now?"

Meg rushed past him in a swirl of skirts and opened the door to a boy in the hallway. He was young and slight, a child still, though he had Tom Callaghan's look about him. When he was older, he'd be the image of his father. He eyed Jake with reserved curiosity. Jake smiled at him in greeting and the boy frowned.

"It's safe, darling." Meg ruffled his brown hair. "Are the others still upstairs?"

He nodded, not once taking his eyes off of Jake.

Meg turned to Jake with her hand on the boy's shoulder. "This is my son, Tommy. Tommy, this is Jake. He's going to look after us. Be nice to him, yeah?"

Tommy wrinkled his freckled nose. "Yeah."

"Good. Now go tell your aunt it's safe to come down."

The boy turned and ran up the stairs. Meg listened to him go before she turned back to Jake.

"He's Tom Callaghan's boy."

Meg nodded. "He is."

When Jake had first seen Meg around years before, she was always with Tom. He'd have taken her out in a heartbeat, except that she'd clearly been spoken for. "What happened there?"

Meg huffed. "What didn't?"

She was clearly irritated. There was more to this than she was saying. He wouldn't press the issue. "Have you got a man, Meg?"

Her eyes widened and her hand drifted to her delicious hip. "Been known to have a few here and there. You asking, Jake?"

Now she was teasing him. "Don't want anyone taking exception to my being here, is all."

She cocked an eyebrow and gave him a long look up and down. Women never looked at him like that, and it made him feel warm from the inside out. "You can handle yourself. Get some sleep. You look ready to fall over. My room's next door if you need anything." She closed the door as she left.

Jake stared at the door. She had left a hint of myrrh in the air as she went. He had smelled it earlier as he helped her down from the bar. Warm, sweet, and a little bit gritty, it suited her down to her toes.

The room was small but tidy, and the bed linens looked to be the finest he'd had in years. Resolved to pack up his apartment in the morning, he locked the door and shrugged out of his coat. As he pulled his shirt over his head, he detected another hint of that myrrh. He undressed with a smile and climbed into bed.

Chapter 3

"Piss," Meg seethed under her breath. "Bloody brilliant start to a lovely day."

Hours after opening the inn, Meg was still attacking the angry red stain from the spilled wine when Jane Virtue floated into the inn with her five beautiful children in tow. Mark Virtue, damn his eyes, brought up the rear carrying the newest addition to their perfect family, another baby girl. Jane smiled at her as though nothing was amiss, one hand on her constantly pregnant belly, while Mark greeted, "Afternoon, Meg! What's in the pot today?"

Meg wiped at her forehead with the back of her hand. As if it wasn't enough punishment for her to have to see her ex-lover happier than ever with her rival, she had to run the inn where they took most of their meals. "Only my pride and the hopes and dreams of my youth," she grumbled.

"What's that?" He laughed, handsome as ever. She briefly fantasized about carefully removing the baby from his overdeveloped arms and slapping him across the face with her mop. It would make a brilliant noise. *Shlurp.*

"Beef," she said louder. "Carrots, potatoes, and a few turnips. That is, if Bess is awake back there. I'll give her a kick."

She leaned the mop against the wall and stormed into the kitchen. Her sister, Bess, was stirring an enormous bubbling pot of stew suspended from a long-suffering hook over the fire. She grinned at Meg as she walked in. "I haven't seen that face in a few days. Virtues in again?"

"They're in here every bloody day." Meg pulled down enough dishes for the whole family and grabbed a loaf of warm, crusty bread from on top of the oven. "You only miss them when you're off with Susan."

Bess' smile was more than a little dreamy. "Oh, right."

"Keep stirring," Meg snapped. "Must be nice to have somebody distract you so you don't notice how rubbish everything else is. Wish I had one."

"Don't you?" Bess asked, resuming her stirring.

She tucked her hair behind her ear, warmed at the memory of Jake's hands on her as he helped her down from the bar. "Jake's just a friend. Not even that."

The spoon stopped and Bess looked up. "I thought his name was Luke. Who's *Jake*?"

Meg cringed. She didn't look up as she began to fill bowls for the Virtues. "He works here now. You'll meet him later."

Bess dropped the spoon in shock. "You hired someone? A man?"

In the all the years the Henshawes had run The Rose and Crown, they had never hired anyone outside of the family to work there. There were so many of them they hadn't needed to. Meg shrugged, feeling defensive. "What of it? Alice and Bel have gone, and lord knows you're only around half the time. I can't do everything on my own."

Meg's hands were shaking. Bess took the bowls from her. "Let me," she said, and for once, Meg did. Bess loaded a tray with stew and bread and ran it out to the Virtues while Meg busied herself by putting away the clean dishes.

Running an inn was no easy task. There weren't enough hours in the day for everything she had to do. She had already scrubbed the floor, hauled coal, and lit fires in the kitchen and the bar. She would still have to put away the dishes, wash the new ones, check the deliveries of bread, meat, and produce as they arrived, order more wine to replace what she had lost, balance the ledgers and pay their bills, all while she was needed behind the bar to serve the few customers they had left. If not for Bess doing the cooking and Judith cleaning everything else, she really would have to do everything on her own, and then where would she be? At least Tommy had school for much of the day to keep him occupied while his mother worked. A plate slipped out of her hands and shattered against the floor with a deafening crash. "Bollocks!"

A broom appeared at her feet and began to sweep up the broken pottery. Meg let out a long sigh and turned, expecting to find Bess behind her. She jumped as she found herself nose to nose with Jake, bending over the broom. "Jake!"

Their faces were inches apart. He didn't move, but lifted his liquid brown eyes to meet hers. "Sounded like you could use some help," he said, his voice barely above a whisper. "Watch yourself, you don't want to get hurt."

Meg blinked dumbly, then realized he was referring to the shards of pottery that surrounded her feet. "Thank you," she stammered, caught off-guard. "Are you all settled in now?"

He smiled and resumed sweeping. "I am. Did you know there's a crack in the wall between our rooms?"

Meg rolled her eyes and turned back to the dishes. She needed to have that fixed, but the only good carpenter left in Southwark was Mark Virtue, and his very existence irked her beyond belief. "No extra charge," Meg joked. His room had belonged to Bess before she moved out, and the crack had never bothered the two of them. It hadn't occurred to her the night before that he would be able to see her dressing if he had a mind to look.

"Meg! You'll never guess who's here! You'll kiss me when I tell you!" Bess' frantic whisper reached Meg as she turned the corner into the kitchen. Meg turned to face her and Jake held the broom to the side to make way for Bess. "It's--" Bess stopped short as she nearly crashed into Jake. She took a few quick steps backward, sputtering.

From Bess' obvious embarrassment, she had been about to announce that Meg's favorite prize fighter was in the bar. She hadn't expected to find him sweeping up in the kitchen. "Joe Ledford," she blurted, obviously trying to cover her tracks. "Joe Ledford is here."

Meg put a hand to her hip. "Joe Ledford is here every day."

"Yes, but I thought you'd be excited because...he owes you money?" Bess shrugged.

That, at least, was true. "He certainly does. Bess, this is Jake. He works here now. Jake, this is my sister, Bess."

Jake greeted her with a pleasant smile and Bess curtsied, clearly flustered. She returned to the pot and began to stir silently.

Emptying the pottery into the rubbish box, Jake put the broom away and excused himself. "There are some people waiting at the bar. I'll sort them out."

"Not like you did last night," Meg teased him. "At least not yet."

His cheek twitched with a smile as he left. When he was gone, Meg let out a long sigh and sunk against the table.

Bess' eyes were huge. "That was Jake Cohen! Well done, you!"

Meg could have throttled her sister. She dearly hoped Jake was out of earshot. "Keep quiet! He works here, is all. I gave him a room upstairs."

Bess scoffed in disbelief. "What's this talk of last night, then? You don't expect me to believe that man stayed the night here and you didn't jump on him!"

"What kind of a girl do you think I am?" Meg deadpanned.

Bess stared at her.

"Fine." Meg looked away. "I didn't, but I would have.

Satisfied?"

"Not by half." Bess laughed. "You will, though, yeah?"

"What do you care? You only fancy girls," Meg spat.

"A preference I've suddenly started to reconsider," she kidded. "I suppose you put him in my room. That crack still there in the wall?"

Meg shook her head. Everybody had thought of the crack but her. "It slipped my mind in a moment of stupidity."

"Stupidity or bloody brilliance." Bess grinned. "Soon you'll be whispering to each other like Pyramus and Thisbe...you'll have to take care to avoid any tigers, of course."

"I'll show you a tiger!" Meg threw a tea towel at her head, but Bess caught it with a laugh.

Bess took the towel and set to work on the wet dishes. "I'll finish up in here. You go check to see how Pyramus is getting on with the bar."

Meg didn't often take the advice of her younger sisters, but Bess had a point. Keeping a bar wasn't a complicated task, but she still didn't know if Jake's mind was as quick as he was. Shooting her one last reproachful look, she left the kitchen to the sound of giggling.

♥

"I've never seen a fight like that in my life," Joe Ledford said over his first gin of the day. "They were outmatched, but the little one got the upper hand. Uppercut?" Joe laughed at his own joke.

Jake nodded. He'd been at that fight, too. Meg had fought the little ginger girl who'd married Mark Virtue. Seven years later, people were still talking about it. "Got lucky, is all. Meg was the better fighter."

"Yes, indeed," Joe admitted, then took a sip. Jake had seen Joe Ledford about for years at different inns and alehouses around London, but had never conversed with him for an extended period of time. For a known drunk, he was surprisingly articulate.

As Meg entered the bar from the kitchen, Joe raised his glass to her. Meg smiled, taking his salute in stride. No doubt she was used to men toasting to her face and form. "Afternoon, Joe. Eating today?"

Joe withdrew a couple of farthings from his worn out coat and slapped them on the bar.

Meg took them and dropped them into a pot under the counter. "Coming right up," she said pleasantly and headed back to the kitchen.

Jake knew the farthings Joe had given her weren't enough to cover a meal, even at the more than reasonable prices of The Rose and Crown. Still, moments later, Meg emerged from the kitchen with a tray loaded with stew and fresh bread. Joe accepted it gratefully, shoveling the stew into his mouth. As Meg turned back to the kitchen, Joe leaned in and said, "No finer woman in five counties. You're a fortunate man."

Jake set to work on the stain on the floor without correcting him. It occurred to him Meg's safety might depend on certain people believing they were a couple, and he wouldn't throw away an advantage like that. Besides, he didn't disagree. He had been fortunate to find another position so quickly.

A clatter of plates at the end of the bar drew his attention and he turned to see Mark Virtue stacking his family's dishes up to help them out. "Cheers," Jake thanked him.

Mark left the dishes and strolled up to Jake with his hand extended. "Mark Virtue," he introduced himself.

Jake shook his hand. "Jake Cohen."

Mark grinned as though he knew a brilliant joke and no one else was in on it. He and Meg had a history, and if the stories were to be believed, Meg had lost him in that infamous fight.

"Pleasure," Mark said. "I was there the night you knocked out Tom Callaghan. Bloody good fight."

Jake nodded. "It was. I was there the night Meg fought your

wife."

Mark paled a little, but he smiled just the same. "Lose any money?"

"I bet a crown on Meg." Jake shrugged. "It was a lucky shot."

Mark glanced at his wife over his shoulder. "Yes, it was. What are you doing around these parts?"

Though Jake had lived south of the river for a few years, his old apartments had been in Bankside and he'd never been a regular at The Rose, a fact he was beginning to regret. "Helping Meg out for a while, is all."

"Welcome to Southwark," Mark said pleasantly. "If you ever need aught fixed, I'm just down the road. Big old house with the sign of the coffin."

Jake nodded, remembering the crack in the wall that separated his room from Meg's. "Let you know if I think of anything."

Meg finally emerged from the kitchen once Mark and his family had left. "What did he want?" she asked, collecting their dishes.

Jake raised his eyebrows. Though years had passed, there was clearly still some tension between Meg and Mark. Mark seemed happy enough, but Jake wondered how Meg felt about the situation. Did she still have feelings for him? "Came over to introduce himself. Talked about boxing."

Meg put a hand on her hip, drawing his gaze down the length of her body. Did she know the gesture had that effect? She was tall for a woman, though she barely came up to his chin, and had a body made to worship. She was no shrinking violet but a rose in glorious bloom. He could not for the life of him imagine her being anyone's second choice.

She sneered in distaste, an ugly gesture her face somehow rendered enchanting. "Mark Virtue has never boxed in his life." She turned to Jake, her gaze resting on the bridge of his nose. He fought the urge to cover it under her scrutiny. He knew he was othing to look at, and he'd been hit in the face so many times the shape of it had changed. It was by stubbornness alone he still had all of his teeth.

Meg surprised him by reaching out and touching his nose, her thumb caressing what was left of the bridge. He almost jumped. He couldn't remember the last time a woman had touched his face. "How many times your nose been broken, Jake?" she asked, her voice husky.

He swallowed, suddenly feeling much younger than his years. "Seventeen. That I know of."

Her eyes widened and she dropped her hand. "I'm surprised you've got one left."

"So am I," he said, already missing her touch. "How'd you break yours?"

Meg glared at the door. "Jane bloody Virtue is how. Thought you said you were there."

"I was." He remembered that fight well. He'd bet on Meg because she was the clever choice, but knowing the prize was Mark Virtue, no small part of him had hoped she would lose. When she did, he had handed over his money with a smile on his face. "And the second time?"

Meg looked at him, caught off guard. "The second?"

He hesitantly raised his hand to her face, stroking the bridge with his thumb where it deviated slightly on the left side. The difference between the sides was so slight it would take a physician to notice, or a lover.

The contrast of his tan, broken hand against the satin perfection of her cheek was too stark, it was almost perverse. Men like him were never meant to touch the flawless beauty of Meg Henshawe. She couldn't possibly enjoy it. He dropped his hand and clutched the mop instead.

She touched her own nose, remembering. "Parting gift from an old lover, is all." She looked away.

Jake's heart dropped into his stomach. "He hit you?"

Meg shrugged and gave a small smile that didn't reach her eyes. "Don't shed a tear for me. I'm a big girl, I can handle myself."

"You shouldn't have to."

"There are a lot of things I shouldn't have to do, but here we are," she dismissed, her voice flat.

From the other side of the pit, Meg Henshawe had appeared to lead a charmed life with a beautiful face, a steady job, and a healthy family. What else had she had to do?

"Anyone raises a hand to you, Meg, you tell me and I'll sort them out," he pledged, deadly serious.

All but forgotten, Joe Ledford raised his glass. "Amen!"

Meg shook her head with a sigh. "You tossed forty-odd madmen out of here last night. What do you reckon they'd do to me if they saw me as an easy mark?"

"There's nothing wrong with asking for help."

She eyed him up, taking his measure. "You ever ask for help, Jake?"

He pressed his lips together. He'd likely be in a very different place if he had.

Her smile was sad, but not unsympathetic. "That's what I thought."

Chapter 4

The Rose and Crown was not what he expected. While most of the inns, taverns, and alehouses south of the river were dank little hovels reeking of piss and misery, The Rose was sprawling, tidy, and remarkably warm.

The warmth of the establishment had as much to do with the Henshawe sisters as the roaring fire between the bar and the door. Bess was a cheeky, toffee-haired woman who kept biting the inside of her lip when she looked at him, as though he had something stuck to his face and she was trying not to laugh. He'd caught himself checking his reflection in a knife just in case. Judith was the youngest. She was shorter than the others, with hair so fair it was nearly silver and alarmingly bright sapphire eyes. Shy but sweet, she shrugged off the attention from the local boys with remarkable patience. She was little more than a girl, really. It was hard to believe she already had an infant of her own.

In the middle of it all was Meg.

The inn was full to capacity. Those who had not exhausted their wages the night before were back again, drinking and having a laugh as though the brawl had never taken place. He'd have thought he dreamt it if not for the clumsy bruises on faces and even around a few throats. He hadn't caused those, at least. He'd been able to chuck enough of them out without properly striking anyone, and even then, he was holding back.

Meg didn't seem to notice the bruises as she saw to the tables, serving drinks with careless grace. She had a smile for everyone, and they repaid her tenfold. She joked with them easily, raising laughs wherever she went. She was poised as an actress, and he wondered how she kept it up without getting tired.

As she approached the bar with an empty tray, she had a smile for Jake, too. It was different from the others, a coy little twitch of recognition, and he suspected that one was real. She set the tray on the bar. "Four more."

He took the mugs from the tray and refilled them from the barrel. He got through two and a half before the barrel ran out. Setting the mugs out of the way on the bar, he lifted the empty barrel from the low, deep shelf that held it. "Got any more of this?"

"In the cellar." She tucked a long piece of hair the color of undiluted gold into the messy knot on top of her head. A ridiculous way to wear it, born of necessity rather than fashion, but hopelessly charming. She'd still be cripplingly beautiful if it was full of twigs. She arched an eyebrow at him flirtatiously. "Think you can lift it on your own?"

He shot her a dark look and she responded with a rather dirty-sounding laugh. With a shake of his head, he went into the cellar, his bad leg dragging a little. He tried to compensate with the other. The last thing he needed was Meg thinking he wasn't up to the task.

When he emerged a long moment later with a fresh barrel over his shoulder, half a dozen women had appeared near the bar. Where had they come from? Each and every one of them watched him like a hawk as he lowered the barrel from his shoulder and fit it into the shelf, their companions forgotten.

He finished filling the mugs Meg had brought to him and returned them to her. She collected them with an expression that was slightly glazed. "Getting tired?"

She blinked and shook her head, as though trying to wake herself. "I'm fine." she snapped. "I could go for hours."

He smiled at her.

Meg visibly trembled. She seized the tray with a deep breath and put her hostess expression back on before charging into the crowd.

Jake scratched his head. *What an odd reaction.*

He felt eyes on him before he heard the muttering. Not two yards away, a cluster of local men too young to know any better was grumbling about Jake's presence in their local boozer. Covered in bruises or nicks, they had clearly been among those he'd thrown out the night before. Jake tensed, wary of another confrontation.

A weedy young man whipped them up into a sloppy furor made all the more feeble by the amount of gin they had consumed. Jake had tried gin once or twice in Amsterdam, but the concoction they served at The Rose bore little resemblance to the refined Dutch spirit. From the smell alone, he reckoned it was strong enough to strip paint. Much more of that and they'd not be able to see him at all.

"Who does he think he is? Coming in here and throwing us out of our inn like he owns it. Bloody porker." He glared at Jake, sizing him up.

Jake dropped the rag he'd been using to shine the brass on the counter and met the boy's stare. He had nothing to prove. Like so many English boys, this one tried to act hard when his mates were about, but left alone with Jake, he'd piss himself.

The boy broke eye contact first.

Swallowing the irritation that rose in his throat, Jake took up the rag and polished the brass with renewed vigor.

Joe Ledford woke with a jolt at the motion inches away from his head. He wiped the drool hanging from his leathery lip with confusion. "Trying to get the dent out?"

Jake raised his eyebrows. "I beg your pardon?"

Joe nodded toward the brass. "You'll polish that dent out if you go much harder."

Jake laughed self-consciously. "Figured I'd do Meg a favor."

"You do that. Gin?" He pushed his glass toward Jake.

The smell of the empty glass was strong enough to make his head spin. "Take it easy, mate. If I throw out these tossers, I'll need you to have my back."

Joe's laugh was half-wheeze but completely genuine. His sallow face lit up like the moon when it was yellow. The gaps in his smile were a familiar sight. Some of his teeth had rotted out, others had been torn by a barber or knocked out along the way. He was a slight man, worn out from life and drink, with a bit of long gray hair curling beneath the brim of his cap. He likely weighed about as much as Judith did, soaking wet. If he sneezed too hard, he'd break a rib. "I could throw a punch in my day, make no mistake." His laughter ended in a series of wet-sounding coughs. "Used to work the docks, before my wife died."

"I'm sorry," Jake offered his condolences. "How'd she pass?"

"That one?" Joe scratched his head, drawing attention to his mutilated ear. It had likely been nailed to the stocks at one point or another and it was missing a large chunk. "That one was plague. I survived it. Sick as a dog for weeks, but here I am."

Jake nodded, remembering. "We were shut up in the City, me and my family. Missed us, but we couldn't leave for months." It was only their proximity to the bakery that had kept them from starving.

Joe frowned. "Married?"

"Almost, once."

Joe raised three dirty fingers. "I had three women, me. First died of a cough, second plague, last one fire."

"My parents went in the Fire. Survived the plague only to burn in their beds. What do you make of that?"

Joe shook his head. "Sorry business. My wife died in a house fire, sometime later. Skirt caught when she was making the coffee.

Found what was left of her when I got home. Mug was still in her hand. Haven't drunk the stuff since."

"I don't blame you." Jake refilled the man's gin. He'd earned it.

Joe accepted it with a sad smile. "Meg's all I've got these days. Looks after me, she does. I'd be dead without her."

Behind him, Judith floated from table to table, pale as a ghost. It was easy to imagine these women of Joe's, but harder to picture him as a young man. The way things were going, Jake would be alone as Joe was in a few years, sitting on the other side of a bar. Perhaps this one, if Meg didn't tire of him in the meantime.

A man walked into the bar and glanced around with uncertainty. He twisted his hat in his hands and approached Jake at the bar. "Are you Mr. Henshawe?"

Jake shook his head. "Not me. How can I help?"

Joe cleared his throat noisily. "That'll be me, squire. Charles Henshawe at you service."

Jake kept his mouth shut.

The man appeared to relax. "I've been sent by your cousin to inquire after your health."

"Right as rain, as you can see." This was punctuated by a rather wet-sounding cough. "Give my best to me, erm, cousin."

"Yes, sir." The man nodded to Jake and turned to leave.

The boy who'd been stirring trouble careened into his way. "Did I hear you say you was looking for Charlie Henshawe?"

"Luke," Meg warned from across the room.

Jake tensed, sensing a fight in the tone of her voice.

Luke laughed and Jake could smell the drink coming of him at ten paces. "Charlie Henshawe's been dead for years. Hasn't he, Meg?"

Jake had never seen anything like the horror on Meg's face. She looked as if she might faint. He went toward her, ready to catch her if need be.

"That's a bit out of order. I'm sitting right here." Joe chuckled and offered an uneasy smile.

The man looked from Joe to Luke in confusion.

"That's very amusing, *Joe.*" Luke laughed and elbowed the man. "That's Joe Ledford, that is. He's the town drunk."

"Luke," Meg snapped, panic in her voice. "Do not speak to my father thus."

"Your father is dead, Meg." Luke had dug his own grave, but he just kept shoveling. "You think he'd let you carry on the way you do if he was alive?" He addressed the bar, "She'll take all sorts, this one. Noble or otherwise. Don't have to be English. Don't even have to be *human.*"

Meg did not faint, but gave Luke an ear-splitting slap. "How bloody dare you!"

No few people shot him speculative glances, no doubt wondering if the gossip was true.

All but forgotten, the man who had come looking for Meg's father put his hat back on and slipped out into the night.

"Do you have any idea what you just did?" Meg demanded.

"Me?" Luke feigned innocence. "I'm only being honest. If you ask me, you ought to try it sometime. You ought to send that one--" he pointed at Jake "--back to bloody Amsterdam. If you ask me--"

"Nobody's asking you, you loathsome little toad," Meg snarled, and the resulting laughter turned his face from a heated red to an enraged scarlet.

His eyes glassy with drink, he puffed out his chest like a pigeon. "You didn't find me so loathsome last week!" he bragged, his pathetic friends tittering like girls. "Or little!"

Nonplussed, Meg put her hands on her hips, meeting his challenge. "I find you loathsome every day. Don't mistake my boredom for favor. Tell me, why is it that every piss-proud ninny with three inches has got to wave it around like it's God's bloody gift? You think I haven't seen enough to know better, do you?"

The bar fell silent but for a robust cackle from Joe. Jake bit his lip to keep from joining him.

Put on the spot and utterly humiliated, Luke made the mistake of raising his hand to Meg.

Jake was halfway to him before Luke struck at her. She caught his hand easily and twisted his arm behind his back. He cried out in pain. "Bloody whore!"

"Bloody whore, he says," Meg muttered to herself as she pushed him past Jake to the exit. "Cream-faced weasel. I eat better men than you for my bloody breakfast. Off you go back to your mother, now. Don't come back until you can grow a beard." She tossed him into the gutter and slammed the door.

The bar was silent when she turned around. Flushed with anger, she threw her arms wide. "If you're waiting to compare pricks, I can assure you, I've seen bigger."

Joe laughed as Jake resumed his place behind the bar. "No finer woman alive, mark my words."

Jake relaxed his fists. She hadn't needed his help at all. "No, indeed. What was all that about?"

Joe lowered his voice. "Men come asking after Charlie Henshawe from time to time. Whenever they come by, I'm him."

"So I gathered. Why?"

Joe finished the last of his gin. "Best not to ask. I don't."

Meg brushed past him behind the bar, blowing a loose strand of hair out of her face. She poured herself a glass of wine and downed it. "You want one?"

Jake shook his head.

She narrowed her eyes, sharp and clear as emeralds. "You judging me, Jake?"

He raised his eyebrows. Her blood was running hot, and she was still looking for a fight. He knew the feeling well. "Disappointed, is all."

Again, her hand climbed to her hip. "What have you got to be disappointed about? You know what I am."

While most men would have cowered in the face of her rage,

he knew it as he knew his own. Its highs, lows, and its limits. He stepped into the heat of her gaze and slowly, carefully raised his hand to tuck the errant strand behind her ear. "I was disappointed I didn't get to see that cross of yours. I'd have had to carry him out."

Her posture relaxed and her eyes softened. He wasn't the enemy, but he'd let her take out all of that energy on him, if she wanted to.

She swallowed, her eyes widening by the moment. The way she was looking at him, he felt like dessert. "Night's not over yet." She swept past him into the kitchen.

It took him a full minute to realize Meg had meant she might yet hit somebody in the hour or so left before they closed the bar. Though his mind knew the comment was not an invitation, other parts of his anatomy were less convinced.

Joe Ledford grinned at him as he returned to the brass. "You're a lucky man," he slurred. "You ought to speak for that one, 'fore she gets away. Make an honest woman out of our Meg!" He laughed so hard he lost his balance, catching himself on the bar top and erupting into another coughing fit.

"I suspect Meg's the most honest woman I've met."

"That she is." Joe chuckled. "She could use someone like you around."

"Meg can look after herself."

Joe waved a hand. "She's a kitten, really. Just needs someone to calm her down. Virtue couldn't do that. Just wound her up until she was ready to scream. Same with Tom. Like oil and water."

Jake nodded as though he knew, though he was less familiar with her history than everyone else. "Did she love them?" he asked in spite of himself.

"Not possible." Joe shook his head. "That girl don't love anything but her sisters, her boy, and her bar."

♥

After she had thrown Luke out, it was all Meg could do to keep from screaming. Her blood raced and her pulse pounded in her temples. If anyone so much as looked at her wrong, she'd bloody *end them.*

That whinging little prick had called her a whore in front of everyone, as though they didn't already know. They knew and it was likely the only reason the inn was still in business. God knew it wasn't the ale. He'd told Davey's spy her father was dead, and now her cousin would probably try to visit, ruining the blissful estrangement they'd enjoyed for nearly a decade. No doubt the blackguard would want something.

Worst of all, he'd gone off on one over Jake. The last Dutch war had only just ended and she didn't need them trying to stir up another. Jake could defend himself, but his fists couldn't save them if they burned down the inn.

A lot of the aggression dissipated with Luke's departure. The punters returned to their drinks and their cards as though nothing had happened. Meg took a deep breath and forced herself to smile. No one wanted a scowling barmaid.

Meg passed half a dozen beers around a table covered in cards for All Fours. When she appeared, all but one of the five looked up immediately, not bothering to disguise their hands. Without looking too carefully, she could see Rob had a pair, Michael had three, and Jerome had shit.

"Would you look at that? The Queen of Hearts," Geoffrey announced as he turned over a card. He held it up beside Meg's face and pursed his lips. "You ought to sit for these, Meg, you'd make a much better queen. You're so…" His eyes raked over figure with appreciation. "Heart-shaped."

Meg blinked to keep herself from rolling her eyes. "Five sisters, four queens. You ought to find a card for each of us, and then we can talk," she challenged, leaning over the table and peeking at Geoffrey's hand. He had two Knaves. She winked at him. "You'll never win with that hand, sweetheart. Can I bring you lads aught else? We just opened up a new cask of whiskey…"

Moments later, she was back behind the bar, pouring five glasses.

Meg almost dropped a pair of them as Jake emerged from the cellar for the second time, now with a cask of wine over his shoulder. It took her both arms and a good deal of heavy breathing to get those up the stairs, and here he balanced it with a single hand like a basket of bread. "More whiskey? I didn't think that one was any good."

As he bent to fit the cask into the low shelf, his thin shirt glided over a half-remembered pair of shoulders. He looked different with his clothes on. The clean linen was a far cry from the dirt, sweat, and blood he wore in the pit. Why had she stopped going?

He stood, his head a hand's breadth short of touching a low beam. He raised his eyebrows as if expecting a response to something.

Right, the whiskey.

"It's rot-gut," Meg agreed once she'd gathered her wits. "I wouldn't use it to polish the brass. I'm trying to get shot of it."

His cheek twitched with the hint of a smile. "Do people just do whatever you tell them to?"

"More or less. Unless it's important."

"Good talent to have."

"What, spinning rubbish?" Her eyes watered at the smell of the whiskey as she finished pouring the glasses. Too many of those and they wouldn't be able to see their cards.

"I was going to say persuasion," he said gently, his gaze softening like burnt-out coal. She could almost see the ashes rising to the rafters. A woman could use a man like that to warm her through the winter.

She gave him her most *persuasive* smile, a slow, knowing look that had gotten her out of trouble more than once. "Reckon I could persuade you to do a thing or two for me?"

His eyes did not wander from her face, but they burned a little brighter as he held her gaze. "All you have to do is ask."

Meg licked her lips and his eyes dropped to follow the tip of her tongue. She smiled. He fancied her. She felt it burning in her gut like that rancid whiskey.

His hand rested on the bar and she walked her fingers toward it. "What can I get away with?" she asked, only hesitating a moment before she tentatively brushed her fingers over it. If she had anything to say about it, she would not be going to bed alone tonight.

He took his hand back as if he'd been shocked. His face fell and a crease appeared between his eyebrows. She had never caused *that* reaction before.

He hesitated before he spoke. "I don't want you to play your games with me."

Meg could not have been more shocked if someone had tossed a bucket of freezing water over her head. It felt like her heart stopped beating as she wrestled with his words. Her *games*?

He'd heard what was said about her. She'd said as much about herself. He knew what she was.

She was a strumpet, and he didn't want her.

Her face flamed with humiliation. He hadn't said as much, but his meaning was clear. He thought he was better than her, and he was right.

Pride eviscerated, she took the whiskey back to her admirers.

Chapter 5

Four candles still flickered on the windowsill when Jake returned to his room. Curtains fluttered as though tickled by a ghostly hand, the smell of ice riding the rain through the crack in the glass. The room was cold as a larder and nearly as dark; when he caught his reflection in the mirror, he was little more than a shadow in the shape of a man. Perhaps that was the truth of it, after all. Twelve winters had come and gone since the Fire, each one freezing another piece of him until he no longer felt the snow.

His leg felt it, though. Hours on his feet had taken their toll on the frayed sinews and crooked break. He'd done a good job of hiding it, he knew. As much as it had pained him to do so, it would have pained him worse to see pity in their eyes.

Squaring his hips, he lowered himself to a seated position and rose again, the muscle stiffening in protest. He bit his lip and did it again. Sweat beading his forehead, he worked through his daily rigors slowly, deliberately strengthening his legs through the pain.

By the time he'd finished with his legs, a slow burn had spread beneath his skin and the draft was almost welcome. He tugged off his shirt and stretched out on his belly on the floor like a snake. Drawing his hands beneath his shoulders, he pushed himself away from the floor. After the struggle with his legs, this was such a relief that he moved through several dozen effortlessly and only stopped when a bead of sweat dripped off his nose and struck his hand.

Hovering above them in half light, his hands looked like someone else's. They had always been cumbersome, but hundreds of fights had rendered them monstrous. Gnarled with countless breaks and covered in a patchwork of ugly scar tissue, calluses, and fresh, bloody cuts, it looked as though they'd been torn apart and sewn back together again, over and over until there was not an inch of flesh he recognized as his own.

Ugly as they were, they were twice as useless. The precision he had honed through his trade was a thing of the past; these days he could barely sign his name. All they were good for was inflicting pain in a job he'd neither asked for nor wanted. Now that was gone, what use was he to anyone?

He lowered himself to the floor, his heart slowing. Beneath the bed, he could see the rolled up portrait of Meg Henshawe he'd taken from Larry's office. It was too good to keep stashed away with his shoes, but he reasoned Meg might take exception to him putting it on his wall.

The floor was cold beneath his cheek. A rustle from the next door drew his attention and he sat up. The crack in the wall glowed with an inviting warmth. Meg was in her room. He caught a glimpse of something white as she took off her dress. Not wanting to intrude on her privacy, he leaned against the bed and closed his eyes.

It was quiet; she was alone. The floorboards creaked under her feet. As she sat down, the bed sighed as though it had been waiting for her return all day. A comb whispered through her hair, only interrupted by a muttered curse as she attacked a knot. He smiled to himself, imagining what her hair must look like when it was down. It was long, he knew. Would it touch the curve of her waist, the impossible flare of her hips?

Distracting as the thoughts were, there was something comforting about hearing her so close. With his eyes closed, he could hear her so clearly she might have been in the same room.

Had things gone as planned, he'd be long since married and listening to another woman comb her hair tonight. He chased her features in his memory, not as clear as they once were. Her chestnut-colored hair shone by the light of a long-extinguished fire, her cinnamon-colored eyes filled with regret after all these years.

I'm sorry, Jakob.

He tried to remember the dress she had been wearing when she left him but this last remaining image of her in his mind fractured at the sound of a sneeze from next door.

It was a funny little sound, Meg's sneeze. She stifled it as if she was afraid of being heard, so it came out like a quack, caught in her throat. He smiled to himself. He might have said something, but he didn't want her to know he'd been listening. He had been alone for so long he hadn't realized he'd missed the company until he heard her through the wall. The idea of being alone again in the silence made him sadder than he could say.

She had flirted with him shamelessly that night and he'd fallen for it like a fool. Just as he'd been about to pledge fealty to her, her words to that boy she'd chucked out rang in his head.

Don't mistake my boredom for favor.

He wouldn't.

The sweat cooled on his skin and he shivered.

Chapter 6

"She's got some bloody nerve showing her face here."

"We're all sinners, Mary."

"Some more than others, eh?"

Meg gritted her teeth as she filed through the door of the church, her hand guiding Tommy's slight back through the crush.

"I don't want to be here, either, you miserable old bat," she muttered.

Tommy glanced up at her with sorrowful hazel eyes.

"Sorry, love," she whispered.

Meg rarely enjoyed attending church, and only went often enough to assure the minister that she had not, in fact, made a covenant with Beelzebub, as the nosey old women seemed to believe. A jovial old man particularly fond of his drink, the minister had never given her any bother and had even judged some of the fights she'd boxed in. Unfortunately for Meg, he'd taken to his bed with gout, and the curate brought in to replace him was altogether less forgiving.

After what felt like hours of listening to the curate bang on about women of ill repute and the sin of fornication, Meg couldn't get out of there fast enough. She took Tommy's hand, needing his comfort more than he needed hers. Her son, whom she loved more than the entire miserable world, was the result of this dangerous fornication, a bastard born to a married boxer and a harlot who had the gall to run a business like a man. She straightened her back and raised her chin defiantly as she waded through the whispers, feeling like the Whore of bloody Babylon.

"...he's only just arrived and he already lives there?"

"She tossed Luke Leighton out on his ear…"

"No use fighting over her. She'll have them both, she will."

"Disgraceful!"

"Someone needs to take a firm hand with that one."

Meg's head ached under the weight of all the profanity she was holding back. Her eyes throbbed with it and she bit her tongue hard enough to draw blood until they passed through the doors into the cold winter sunlight.

"Ought to stick to her own kind. None will want her now that Jew's had her."

"Those girls will have a blackamoor down there next."

The dam burst. "I'm right here!" Meg spun on her heel and faced the people talking about her. Half a dozen old busybodies gaped at her. "I can hear you! You drink in my bar, you eat my food, and you slag me off in a church in front of my son? You're not so high and mighty yourself, you bleeding hypocrites! Mary, you've been in the Clink more times than I can count, and Freddy, you tried to pay me a crown to suck your cock *last week*!"

Freddy turned greener than the river. His wife snarled at him.

Meg focused her anger on her. "I *didn't*, but you mind your miserable manners or I might next time. To hell with the lot of you!"

The church had emptied and the dozens of people milling outside had heard her tirade. They wouldn't have heard what the others had been saying about her, so they no doubt thought she was mad. Fearful of winding up in Bedlam, Meg grasped Tommy's hand and marched down the street toward the inn. Within the hour, the lot of them would come in expecting dinner as though nothing had happened. She had a mind to piss in the stew.

"I'm sorry, Mum." Tommy said in a small voice.

Meg frowned, sidestepping a particularly nasty-looking pile of manure. "Whatever for, darling?"

"I'm sorry people are cruel to you. Is it because of me?"

Meg stopped in her tracks and looked at him seriously. He was barely ten. She'd been trying to be a good mother by taking him to church, but if he came out of it feeling guilty for his existence, they'd stop going altogether. The recusancy laws were rarely enforced in Southwark, and they couldn't say anything worse about her family. Her eyes clouded as she hugged him.

She fought the tears with everything she had. She would not let those cretins see her cry.

"No, darling. Your old mum was making vicars blush years before you came along." She held his shoulders and looked into his eyes, so much like Tom's, but kind. "Why on earth would you think that?"

He sniffed. "Mrs. Fletcher said I don't have a father."

Meg mentally added another name to her shit-list. "You do have a father, he's just a prick." She wiped a tear from his freckled cheek with her sleeve. "You are a good boy and you mean everything to me. I don't want you worrying about every nasty thing that's said, because it doesn't matter. They don't matter, you understand me?"

Tommy nodded gravely. "Yes, Mum."

"Good." She straightened. "Let's get back and check on the food."

The walk was mercifully short, but over the few streets between the church and the inn, several people cast her meaningful looks. Obviously they'd already seen or heard about her rant at church, though not one of them dared to say a word.

"Meg?" a woman's voice called.

Meg turned toward the sound. "What?"

Jane Virtue jumped at Meg's angry reply, clutching her pregnant belly with one hand and her daughter's hand in the other.

"I'm sorry, I didn't mean to disturb you. I only wanted to say that your hair looks lovely this morning."

Meg touched the knot self-consciously, feeling bad for barking at Jane. Reeling from Jake's rejection, she had spent longer on it that morning. "Thank you," she said tersely. "How's the baby?"

Jane rubbed her belly, breaking out into a smile like pure sunlight. Half a dozen children and she kept getting prettier. She must be near thirty by now. Meg had doubted she'd ever looked so radiantly happy in her life. Envy rose like bile in her throat.

"Good," she said cheerfully. "Won't be long now. Keeps kicking me. I think he wants to be out!"

"Reckon it's a boy?" Meg asked.

"Bound to get one sooner or later." Jane shrugged a shoulder. "All girls so far. Apart from Hugo, of course."

Meg nodded. Jane had half a dozen beautiful little girls with amber hair and clean, perfect little gowns. They had taken in Harry Townsend's boy and despite Jane's best efforts, the child always seemed to be ruffled, much like his charming reprobate father.

She glanced down at Tommy's worn shirt and his jacket with holes at the elbows. Meg couldn't sew to save her life, and with Jane half-running the only tailor's left in town, Meg had avoided going and many of their things had fallen into disrepair. "I hope it's an easy birth," Meg said, though she knew it couldn't be anything but. Everything seemed to come so damned easy for Jane.

"Thank you," Jane replied without a hint of wrath or envy. What did she have to be angry about, anyway? She'd won. "Probably see you this evening. Good bye, Tommy."

"Bye, Missus V," Tommy said pleasantly.

Meg tugged at her threadbare skirt as they walked the rest of the way to the inn. The morning was bright but blisteringly cold. A hint of pine hung on the air. Too poor a street for Christmas decorations, it was probably just wood for another coffin.

"Why didn't Jake come to church?" Tommy asked her, pulling her out of her thoughts.

"He's Jewish, sweetheart. He goes to a different church."

Tommy nodded, accepting this new information without question.

"You like him?" Meg asked, knowing it might be too soon for Tommy to have formed an opinion.

Tommy shrugged. "He made Luke angry."

"You heard that?" Meg frowned, wondering what else he had heard.

Tommy nodded. "Luke's a rat bastard," he said seriously, borrowing a colorful term from his mother.

Meg smirked. "Wherever did you pick up such language?"

Chapter 7

Perhaps it was the smell of the burning pies or the wailing of Judith's baby, but Meg was wound tighter than a spring. She pulled the pies out of the oven and almost dropped the tray as she bumped into Bess' arse. Jostled, Bess dropped the long spoon into the bubbling pot of stew.

"Piss!" she cursed, searching for something to use to fish it out.

Another burning smell filled the room after the smoke from the pies had dissipated.

"Bess," Judith shouted over the baby, "Bess!"

Bess cursed as she burned her fingers on the stew. The spoon dropped back into the pot and Bess sucked on her fingers, her face flushed with pain.

Meg threw open the back door to clear the smoke in time to see a gull swoop in to snatch a piece of bread out of Tommy's hand. Shocked, her mild-mannered little boy let out such a stream of foul language that she would have been surprised had she not known precisely where he'd heard it. As she turned to grab him another piece, Bess emitted a scream so close to her face that it rattled Meg's skull. Flames licked at Bess' ankles, rising toward her knees.

"Your skirt's on fire!" Judith held the baby with both arms, unable to help apart from stating the obvious in an increasingly high pitched voice.

"We can see that!" Meg stomped on the hem as Bess screamed her face off. "Untie it!" Meg commanded her.

Oblivious to the drama inside, Tommy moaned. "Mum, he's eating it on the roof! He's trying to wind me up! Bastard seagull."

Judith shifted the baby to one hip, grabbed the nearest broom, and swatted at Bess' skirt as it fell away from her hips. No sooner had Bess dashed away than the dry bristles of Judith's broom went up like kindling. She waved it about madly, looking for a safe place to drop it.

Meg grabbed the mop bucket and thrust it at Judith, casting filthy water across the stone floor. "Damnation!"

Tommy noticed the commotion in the kitchen and turned away from the taunting seagull. He took off his hat and waved it through the smoke, which only fanned the fire eating up Bess' skirt. Bare-legged and ruffled, Bess pumped another bucket of fresh water and ran with it into the kitchen. She threw it onto the fire and missed most of it, but succeeded in soaking Meg from the waist down.

When Jake walked in, the kitchen smelled of two distinct kinds of smoke. The floor was covered in filthy water and ashes, and both Judith and the baby were screaming. Bess was half naked, Meg held her skirt around her hips and stomped on the burning skirt with soggy stockings slipping down over her knees. The broom in Judith's hand burned like a torch, and the spoon was still at the bottom of the stew.

Tommy cursed from the garden as the seagull dropped a chunk of the bread onto his head.

For a split second, Meg was acutely aware of how ridiculous her life must look to him. After thirty-five years living in it, she had stopped noticing the absurdity. A sinking feeling that might have been shame weighed down her gut, and she banished it with anger.

She had *nothing* to be ashamed of.

Jake didn't miss a beat. He pointed Judith toward the door, took the flaming broom from her hand and extinguished it in the puddle on the floor. He kicked the skirt into the same puddle, opened the window, and set the pies beneath it. Taking up a mop, he set to work on the floor while Meg clutched her dripping skirt, blinking away the smoke in her eyes.

Bess smacked her own forehead as she remembered. "The spoon! It's still in the pot."

Without slowing, Jake plucked a set of tongs off the hook on the wall and handed them to her.

Bess pulled the spoon from the pot without further incident and took it outside to wash.

As the mop brushed Meg's toes, she realized he had run out of floor space and she would have to move. Without asking, he took her hips in his hands and set her on the edge of the table.

She was too dumbstruck to complain. He cleaned the last of the floor and tossed the remains of Bess' skirt onto the scrap heap. Everything had been undone as quickly as it had happened, and there was little evidence left to suggest it happened at all.

Except for Bess being half-naked, that is. "Mind if I borrow a dress, Meg?" she called from the doorway.

Meg nodded, distracted.

Jake tossed the mop water into the back garden and took over stirring for Bess with a new spoon.

Order restored, Tommy snuck in and stole two rolls from the basket.

"Tommy, run and get your aunt a skirt from my room."

"Yes, Mum," he replied, his voice muffled as he shoved a roll into his mouth.

Jake bent over the pot, stirring in silence. He had just put out a fire and prevented any number of humiliating horrors, but he was still remarkably composed while she probably looked like she'd been caught in a storm. His hair was neat and freshly washed, his clothes were clean, and he didn't smell remotely like liquor. He was about as far away from a local as he could be. Did he feel as uncomfortable being here as Meg did, watching him wade through the mire that was her life?

The silence was deafening. Meg tested her suspicion. "Itching to leave yet?"

♥

Jake frowned over the stew. "Tired of me already?" he asked, only half-joking. Meg had been short with him since the night before and he couldn't think why, unless he'd made some mistake she didn't want to point out.

"You've been here all of two days and you're already putting out fires. Can't be what you expected."

His employment had been so sudden that he'd not had time to form any expectations about it. Granted, he'd never walked into a room that was both burning and flooded before. He shrugged. "I'm sure it's not like this every day."

"It is exactly like this every day." Meg's voice was so soft, he might have imagined it. Heavy with resignation, it said more about the state of affairs than words ever could. He turned to see if she needed comforting, and had to catch himself from falling backward into the pot.

Meg still sat on the table where he'd left her, her damp skirt hiked up around her hips. With one heel balanced on the edge, she rolled a sodden blue stocking over her knee and down her calf, tugged it off her foot, and flung it across the kitchen. As she stretched out her bare leg--there seemed to be miles of it--and pulled her other heel up to remove the stocking, he caught a fascinating shadow between her lush thighs and wondered, briefly, if she wore anything at all beneath that skirt.

His blood surged downward so quickly he felt the room spin. His gaze ate up every inch of exposed flesh from her ankle over her bent knee to the smooth expanse of her inner thigh. *Verdomme.* Her skin was white as cream; would it taste as sweet? He licked his lips, curious.

If she knew he was looking, she gave no indication. Her every movement was efficient and unselfconscious, as if she'd forgotten he was even there. The stocking made a wet, sucking sound as she yanked it off her toes. She curled her lips in disgust and lobbed it across the room.

Meg Henshawe was surly, unkempt, immodest, and utterly charming.

Her eyebrows drew together as she caught him looking. "What?"

Jake shook his head, trying to banish the thought of his mouth on her thighs. "Nothing." He cleared his throat. "Are you cold?"

She studied him with pursed lips and he wondered if she could see through his skin to the degenerate lurking inside. He turned back toward the pot before she noticed how tight his trousers were fitting. He let out a long breath as he stirred the stew, trying to think of anything else.

"Warm, if anything," she said, distracted.

Bess' voice rang through the kitchen from the doorway. "I'm freezing my fanny off. Do you mind if I come inside?"

The flesh of her exposed hip was so white it was almost violet, and iridescent as a pearl. Not at all the shade a living woman should be. Meg eyed him warily, and he realized they must be waiting for his response. "By all means. I won't look."

Bess rushed inside gratefully and took the chair nearest the fire, rubbing her bare knees over her stockings. Oddly enough, he didn't have the same reaction to seeing her legs, and rather more of her was exposed. She tugged her short chemise down over her lap as far as it would go, but there was no disguising the fact she was not wearing undergarments. "Christ wept, that was close. You'd have had to send me home in a box." Her voice caught as she giggled with nervous relief. "All I need is something to cover my bits and we'll be in business. Tommy's taking his time, isn't he?"

She was clearly uncomfortable. Without thinking twice, Jake tugged his shirt over his head and offered it to her.

Bess made no move to take it, but stared at him in stunned silence.

"It's clean." He shrugged.

With a little snap of her head, she reached out and took it. "Cheers. You don't need it?"

The chill of the December air pricked his chest while his back tingled in the heat of the fire. "You keep it until Tommy returns."

Bess tucked it around her lap like a blanket and it covered her almost to her feet. "I don't know that Meg'll let me give it back." She gave a particularly dirty laugh.

His eyes darted to Meg, all but draped over the table. She leaned back on the heels of her hands, her gaze focused just south of his navel. He could almost feel it as it slowly climbed his chest, bright and hot as the hearth at his back. As their eyes met, her expression was more fearful than inviting. He lifted his eyebrows and she squirmed.

Interesting.

"Do I pass muster?" he kidded, acknowledging her appraisal.

She bit her lip, a little line appearing between her eyebrows as they drew together.

Bess cackled. "She's never been this quiet in her life. Can you stay awhile?"

Meg lobbed a rag at the back of Bess' head, flushing a brilliant scarlet. Bess squealed as it slapped the back of her neck, and she bubbled over with laughter. She threw it back at Meg, but Meg caught it easily. "I'm thinking, is all," Meg insisted.

Jake crossed his arms over his chest.

Her gaze met his for the briefest of moments before she looked away. "You might be what we need to bring more women in to drink."

Jake frowned. It probably wasn't a good sign if the sight of him made her think of drink.

The baby's cry announced Judith's return to the kitchen. She rushed in, wild-eyed, as though the hounds of hell snapped at her heels. "Meg--"

A portly man followed Judith into the kitchen and all but shoved her aside in his haste.

His took in the scene in the kitchen with barely contained revulsion; Meg's bare legs hanging off the table, the shirt wrapped around Bess' hips, the fading violet bruises that spotted Jake's naked torso. The room was a mess, the pies were burnt, and God only knew what it looked like the three of them had been doing.

Meg's mouth dropped open, her face whiter than death. "Davey!"

The tense silence was broken by Tommy skidding into the man with a skirt streaming behind his fist like a flag.

The man shot Tommy a poisonous look before aiming the full force of his ire at Meg. "When you've dressed yourself, I'll be waiting for you outside."

Chapter 8

Meg charged out into the street to find her cousin standing in front of the inn, pointing at the sign. She'd known he would darken her door after his lackey had been by, but she'd never dreamed it would be so soon. He gave some direction to a painter who then climbed a ladder propped against the side of the inn with a bucket and brush in his hand.

"Stop," she commanded with such force that the painter dropped the brush. It bounced off of Davey's wide-brimmed hat and fell into the ditch.

Davey greeted her with a tight smile, his gaze following the low curve of her neckline. "Meg, how lovely to see you. You're looking...well."

"Spare me the shit, Davey. What in God's name do you think you are doing?"

All but forgotten, the painter cowered at the top of the ladder.

Davey crossed his arms across his flabby chest, his jowls tinged pink beneath his patchy stubble. "I was most distressed to hear you had been obliged to run this place on your own since my uncle's death, but never fear, good cousin. I am come to relieve you of your plight."

Her father had been dead for years and they hadn't heard a

word from Davey about it. How had he found out? "Plight, hell! This is my inn and you've got no right to be here. Piss off or you'll find yourself at the bottom of the bloody river."

She felt Jake's presence as he stepped behind her. The look Davey cast over her shoulder was arrogance tempered with fear.

He opened his mouth in feigned shock, his soft-looking lips more suited to an infant than a grown man. "I think you'll find this is my inn, cousin." He produced a letter from inside his coat and held it open for Meg. "Forgive me, I suppose you can't read. Allow me to assist. Your father sold me the inn."

Meg almost laughed at the absurdity of this statement. She snatched the letter out of his hand. "Of course I can read," she snapped, and did just that.

I, Charles David Henshawe, being of sound mind and body, relinquish The Rose and Crown to my nephew, David, upon my death for the sum of ten guineas…

Ten guineas.

Her father had sold the bar, and he'd done it for the pathetic sum of *ten guineas.*

Meg's stomach lurched and she felt as though she might faint. Was it possible to die of horror?

The fool just kept right on talking. "I settled some of your father's debts years ago and in return, he agreed to give me the inn at the time of his death."

Meg shook her head. "It's ours. He had no sons, so everything was divided equally between the five of us."

"Everything but the inn," he insisted, his smile stretching into his jowls. "The inn is mine, as is the wardship of you and your unmarried sisters, of course. I will being seeing to your welfare from this day forward."

A hundred ways to murder him filled her mind so quickly that she came up blank, torn between choking him and chasing him into the river. Heat flooded her cheeks and she heard her heart hammering in her ears.

A big hand settled at the base of her spine, more of a pleasant distraction than anything else.

Davey's eyelid twitched as he glared at Jake, sizing him up for a fight he was certain to lose. "Who are you?"

"I'm Jake Cohen," he asserted in a calm voice, pulling himself up to his full formidable height. "I work here."

Davey snorted his laugh. "Yes, I believe I get the idea of what my feather-brained cousins keep you for. I suppose I should be grateful there's a man here to keep them in line."

If Meg's blood was any hotter, she would have melted all of the snow for yards. "I am thirty-five years old, you swine. I've been all but running this place for twenty years. If you think you'll be seeing to my welfare, you're in for a surprise. I'll see you into a box before I take orders from you. Leave."

He sniffed, looking down his piggish nose at her. "As you wish, but if I leave here, I'll be returning with a magistrate. I have more copies of that letter, and I think you'll find the sale quite legal. You can stay here and work for me, if you wish, or I'll toss the lot of you out on your arses."

Terror gripped her heart. She had nowhere to go. Her home and her job were one and the same, and her whole family depended on the inn. Bess and Bel were both kept by their lovers, but Meg, Judith, Tommy, and the baby would be homeless with no prospects in the dead of winter. She'd be forced to walk the streets to feed her son. No doubt half the town would love to see her brought so low.

She jumped at the sound of Jake's voice. In her distress, she had almost forgotten he was there. "There's no need for that. The girls run a good business here, and you'd do well to keep them on. Meg does the work of three men, easily, and you'll not find a replacement half as competent anywhere. I'm sure we can come to an agreement."

Meg gaped at him. How could the man be so calm? Couldn't he see her life was over? "Agreement?"

Davey ignored her and addressed Jake. "Coyne, was it?"

"Cohen."

"I've heard that name before." He frowned. "It's not Hebrew…?"

"It is." For all he sounded calm, he was clearly on his guard. Of all the people Meg would like to see him hit…

"You're a bit of a brute, aren't you?" Davey laughed. "I don't suppose they're keeping you for your face. Very well, I could use a man's help with these harridans. And Hebrew, as well! You take care of the money and the day-to-day, and the girls will answer to you."

Meg opened her mouth to protest that Jake had only been there two days and hadn't the slightest idea of what went into managing an inn, but her words were cut off.

"Done."

A knife to the heart would have been quicker. Twenty years of running this place on her own and he gave the care of it to a man who'd been there *two days*? She'd burn this place to the ground before she let Davey have it.

As they shook on it, Davey warned Jake, "From now on, if you want to avail yourself of any of my cousins, you'll pay me for the privilege."

"Fat bloody chance." Meg turned on her heel and charged back toward the bar.

♥

Jake found her in the kitchen, trying to start a fire on the floor. Fortunately, most of the room was still too damp to catch. "Meg."

"Bloody traitor," she snapped. "I hope you like running the day-to-day for a heap of ashes!"

His leg screamed in pain as he knelt beside her. She smacked him as he took the smoldering rushes from her hands, her face streaked with anguish. He threw them into the mop bucket and caught her flying hands. She struggled against his grip, so he gathered her to his chest in an embrace he hoped was calming. He ran a hand down her back. "Nothing has changed," he whispered in her ear. "I'll do whatever you say until we decide what to do. It's going to be all right."

She pulled away far enough to look at his face, searching for a lie. "Why?"

"I said I'd protect you."

She sniffed, her eyes glassy with the promise of tears. "You don't know me."

He shrugged. "You took me in when I had nowhere to go. Perhaps we can help each other."

The quiver of her lip was all the warning he had before her rage gave way to despair and she collapsed against his chest. He waited for the tears, but they never came. The only hint she was upset was a faint hitch in her breath.

He didn't know how long he held her there, on his knees on the kitchen floor. He knew what it was to lose home and livelihood at the same time, and he wouldn't wish that pain on his worst enemy, let alone a woman like Meg. At least she still had her family. He had lost that, too.

He wrapped his arms around her back so she would feel supported from all sides. It was a desperate gesture. Who was he to her, anyway? He barely knew her, but surely kindness from a near-stranger was better than none at all.

He'd been alone when his world had fallen apart.

Her cheek fit neatly into the hollow beneath his collarbone and he was struck quite suddenly by how remarkable it felt to hold a woman in his arms again. He'd been with plenty, but he never got to just hold anyone. Her back was long, graceful, and obviously strong, and her hair smelled of roses and myrrh. The way her soft, warm curves pressed against his chest and his belly had him wondering how they'd feel under him.

Disgusted with himself, he let her go. He could see why so many men made fools of themselves over her. Everything about her was so perfectly, exaggeratedly feminine that God could have made woman in *her* image. He would have gladly donated a rib.

She sat back on her heels, looking faintly dazed. She pinched the bridge of her nose, and all hint of impending tears was gone. "Day's not a complete disaster. I got to feel that chest of yours for myself," she kidded.

He almost smiled. The way he remembered it, he'd been the one doing the feeling. He opened his arms to her. "Got to be worth something. I'll let you feel anything you'd like if it'll make you smile."

As soon as he uttered it, he realized how lascivious the offer sounded and regretted it. He'd only meant to tease her in kind, but had inadvertently spat out the truth. He cringed inwardly. *Why not ask her if she's wearing knickers, while you're at it?*

After a moment of stunned silence, she laughed abruptly and stood. "Don't tempt me, Jake."

His leg shook as he tried to stand, his knee buckling as soon as he shifted his weight onto it. "*Kut*," he muttered, clenching his teeth.

Meg's hand appeared in front of his face, lily white and work roughened. He took it and allowed her to help him up, holding it for a perhaps a beat longer than necessary. She took her hand back and tucked a long strand of hair behind her ear. "Where's Davey now?"

Jake blinked, trying to remember who she was talking about. Oh right, the cousin. "He's moving some things in upstairs. He wanted your room, but I talked him into taking the vacant one at the top. I suggested it was bigger, and that was all he needed."

As she cocked her head and studied him, he felt as though he was being tested. "That room has a view of a cesspit."

Jake shrugged. "I told him it's quieter facing away from the street."

The mischievous grin Meg gave him felt like a gift. "You do catch on, don't you? Perhaps we can pull this off. We could use more help around here."

Chapter 9

"*Heb je enig bedden?*"

The sound of Dutch being spoken was so out of place, Jake thought he'd imagined it. Many languages were spoken around the docks, but it felt like an age since he'd heard anything other than English or French.

"I'm sorry, what was that?"

"*Heb je enig…* bed? *Een bed?*"

Judith's sigh reached him from the end of the bar. "A bed? You're looking for a room?"

Jake finished pouring Davey's eighth glass of the good wine and left it for him at the edge of the bar. He'd only known the man half a day and he was already tired of him. If he insisted on drinking the best without paying for it, he could bloody well come get it himself.

"*Alstublieft, twee bedden voor de kinderen.*"

"You've lost me," Judith muttered, looking hopelessly around the bar.

Across from her, a young family with two small children looked ready to drop from exhaustion. "*Goedeavond,*" he greeted them. "They want a room with two beds," he explained to Judith.

"Davey took the last room we had free," she grumbled,

shooting daggers at her cousin's corpulent form roasting in their best chair beside the fire.

He grimaced. "I'm sorry, we have no free rooms," he told them in Dutch.

The woman looked ready to weep. The youngest child slept draped over her shoulder, while the older one looked up at Jake with sorrowful blue eyes.

"Could we stay the night here in your bar?" the man begged. "We have come a very long way and my wife is unwell. We won't be any trouble."

He translated this for Judith and added, "Let them have my room. It's cold, but it's better than nothing. I'll stay down here."

Judith shook her head and set her jaw. "Mine's the only one with two beds. Me and Pea can sleep in Tommy's room tonight. Tell them to give me a minute to clean it." Without waiting for his answer, she marched up the stairs.

"We're going to make room for you," Jake assured them. "Judith is cleaning a room for you now."

The man's shoulders dropped in relief. "You are kind."

"Are you hungry?"

"Famished."

"We'll have something brought up to your room. You make yourselves comfortable and let us know if there is anything you need."

As Judith returned to lead the family up the stairs, Jake felt a sense of satisfaction he'd thought was gone for good. It had been years since he'd been able to help someone in any meaningful way. Sure, he'd helped people win money, and he'd helped people lose it. He'd helped a good few rearrange their faces, but he hadn't been able to offer anyone comfort in quite some time.

The smell of roses and myrrh floated past him and he remembered holding Meg on the floor of the kitchen hours before.

Well, not in a *professional* sense, that is.

"You're rather useful, aren't you?" She asked from behind his elbow.

He turned to find her filling two large glasses of ale to add to a tray of food that seemed to come out of nowhere. The idea of his being useful warmed him more than words could say. He smiled. "I do what I can."

"May have to keep you around." She took the tray and headed to the stairs.

"Is that for them already?" he asked. "That was fast."

She shrugged one shoulder. "It was for someone else, but I reckon he can wait." She winked and went up.

Jake watched her until she disappeared. When he turned back toward the bar, Davey was frowning at him. "Where's she gone with my supper?"

"Yours is still coming," he assured him, biting his lip to hide his smile.

Davey settled deeper into the chair, muttering to himself. Right there in front of the fire was the warmest spot in the bar and he'd been holding it for hours. They had nailed a blanket over the shattered window, but the cold still seeped inside until even the drunks were shivering.

When Judith returned from showing the guest to her room, she went straight back into the kitchen, and Jake couldn't blame her. He wouldn't say no to a few minutes beside the fire. He wasn't looking forward to trying to keep warm in his room without a serviceable hearth.

Happy to have been some use, Jake busied himself with cleaning up the bar and serving customers. The supper rush was long since over, but those who worked longer hours were still bringing their families in to eat. He served a dockworker, his wife, and six children, and called into the kitchen for bread for them. They clearly weren't well off, but the bread would hold them over until morning.

When Meg brought it out, he watched her serve it to them,

and he wasn't the only one.

"What will a crown get me?"

Jake reluctantly pulled his gaze away from Meg's downcast eyes long enough to address another man that had appeared beside the bar without him noticing. His sleeves were pushed up and his arms were colored a murky green up to the elbows, a telltale sign of a dye-house worker. "Most anything. Supper, ale, beer, wine, gin. Take your pick."

The man gave a suggestive laugh. "I fancy something sweet for my pudding, if you get my meaning." He nodded toward Meg. "I hear this one can perform miracles for a crown."

Jake swallowed the bile that rose in his throat. "She's not for sale."

"Very amusing." The man tapped his coin on the bar impatiently. "Meg's been renting out her front room since I was in school. My money's good as yours."

He crossed his arms. "She's not for sale."

Either he didn't hear the warning in Jake's voice or he chose to ignore it. He laughed and leaned in. "Don't be a glutton. There's enough of that arse to go around, isn't there? I'll give it to her in one end and you can take the other. Don't matter which. Come on, mate. Half of bloody London's already beat you to it. What's one more?"

Without thinking, Jake reached out, grabbed the man's hair and slammed his face into the bar. The impact of bone colliding with wood made such a resounding smack that it drew the attention of every person standing within a few yards of the bar, including Meg.

The man stood, clutching his bloody nose with a stunned look on his face. "Mad bastard!"

Jake shrugged. He didn't feel mad. The response had been automatic, as easy and obvious as pulling on a pair of trousers in the morning. "Piss off."

He clambered off the bar, cursing all the way. The punters in his wake turned to Jake with guarded alarm, as though he'd turned into a bear and they'd only just noticed.

Meg darted to his side, her face flushed and looking more distressed than the man he had injured. "What in God's name was that?" she whispered frantically.

Jake shot a look of disgust toward the door. "He tried to buy you."

"You do realize we're molls?" Meg's hands rose to her hips. "Men might try to pay for us from time to time."

Jake felt his jaw tightening. If brokering the Henshawe sisters was to be one of his new duties, he didn't have the stomach for it. "Should I have taken his money and sent you off with him like a bloody pimp? Is that what you want?"

She colored, clearly uncomfortable. "No."

"Tell me what you want, Meg."

Her neck flushed and she fidgeted with her hair. Hadn't anyone asked her to before? She crossed her arms, looking torn between anger and tears. "I don't want to do it anymore," she blurted. "Not for you, not for Davey, not for anyone. But that's up to me, do you understand? I'll not have you making decisions for me. You ask me next time."

"You want me to ask you before assaulting men who disrespect you?"

She blinked. "Yeah. Well, not always. Use your judgment."

He smiled.

She started to smile back before she caught herself. "You don't own me," she asserted. "You don't get to push me around."

"I'd never try," he pledged, surprised by her reaction. "But if someone talks about you like that, I'm going to break their nose."

Her eyes widened in surprise. He could almost believe she was not accustomed to men standing up for her. "Good." She gave his shoulder a playful push on her way back into the kitchen.

Jake had heard legends of Meg's prowess for years. He didn't have to like it, but he accepted it. Most women he'd met from the lowest classes had been strumpets, at some point in their lives. There were sixteen brothels between Bear Gardens and The Rose and Crown, and they were always full to capacity of willing women. He wouldn't look down on her for it, but if she didn't want to do it anymore, he would make it clear to all and sundry that they would have to find their entertainment elsewhere.

If Davey said otherwise, he'd make it clear to him, too.

"--cripple."

The word, overheard, startled him to the present. Had someone noticed his limp?

Jake looked around the bar until he found the conversation in the least likely of places. The dockworker's family was finishing their dinner beneath the broken window. The eldest of their children, a slight lad perhaps a little older than Meg's boy, was in tears. He sat awkwardly on a bench, his left leg extended and unnaturally stiff.

"Docks won't take him. He'd drown if he fell in." the boy's father said, not unsympathetically.

His mother smoothed his hair over his freckled forehead affectionately. "Carpentry is out. We'll never get the money together to apprentice him to a tailor."

The father, himself a large dock worker, shook his head. "Can't afford to apprentice him to anyone, love."

"I don't want to beg," the boy sobbed.

His mother hugged him close. "I know, darling. We'll think of something."

If his leg was useless, the boy would be fortunate to get any work at all. With no money for skilled training, he'd likely die a beggar. His disability might inspire generosity, but London had countless beggars who were worse off. Missing eyes and teeth, with scabies, scrofula, or leprosy, their lives were miserable and short. Seemed a harsh fate for a boy with a busted leg.

Jake was across the bar before he realized what he was doing. "Boy."

The boy and his family looked up, surprised.

Jake looked him over as if to size him up. "How old are you?"

The boy wiped his nose. "Twelve."

Jake nodded. "What's your name?"

"Chris Cooper."

"How'd you like to work here for a while? The girls could use the help. You could come by in the day and we'll show you how to keep a bar, help out in the kitchen. What do you reckon?"

Chris' face lit up and his parents looked close to tears themselves. "Really?"

Jake nodded sharply. "You'll have to keep up. We'll not take it easy on you."

The boy grinned. "Yes, sir. Thank you, sir."

"We can't pay you," his mother protested meekly.

Jake shrugged. "I should think not. Not an apprenticeship, so we'll pay him. Imagine you could use the money."

That did it. His mother wept tears of gratitude. Chris' father stood and enfolded Jake in a firm embrace. "I can't thank you enough. Kit Cooper," he introduced himself.

After he introduced himself to the Coopers, Kit cocked his head, trying to place him. "Have I seen you somewhere before?"

Jake nodded. No one seemed to recognize him with his clothes on. "Yeah."

They arranged for Chris to come by the following day to begin work at the bar. Jake wasn't altogether certain how much work the boy would be able to do, but he wanted to get a look at his leg. Leg injuries were something he knew a bit about, and if he could build his strength and walk after what had happened to him, perhaps Chris Cooper could, too.

He had barely made it back behind the bar before he felt the hard tug on his shirt. Meg pulled him forcefully into the shadow of the storage cupboard and pushed him up against the shelves. She was remarkably strong for a woman. "Who do you think you are?"

He blinked, surprised by her obvious anger. Her cheeks were flushed, her eyes were bright, and her chignon was lopsided. She was quite breathless. Her hands were on his chest, her breasts pressed against him in the cramped cupboard. Far from intimidating, he found her fury strangely arousing. His hands found themselves resting on her hips. *To keep her at a safe distance*, he told himself, ignoring the wicked whispers in his mind.

She looked as though she was ready to scratch his eyes out. "First you break Pat McCormack's nose, and now you've hired the Cooper boy?"

His gaze rested on her parted lips, and he was overcome with the desire to kiss the rage right out of her. He licked his lips, tempted. "Pay the boy out of my wages," he said huskily. "You said you wanted help. No one should be forced to beg."

Her anger diffused into something else entirely. Caught somewhere between confusion and contrition, her eyebrows drew together. She was in his arms now. Either she hadn't noticed, or she didn't mind. "This is my inn," she protested firmly.

"I am at your command," he agreed, quite breathless himself.

Her gaze softened, the cold emerald melting into a warmer shade of bottle green. Remarkable. He felt his cheek quirk in an involuntary smile.

Meg flushed a brilliant shade of scarlet. "Don't forget it," she sputtered, slipping out of his grasp and back into the bar.

The door swung shut beside her, and he was grateful for the darkness as he took a long breath and tried to get himself back under control.

Jake could still smell her after she was gone. Myrrh, roses, and rage.

He smiled.

Chapter 10

Safely contained in her room, Meg stabbed at the coal in her fireplace, displacing a layer of ash to reveal the amber glow beneath.

Even when the flames were extinguished at The Rose, they raged on in her breast, consuming everything in her path without prejudice. She thought she would have accepted her lot in life after nearly four decades of thankless toil, but try as she might, she could not make peace with it. Her life was lived in halves; she had the responsibility of running the inn without the security of owning it or the ability to sell it. She had children without the comfort of marriage, and all the sex she could wish for without a hint of love.

The older she got, the less likely it was she would ever have the kind of life she wanted; a home, a husband, the chance to raise her own children. She was not the sort of woman men married. Men married women like Jane Virtue.

Meg propped the poker against the wall, fighting tears of frustration. Jake's reaction to Pat McCormack trying to buy her had shocked her out of her acceptance of her situation and had forced her to take another look at her life. He had reacted violently, and he was right to. The question she'd been asking herself all night was, *why didn't she?*

She had long since learned her only real commodity was her beauty. While that in itself hadn't been enough to inspire anybody to marry her, she had used her only weapon to build a life for herself and her family. People came from far and wide to see her for themselves, a fact she took no little pride in, but it was only the best of the worst situation.

Meg was bloody tired.

There were only so many doomed love affairs a woman could be expected to weather before she threw in the towel for good. Now when she took men to bed, it was because she fancied them, not because she needed the money, and certainly not because she wanted anything from them. She had been disappointed too many times to put her faith in anyone but herself.

Meg tugged the laces loose down the front of her dress and pulled it off, tossing it over the foot of her bed. She filled her basin with rose water and washed her face in it, splashing it over her neck, her breasts, and under her arms. She yanked the pins from her high chignon and her hair tumbled down her back in heavy waves. She had been too busy to look after it properly and it had gotten bloody long, brushing her arse when it wasn't tied up. Feeling a knot the size of a lump of coal near her shoulder, Meg grabbed her shell comb and set to work untangling the whole mess.

Once she had finished, she blew out the candle beside her mirror and climbed into bed. The fire was burning steadily now, casting the room in a mellow, warm glow. She pulled the coverlet up to her chin and turned toward the wall, making a mental list of everything she had to do the next day. Tommy was safely tucked into his bed upstairs, and Meg said a silent prayer of thanks that her son was as serious and responsible as he was.

Meg heard Jake's door close softly through the wall. She hadn't been very pleasant to him, she knew. All he'd done was try to help out the Coopers, but it had felt like he was taking over the bar in earnest and she'd given him a hard time.

Hating herself for doing it, she opened her eyes.

Through the crack, she could see Jake milling about his room alone. She'd half-expected him to have company. A man like him would have no shortage of invitations.

His hearth was cold and his room lit by a few candles in his window. He pulled his shirt over his head, ruffling his short, dark hair. Meg shuddered at the sight of his bare back. A study in shadow and light, the long muscles were so elegantly formed that he could have been sculpted by a master in marble but for their subtle play beneath his skin. He poured fresh water into the basin on his dressing table and splashed his face. His hair curled as he ran his damp hands through it, and she wished she was running her hands through it, too.

Meg let out a long breath. She knew she shouldn't be spying, but she couldn't bring herself to look away.

A sharp knock sounded at her door. He looked up as he heard it.

"Meg…" Luke Leighton called, scratching at the wood like a cat.

She cringed. Who had let him back in? She closed her eyes and pretended to sleep, as if Luke could feel her deception through the door.

"I'm sorry for last night, I was beastly. I've missed you. Open the door, darling."

Meg threw her arm over her eyes. "Piss off."

"There's no need to be rude. I've forgiven you for all the nasty things you said to me. Would you show me a little…kindness?"

She screwed up her face and raised her voice. "I'll show you my bloody foot in a moment! Leave!"

"Come along, Meg, have mercy! My bollocks are bloody indigo out here. I won't be long, I swear."

If her cheeks burned any hotter with humiliation she would have set her bed alight. "Your miserable bollocks are not my concern! Fuck off and have a wank!"

She heard a thunk as Luke's head hit the door. "Don't be like that. You can't expect to wear what you do and be left alone. Your cousin said--"

The already high level of rage Meg barely contained at all times reached boiling point. She leapt out of bed and threw open the door so quickly that Luke lost his balance and stumbled face first into her stays. She grabbed him by his collar and gave him a shake. "Listen here, little boy. The only person you need to trouble yourself with is me, and I said no. It is not my *duty* to fuck you. Now piss off before I toss you out the bloody window. I can't afford to replace another one."

He pulled away from her grasp and threw his wiry arms up, caught between outrage and fear. There was a time she had preferred her lovers younger than she was as they were unmarried and eager to please, but seeing Luke standing there in the hallway, looking as though he was trying to decide whether or not he ought to strike her, she wondered what she had been thinking. He was in his early twenties, but he seemed younger still, a shadow of a man. Had he always been so insignificant, or was it just that she was comparing him to Jake?

"You wouldn't do that," he challenged her.

"I would." Jake said pleasantly as he stepped into the hallway and closed his door behind him.

Luke cowered and backed away. Jake was perhaps a foot taller than he was and had a few stone of muscle on him, all of which was plainly visible as he hadn't bothered to put his shirt back on.

Jake didn't advance. He didn't have to. He nodded to Luke as if passing an acquaintance on the street and to Meg's sincere surprise, slipped past her into her room, snaking an arm around her waist. Meg smiled at Luke's look of shock and flipped him two fingers before she kicked the door shut in his face.

"Bloody Jew," she heard him mutter through the door.

Jake heard it, too. He stiffened behind her and dropped his arm, putting some distance between them.

She went for the door, ready to give Luke a piece of her mind.

"Don't bother," Jake said quietly. "It's not an insult."

"He meant it as one."

"I won't take it as such. It's not unlike me pointing out he's English, or an abject wanker. Not so much an insult as a statement of fact."

Meg's giggle stopped cold as she turned to face him. He stood before her window, nearly nude and utterly unapologetic about that fact. He was more than beautiful, he was *devastating.* A dusting of dark hair covered his broad, hard chest and the taut ridges of his belly, a pair of loose breeches hanging off of the V-shape of his hips.

She forced her gaze away from where the line of hair on his belly led into his breeches and met his eyes. "You were serious about keeping their hands off my tits," she said with some surprise, and her voice sounded strained even to her.

He nodded, giving no indication he had noticed her looking. "You asked him to leave and he wouldn't. Nothing a man respects like the claim of another man."

Anger flaring up again, Meg rolled her eyes so hard her face hurt. "Can't you respect the word of a woman?"

He crossed his arms over his chest. "I can. Can't speak for the others."

She sat on the edge of her bed, feeling oddly shy having him in her room. He was far from the first man she'd had in there, but something about his size made the room feel smaller. It wasn't just that he was bigger than most men, but his very presence was somehow larger than life. He seemed more vital, more alive than anyone else she'd ever met. Meg was not a small woman, but next to him, she felt positively fragile, and as feminine as a box of ribbons. A man like him could break her in half.

Meg tried to pull her shift up beneath her stays. She felt

suddenly very exposed. "I suppose you think I ought to keep these covered up."

He shook his head. "What you wear is your concern."

She certainly thought so. "With tits the size of mine, can't help people seeing them."

The muscle in his shoulder rolled as he shrugged. "You could pour drinks stark naked and they'd not have the right to touch you."

Meg blinked.

He held her eyes with a level gaze. He didn't budge, made no move to touch her. Yes, she had hired him to protect her, but she never would have asked him to scare off tiresome lovers. Why had he bothered?

"What's your game, Jake?" She narrowed her eyes, suspicious from experience.

"Got to have a game, do I?" he asked, clearly insulted. "Thought I'd stand here awhile in case the boy tries to come back. You want me to leave?"

"Don't." Meg shook her head. "I could have handled him."

Jake's cheek quirked in a half smile. "I know."

"You're humoring me."

"I most certainly am not."

They stared at each other for a long moment, the only sound in the room the crackle of the fire.

He cleared his throat. "May I sit by your fire for a bit? The hearth next door needs cleaning. It smokes…"

"Of course," she blurted, dismayed to hear she had inadvertently given him the only room in the inn without a serviceable hearth. It was December and punishingly cold; he'd catch his death without a source of heat. One more thing to sort out in the morning.

He sat on the floor in front of the hearth, between Meg and the door. If anyone else came to bother her, he'd be the first to send them on their way. Not that they'd try now. She gave it until morning before the whole of Southwark heard that Luke Leighton had seen Jake Cohen in Meg's bedroom. If the men in town thought she'd made a conquest of the prize fighter who kept her bar, they'd keep their distance for fear of their lives.

Meg smiled at Jake's turned back. She didn't even mind. She'd like it if they thought she could catch a man like Jake. Better yet, she'd like it to be true. Watching the slight rise and fall of his back, she thought of all the times she'd seen him fight. She had always liked boxers, and Jake in particular, but she had caught Tom's eye first and it was Tom she had taken up with. How different would things be if she had set her sights on Jake?

She was beginning to suspect hiring Jake was one of the cleverest things she'd done, and she didn't want to ruin things by throwing herself at a man who didn't want her. Besides, she didn't know if he had a woman somewhere, or how he'd treat her if he did. The last thing she needed was another fighter using her as a punching bag.

She touched her nose self-consciously. No one else had noticed the break. The only other person who knew Tom had hit her was Joe Ledford, and he had been so deep in his cups that it'd be a miracle if he remembered it at all.

Feeling the weight of her wasted years, she sighed.

Luke wouldn't come back. Bess would be locking up by now, and Jake would have no reason to linger apart from the fire. She'd be alone again before long, trying not to look through the crack in the wall.

Telling herself it was the only the chill that drove her there, Meg sat beside him on the floor. They sat in silence for several long moments until Meg said, "I'm sorry about earlier."

"You don't have to apologize to me," he replied, his eyes on the fire. "I know why you were cross."

Did he? No one had ever treated her anger as anything other than madness. Meg's gaze followed the long line that curved around his shoulder and over his bicep to his elbow resting on his knee. She had no doubt she had been angry, but looking at him, she couldn't for the life of her remember why. "You're not like other men, are you?"

He looked at her, his dark eyes warming her more thoroughly than the fire. "Disappointed?"

She shook her head. *Not in the slightest.* "You have a bit of an accent. Where are you from?"

"Good ear. I was born in Amsterdam. I've lived here for nearly twenty years."

She smiled. "I heard you were Dutch, but I didn't think anything of it until I heard you speaking to that family tonight."

"Do you mind?"

"I don't follow politics." The Dutch were only the latest of England's enemies. If not them, it'd be somebody else. "Twenty years is a long time. How old are you?"

"Thirty-eight."

"I'm thirty-five," she supplied. She'd said as much in front of him before, but her introspection had given her the urge to confess.

"I figured you'd be immortal."

Meg blinked. "I beg your pardon?"

He turned to face her and gave her a slow, lazy smile. "With all the legends I've heard about you, I didn't think you could be human."

She scoffed, afraid of what he'd heard. "King's Evil and all that?"

He nodded. "I've heard you can restore sight to the blind."

"That's a new one." Meg rolled her eyes. "Did someone really say that?"

Jake shrugged. "I believe the story was about an old man whose final wish was to be able to see again so he could gaze upon your perfection once more before he died."

"Gaze on my tits, you mean." She dismissed, disappointed. When she glanced down, they were all she could see. She crossed her arms over her chest. "If he'd stop drinking, his sight might come back."

"That was the upshot, yes." He looked at her without a hint of humor on his face. "You're more than a pair of tits, Meg."

Meg blinked. Was she? He'd certainly been the first man to say so. "You sure about that, Jake?"

He nodded, his eyebrows drawing together. "I'm surprised anyone notices them at all with that hair of yours."

Meg tugged on a long lock of her hair, suddenly self-conscious. "Why?"

"The color," he said, reaching for it. He rubbed it very gently between his fingers, sending a current of energy up the strands and into her scalp. Her toes curled in delight. "It's pure gold. I've never seen anything like it."

Meg closed her eyes, her nerves alive at his touch. "There are lots of women with blonde hair in these parts."

"Not like this," he said softly. "There's not a touch of brass or flax."

"I don't lighten it," she said defensively.

"You couldn't," he agreed, turning it over in his hand. When she didn't pull away, he began to play with it, slowly twisting the strands together. It may have been odd to sit there on the floor in the dark, allowing a man she barely knew to fondle her hair, but she didn't say a word in case he stopped. She'd never felt anything so divinely erotic in her life.

Stealing a glance, she watched his hands move through her hair, winding the curtain of gold into something more, an intricately woven column. His hands were big and almost ungainly, firm and strong with traces of old breaks visible in his fingers. The cuts from his most recent fight had begun to heal, but red gashes still sliced through the violet smudges of his swollen knuckles. She had watched him best all comers with those hands over the years, and the delicacy of his touch seemed somehow unreal.

Feeling the muscles in her neck begin to unwind, Meg stifled a moan. She had always liked her hair pulled, but no one had ever just played with it before. She closed her eyes and gave in to the exquisite pleasure of Jake's hands in her hair.

Too soon, he reached the bottom. Her eyes opened lazily as he stopped. He passed her the coil and she took it, bewildered. It was more than just a plait, he had somehow bound perhaps a dozen strands together in a remarkably complicated pattern, unusual as it was beautiful. She ran her thumb over it, amazed something so precise could be attached to her head. It was a far cry from the lazy twists she habitually employed to keep her hair out of her face. "How did you do that?"

He shrugged, his big frame at odds with the delicacy of his work. "It's just a variation on a chain. It's nothing."

She looked it over carefully, trying to unravel the pattern with her eyes. "What kind of chain?"

"Gold, of course. Or any soft metal, I suppose." He stretched his long legs toward the fire, warming his feet. "I was a goldsmith, once." he said, almost to himself, and she thought she detected a hint of sadness in his voice. Perhaps she was not the only one with regrets.

"What happened?"

"The Fire." He didn't have to say anything else. The Fire had destroyed most of London, starting with a bakery and a row of goldsmiths' shops next to it.

"You were in the City?"

"Where else?" He sighed. "I worked in my father's shop. The Fire destroyed everything. The shop and everything in it, everything we had. It killed my parents, our neighbors. Gone in minutes."

Meg had to catch her breath at the tragedy of his story. She couldn't imagine losing her family all at once.

"I stayed up for days, tearing down houses to try to stop it spreading. Even met the King when he came down to lend a hand. Only stopped when I tore my leg."

Meg's gaze drifted to his thighs, clearly as well formed as the rest of him even through his breeches. "Is that why you limp?"

"You've seen it, too? Perhaps Larry had a point." He ran a hand over his eyes. "Yeah, that's why I limp sometimes. It comes and goes, but it's never been right again."

"I'm sorry." Life was unfair and she wasn't often given to sympathy, but it sounded as though he'd had a harder time of it than most. He had lost everything and now here he was, a highly skilled artisan reduced to keeping bar with an aging strumpet. "Think you'll go back to it? Being a goldsmith?"

"Can't now. Hands aren't up to it. Too many breaks."

It would seem both of them had built their reputations out of necessity. He was more than a boxer. She wanted to believe she was more than a whore.

She took one of his big hands in both of hers and he flexed his fingers in her grasp. The action may have been bold for a lesser woman, but was remarkably subdued for Meg. She wasn't trying to seduce him, but she had felt the need to comfort him. The impulse was so foreign to her that it took her a moment to understand what it was. She knew she shouldn't care whether Jake was hurting, but comforting him felt a little like comforting herself. She saw a hint of the scars that had built him behind those dark eyes, deeper if less obvious than the ones on his hands.

"It must have been something to work with. I've never had anything gold before."

His cheek quirked in his curious half smile as he tucked a piece of her hair behind her ear. "You have more of it than anyone I've known."

Her eyes met his and for the first time in her life, Meg felt almost bashful.

Kiss him! A voice urged her from the recesses of her mind, or perhaps somewhere lower.

He dropped his hand and the moment was lost.

Taking the coil he had woven in her hair, he unwound the

bottom few inches and shook it out. "What would you like? I'll make it for you," he offered with a smile.

"I would have said a ring once," she answered honestly, carried away by the peculiar intimacy of the moment.

His gaze dropped to the thick strands he held between his fingers. "And now?"

"I don't know. Something useful, perhaps. A lock on my door or something to keep the punters in line. I don't suppose you could fashion a weapon out of my hair."

He almost laughed. "Beauty is useful."

She shrugged. "Much good it's done me."

A frown passed across his face and he regarded her oddly, as though he was trying to figure out how she was put together. Bless him. Few men had spent enough time with her to care. "Come here."

Meg stiffened, unsure of what he was offering. Undressed and disheveled in the firelight, she had never seen a more desirable man in her life. It would be no hardship to climb into his arms and stay there for years.

He swung his leg to the side and pulled her halfway into his lap, facing the fire. When he didn't immediately start groping her, she realized with some wonder he had only meant to take up her hair once more. She smiled to herself, settling her hips between his strong thighs. Jake was an odd one, but she'd bite her tongue before she told him to stop. He swept up a section of her hair beside her ear and began to work it much as he had before, adding pieces as he went and following her hairline over the top of her head. Meg savored the feeling, boneless with pleasure and more aroused than she remembered ever being.

"People will talk," she heard herself say. "You being in here with me like this."

"I've been accused of worse," he dismissed, his voice soft and warm as smoke.

"As have I," she said, dropping the notion as she surrendered to the pleasure of his hands in her hair. The feeling was so good it made her insensible, lingering somewhere between ecstasy and oblivion.

She felt herself falling into him a little at a time. Her arse between his legs, the small of her back against his flat belly. Her shoulders rested on his chest before she realized she was there, her cheek on the column of his neck and her head below his jaw. He didn't resist, but supported her weight without complaint, the warm strength of him lulling her into a state of relaxation she had never reached. How could a man so hard-looking be so comfortable?

Convinced she was still in her bed and dreaming, Meg slipped into the deepest sleep of her life.

Chapter 11

Meg had just served the last pie of the dinner rush when Tom arrived. He strolled through the crowd like he owned the place, smelling of whiskey at twenty paces. More than handsome, he was charming as all get out with just a hint of madness in his eyes. Even now, it wasn't difficult to see why she'd fancied him in the first place.

She'd learned her lesson, though.

Tom's smile as he spotted their son was almost predatory. He'd never laid a hand on him as far as she knew, but Meg still wanted to protect Tommy from the madman she knew his father to be. It was one of her greatest regrets that she had not been able to protect herself.

He looked her up and down appreciatively as he arrived at the bar. His grin was more a baring of teeth than a genuine smile, revealing a gap where a canine had been knocked out in a fight years before.

Come to think of it, Jake had been the one to take it. Meg's smile was real as she poured him a glass of whiskey she knew he wouldn't pay for. "Afternoon, Tom."

He took the glass she passed him and raised it to his lips, extending a finger to point at her head. "What's all this, then?"

Meg curled her fingers around the end of her braid

protectively, warmed by the memory of Jake's hands in her hair. When she had woken up, she had found a crown across her head, the length woven into a chain of many strands that looked like something a lord might wear around his neck. She had never felt more beautiful in her life. "Thought I'd try something new."

"I don't like it," he dismissed, his gaze following Judith as she carried bread from the kitchen to a table on the other side of the bar.

"Didn't ask you, did I?"

He ignored her, giving Judith the look that used to make Meg weak in the knees. Judith paled as she saw it and hurried back into the kitchen, looking at her feet.

"Don't touch my sister."

"Bit late, Meg," he said under his breath and sipped his whiskey, calm as could be.

She didn't mind him as much when he was calm.

Jake rounded the corner from the cellar with a barrel over his shoulder. Tom stiffened as he saw him behind the bar, his eyes hard. Jake fit the barrel neatly into the low shelf, only noticing Tom as he stood and turned to Meg. Surprise flickered on his face for only a moment before he set his jaw and crossed his arms, and again he was the hulking terror that had bested all comers, Tom included.

Meg twisted the end of her braid between her fingers, a familiar ache tugging at her belly. *That,* by God, was a man. Her sigh went unnoticed as her past and--she hoped--*present* glared at each other over the bar. Tom held his glass so tight his knuckles were white, the spark of madness in his eyes flaming into full blown insanity.

Jake held his ground. He had nothing to prove. "Afternoon, Tom."

Tom's eye twitched, but he did not blink. One wrong move and he'd smash that glass, and she could only guess at which direction it would go. "Meg. A word."

"I'm busy."

He didn't look at her. "We're all busy, aren't we? I came all the way down here to see you. You can spare a moment for the father of your son." His jaw was so tense his lips barely moved.

Meg rolled her eyes. "Are you addressing me? You're looking at Jake."

Tom forced his gaze to her and she took a step back at the rage she saw there. The last time he'd looked at her like that, he'd broken her ribs. That was not a pain she was likely to forget. "I won't keep you long." His voice was pleasant enough, but she'd be blind to miss the threat.

Her stomach tensed, instinctively preparing for a blow. Jake would see him off, she knew, but they were surrounded by people. If one of them caught wind that Meg wasn't up to handling her own fights, they'd walk all over her when Jake wasn't around. She couldn't hide behind him for the rest of her life. Her heart skipped as she led Tom through the bar into the courtyard out back.

Jake waited inside. She had told him to leave her to sort her own affairs, no doubt he was just obeying her wishes.

She wished he wouldn't, just this once.

Meg's breath was knocked out of her body as Tom shoved her up against the outside wall. "What do you think you're doing?"

She met his eyes even as she gasped for air. She wouldn't let him see that he had rattled her. "You're not my man anymore, are you? I'll do as I please."

Tom scoffed, the bastard. "You think I care who you fuck? You can have the whole navy if that's what it takes to satisfy your greedy cunt. See if I stop you. What's *he* doing here?"

She coughed. "So happens I don't need the whole navy."

He slapped her.

"Prick." She spat. "You come down here for Jake? Call it a hunch, but I don't think he fancies blokes."

His hand closed around her throat, pinning her to the wall. "I will not have that Hebrew bastard staying here. I don't want him near you, do you hear me? Nor Judith, nor Tommy. They're dangerous, you know."

Meg sneered at the nonsense pouring out of his mouth. "What rot," she croaked.

"What did you say to me?"

She slapped his hand to let her go as she saw tiny silver stars begin to twinkle around his head. He loosed his grip enough to allow her to draw the longest, sweetest breath of her life. "I said," she heaved, "I said that's a lot of toss. He's not the one with his hand around my throat, is he? You think he's the first Jew to stay here? You think he's the first Jew I've *fucked?* You don't want him here because he's *better than you.*"

She pushed him. She was lying about her relationship with Jake, but she was so angry she didn't care. Let him think Jake had a reason to protect her. Maybe he'd think twice about hitting her again.

Fully expecting another blow, his laugh alarmed her more than anything else. "*Better* than me? What rot. Before you get too excited, you know they cut the ends off their knobs?"

"And it's *still* bigger than yours. What do you make of that?"

Her head struck the wall before she realized he'd pushed her, her teeth snapping together on her tongue.

He lowered his face to hers, his voice a menacing whisper. "Come along Meg, don't be ridiculous. We both know there's still something between us. Something here." He shoved his hand between her thighs over her skirt and she struck out at him. He dodged easily. "You're mine. You'll always be mine. Have anyone you want, but not him. You understand me? Not him."

She grimaced at the pain radiating from between her legs. "Already have, haven't I?"

"Not bloody likely." Tom laughed. "He's still here."

He let her go and she had to grab the wall to steady herself as her legs buckled beneath her. Tom strolled out of the courtyard without a backward glance, casual as could be.

"*Prick prick prick prick prick!*" Meg hissed as the blood rushed back toward her bruised pelvis.

Crumpling to the ground, she wrapped her arms around her head and tried to scream in frustration, but not so much as a squeak came out. Her tongue had stopped bleeding, but she could still taste copper in her mouth. She'd had more than enough of Tom and told him so, but did he listen?

Mark would have taken care of him, if she'd asked him to. Married or not, he would have, and she'd hate herself for letting him.

Asking for help was never an option. Any sign of weakness would be noticed and exploited. In any case, it was her own bloody fault for taking up with a short-fused boxer.

Meg took a moment to straighten her dress. She took a long, deep breath, put on her hostess face, and headed back into the bar.

Jake polished the brass nearest the kitchen as he waited for her, his shoulders tense. He'd been near enough to come for her if she'd cried out.

She wished she would have. It would have been more than gratifying to see him take another couple of Tom's teeth from him.

Another boxer. *Christ.* When would she learn her lesson?

Jake seemed kind enough, but so had Tom. Hadn't he? Oddly enough, she couldn't remember. She had wanted him, and that had eclipsed everything else.

His eyes lit up as he saw her, scanning her for injury. "Are you well?"

Her hand grasped her braid reflexively, seeking strength in the chain. "I'm fine." Her lies were adding up today.

His gaze focused on her neck and his face fell. "Right. My apologies." He left the rag on the bar and nodded toward the cellar door. "Davey's drunk the wine. I'll get some more before he wakes."

Meg shifted from one foot to the other, disturbed by the chill in his tone. He didn't know what had happened. Was their rivalry so bad he'd think less of her for talking to Tom?

Pewter clattered as Bess hefted a tray of dirty dishes onto the end of the bar. She gave a low whistle. "About time."

Meg looked at her askance. "What?"

"Jake, right?"

She frowned, feeling slow. "What about him?"

Bess laughed. "Your neck! Didn't do that to yourself, did you?"

Alarmed, Meg checked her reflection in the brass Jake had been cleaning. The image was warped, but she could just about make out what Bess had seen.

Tom had left a bruise on her neck and it looked like a bite.

No wonder Jake had cooled off the way he did. It looked like she'd had Tom outside.

"Bloody brilliant," she muttered. "Damn his eyes."

"Bit harsh, isn't it? Looks like you had a good time." Bess grinned.

Meg shook her head. "It was Tom again," she whispered. "This isn't what it looks like."

As Jake emerged from the cellar, she repeated, louder, "This isn't what it looks like."

He shrugged. "It's none of my business." His face was neutral. Passive, even. He didn't care.

Her shoulders sloped beneath the weight of her disappointment, even as she told herself it was for the best. "I suppose it's not."

Chapter 12

"*Godverdomme.*"

Jake popped the pad of his thumb into his mouth to slow the bleeding. Helping the girls hang Christmas decorations that afternoon, he'd been pricked by holly so many times he felt like a pincushion. Between the holly and the dry evergreen boughs hanging from every beam, the bar was filled to the rafters with needle-sharp plants. Who had come up with that nonsense? He much preferred the glow of his candles to the gauntlet of Christmas cheer he had to endure because he was the only one tall enough to reach the ceiling.

The decorations made the girls happy, though. Judith smiled and twirled the baby, her face lit up with what he could only presume was the elusive Christmas Spirit. Bess kept everyone in stitches with jokes as she tied lengths of reddish rag around the poles like ribbons, and Tommy helped his mother spike a dozen overripe oranges with cloves.

Meg was withdrawn, totally engrossed in stabbing the oranges with those sharp little clove spikes. She hadn't been the same since Tom had left. That he could understand; the man had always made him want to stab things, too. He'd never had to deal with him for longer than an hour or two, though. Meg had known him intimately for years.

He shuddered, his mind going somewhere he didn't want it

to. He had no business thinking about Meg's private life. Her affairs were her own, and he wasn't about to get in the way.

As much as he told himself to be a man about it, he still felt like sulking. She'd slept in his arms most of the night. The feel of a woman against his body again--and not just any woman, *her*--was more than welcome, it was a bloody miracle. His back ached and his legs hurt from sitting so long on the floor, but he didn't care. He had shivered when the fire went out, but he hadn't moved. It was only when Meg began to feel cold that he had tucked her into her bed and returned to his room.

Then she had left with Tom.

Jake sighed. He was a fool.

An uneven creak of the door announced Chris Cooper, the little boy with the twisted leg. He peered into the bar and froze, still and frightened as a rabbit sensing a threat. Jake went to greet him with a smile, relieved when the boy did not immediately scamper back home. "Good evening, Chris. Come inside, it's cold."

His face was white as snow with splotches of red in his cheeks and the tip of his nose. As he held the door with one hand, he hobbled around it with stilted steps. It was clear his leg was worse than Jake's had ever been. The poor boy needed a crutch. Jake pushed the door open for him at the top. Freed of the burden of the door, Chris was able to walk inside more confidently.

Which wasn't saying much.

The boy looked at the decorations with open wonder, as one might admire a palace or a work of art. Most were salvaged scraps or castaways, but the boy had likely never seen anything so grand in his life. With his parents working all hours to keep their children fed, they wouldn't have money to barter or time to sift through the scraps at the Royal Exchange for broken pine boughs.

He sneezed.

"Chris," Meg called. "Come here and help Tommy."

"Yes, Miss Henshawe." He set off to join their table as quickly as he could.

"Call me Meg, sweetheart. There are too many Miss

Henshawes for all that nonsense." She rose to meet him halfway there with a frown that could freeze water. Pressing her hands to his scarlet cheeks, she muttered a colorful curse. "Tommy, bring those down here. You two are gonna sit by the fire."

Tommy gathered their supplies and took them to the table beside the bar. Joe was tucked into the corner of the best high-backed chair, snoring peacefully. Tommy offered the other chair to Chris and took the stool for himself, and within moments the boys were studding oranges together.

When Meg brought the boy a bowl of hot broth the size of his head, Chris looked like he might just weep. Meg didn't say a word, but she squeezed his shoulder, and this small gesture warmed Jake to his bones. For all her assertions to the contrary, she was generous and kind, a natural mother. She might not have chosen to hire Chris herself, but now he was here, Jake knew instinctively she would look after him the way she looked after everyone else.

His gaze kept finding her as he helped Bess pack up the scraps before the supper rush. Her every movement was confident and graceful, a sort of dance of putting away the pewter. Oddly subdued, it was clear her mind was somewhere else.

Another sprig of holly impaled his finger.

Her head shot up as she heard the pained sound he made.

Bess gave a low whistle. "You'll want to wrap that. You're bleeding all over the table."

Meg produced a roll of tightly wound linen from beneath the bar and beckoned to him with it. He took the stool opposite her and reached for the linen. She stopped him, seizing his hand. "Christ, Jake. Look at you!"

She turned his hand over in hers to reveal a constellation of punctures across his fingertips. The scratches were like red comets, a veritable shower of apocalyptic portent. She wrapped the only finger that still bled, hesitating over the others. "You can hardly have all of them bandaged, can you?" her voice was low, the same velvet purr from the night before.

"They don't hurt anymore," he confessed, though he wasn't

sure if the pain had passed or if it was just that she was touching him.

"Let's see the other one," she ordered him, and he gave it willingly, turning over his palm like a beast shows its belly. He felt absurdly vulnerable with his hands under her scrutiny in a way he hadn't when she'd seen him half-dressed. Half the city had seen him without a shirt, but he'd never shown his hands to anyone.

Her fingertips drifted over his, pale as petals and scored rough with years of labor. For someone who worked as hard as she did, they were remarkably even and soft; he'd seen women her age with cracked skin as red as meat.

Curiosity getting the better of her, she turned his hands over on the bar to examine the grotesque patchwork of his knuckles, tan and thick as leather perforated with new wounds just beginning to heal. To her credit, she didn't so much as gasp, but covered his hands in hers. It was a gesture of comfort, and it moved him more than he could say.

He met her gaze over the bar and saw nothing but kindness in her eyes. He hadn't realized until that moment how much he'd needed it.

A man should not be alone.

He'd heard the words so many times he could still hear them in his father's voice, clear as if the man was standing behind him.

He wished he could see him again.

Jake had been raised for family life. Since he was a child he'd looked forward to marriage with anticipation. He thought he'd find his *bashert* and together they'd have a big family and a happy, peaceful life. More than success or wealth, love was what he wanted, and as a rather romantic adolescent, he'd never imagined for a moment he wouldn't get it.

He'd almost had it. He still felt its loss.

Meg made it worse. Comforting as it was to smell her hair or hear her laugh, she made him all the more aware of what he was missing.

"Your hands are soft," he said, like an idiot.

"Bess makes a rose salve we all use after scrubbing the pots," she explained, a hitch in her voice.

"Do you think it would work for me?" he kidded. No ointment on earth would fix his hands.

"Aren't you sick of the smell of roses yet?"

When she was near, the heady sweet smell of her sent him into a daze. Whatever it was she used, the scent of roses mixed so naturally with her own feminine chemistry that it seemed to come from within. "Never."

Her smile was knowing, and more than a little wicked. There was an invitation in her eyes he was dying to accept. The only thing that kept him from doing just that was the idea she didn't mean anything by it. Perhaps it was something she couldn't turn off.

Or worse, it was *pity*.

His heart tugged as surely as if she had it on a lead. What did he care if she was feeling charitable or bored? Her motivations were her own. She didn't have to love him, but by God, he'd love her. He'd love her so thoroughly she'd forget Tom Callaghan and anyone else she'd ever given the time of day to.

His gaze involuntarily dipped to the mark on her neck.

Her eyes dimmed and she took her hands back. "Why are you looking at me like that?"

Jake shook his head as if he could physically cast the distraction from it. "When's your next day off?"

She frowned. "Day off? You mean away from work?" She laughed. "I haven't had a day off since Tommy was born."

"He's ten years old."

"Yes, he is." She glanced toward where he sat with Chris by the fire.

"Shouldn't you get one every week, at least? We have Shabbos, but I thought yours was more or less the same. You don't ever take Sundays?"

Meg shrugged, a languid roll of her shoulders. "Inns don't. Never close, do we?"

She seemed to accept it as a given that she would never have a day off. He couldn't wrap his head around the bleakness of it. "You must be exhausted."

"You have no idea. When it's not one damn thing, it's another. Why do you ask?"

Because I want twenty-four uninterrupted hours with you in my bed. "Might be good for you to get out of here for a bit." *With me.*

Her eyes brightened with interest. "What are you suggesting?"

What *was* he suggesting? "What would you do if you got a day?"

"Sleep, like as not," she blurted. "Stay in bed, either way."

My thoughts exactly. "Sounds nice."

"Does it?"

He'd thought she was flirting with him, but now he wasn't so sure. Her expression had lost all of its sauciness, and she looked younger, oddly vulnerable. He didn't know what to make of it. "I'll open the bar for you, if you ever want to sleep late."

Her shoulders sagged. "Thanks." Her voice was flat and lifeless. She turned toward the door. "Would you look at that? Here they come."

Jake stood and busied himself serving customers until everyone had been fed, and then he fell into the now familiar routine of pouring drinks and changing barrels. Every chance he got, he stole a glance at Meg.

She ignored him.

♥

There were two of them now. Anne Moore and Kitty Hart, both a good deal younger than she was but old enough to know better. They were barely out of the bloody schoolroom and here they were, draped over her bar giggling like Bedlamites over every single thing the man said. Anne cradled her face in her hands, starry eyed and more than a little pissed, while Kitty played with her thick ginger braid. As he turned to top up their glasses, the girls leaned further over the bar to get a better look at his arse.

"You'd think they'd never seen a man before," she muttered to herself, though she couldn't find it in her heart to blame them for looking. Every last inch of him was rather spectacular.

All the inches she'd *seen* at least.

She passed out a round of ale without thinking about it and moved on toward the next table before a man stopped her. It was Sam Turner, a fishmonger from down the road. "Beer, it was. Have you left mine behind the bar with your brains?"

"You'll drink what I put in front of you," she snapped.

Sam balked, emitting an incredulous laugh. "Is that how you speak to your customers?"

She cocked an eyebrow, taking his measure. "Piss off, Sam. You haven't been coming here all these years for the drink. You're here for the view."

He curled his lip as his gaze dipped to her breasts. "A view that suffers a little more with each passing season. You ought to be sweet to us, or we'll take our business to the Hanging Sword."

"Go, for all I care. I hope you get your throat cut." She took the ale back to the bar to switch it out for beer, taking a long gulp as she went. Sam Turner was an idiot and a pisshead. She could have smoothed things over with a little flirtation, but goddammit, she didn't feel like simpering for fools tonight.

The ale splashed as she all but dropped it on the bar. She poured a beer from the barrel, and as she turned, noticed Jake leaning against the bar to better talk to the girls. He was still far enough away they'd have to leap to reach him, but the way he stood elongated his body even further--the man was a bloody giant as it was--and the flex of his hands supporting his weight emphasized the sloping muscles of his forearms in the most fascinating way. They leapt under his skin as he shifted his weight.

It was the kind of detail that rendered her incapable of rational thought. Had Tom's ever done that? Is that why she'd gone to bed with a lunatic?

Jake smiled at her. It was a funny, crooked smile of bemusement, as if something she'd done were funny, or worse, he'd caught her looking.

She spun on her heel and took the beer back to Sam.

"It's about time--"

"Don't start, or the next one's going in your face."

Sam shook his head. "You're not pretty enough to be such a bitch."

She snarled at him. "Yes, I am." She marched back to the bar, blood racing. For all her brave words, she felt bruised as a rotten apple, and about as physically appealing. Who was Sam Turner to judge her?

"Bastard reeks of rotten oysters," she muttered, pouring herself a glass of wine with shaking hands.

She felt Jake's hand on the small of her back before she heard his voice in her ear, a caress that shot straight down her spine and set light to her belly. "Are you all right?"

Caught off guard, she met his gaze. It was deep and dark as the night outside, and likely presented as many dangers to her person. "Fine." She sipped her wine.

I'll open the bar for you if you ever want to sleep late. She should be grateful for his offer, but she was spitting tacks. The way that conversation had gone, she'd half expected an offer to shag her into next week, but no, he was just looking after her welfare again. She had no idea what to do with that. Every man who'd ever wanted her had always wanted to hurt her a little bit, to take with no regard for her comfort or wants.

Jake wanted to *give*. Give her a hand in the kitchen, a morning to sleep in. That was all well and good, but the only thing she wanted him to give her didn't seem to be on offer.

Probably something to do with those two little biters at the bar. Why should he limit himself to her when he could have two under twenty?

He took her empty glass from her and set it aside. "You're upset," he observed. "Here, hold still."

She froze, still as a piece of furniture as he caught a loose strand of her hair. He stepped towards her so she was staring at his chest above his open collar. The warmth of him was enough to make her forget the broken window. The noise of the bar receded beyond the sound of his breath. She was still smelling citrus and cloves. Either she was smelling them from the kitchen or Jake had some remarkable soap.

Meg closed her eyes as he carefully worked the hair back into the braid that crossed her head. He wasn't unlike those oranges, himself. He was a rare, delicious treat she was desperate to taste.

When he finished what he was doing, he dropped his hand and it caught in her hair, pulling her braid hard. The tug shocked her, fanning the fire his voice had lit in her belly. She gave an involuntary moan.

He noticed. "Sorry?" His apology sounded like a question, as though he wasn't sure he ought to give one.

"No harm done," she managed, breathless.

A noisy belch heralded Davey's arrival. Jake took two steps back and she noticed there were people at the bar waiting to be served. How long had they been there?

Meg hadn't seen Davey all day, but from the look of him, he'd already been drinking. She'd have to check the inventory to find what he'd stolen later.

He waded through the crowd and kicked the chair Joe was still sleeping in. Joe snored louder, the flicker of his eyelids the only hint he was faking it. "Get up," Davey commanded. "You're in my chair."

Meg launched herself at him, the bar restraining her like a caged animal. "That is his chair."

"I own the bar," Davey insisted.

"He's been sitting in it for twenty years," she spat. "We may as well carve his name into it. Find another seat."

Chris was cheerfully polishing cutlery in front of the fire. Davey addressed him, "You, boy. Move."

Chris moved to obey him, his leg shaking as he attempted to stand.

"Sit down, Chris!"

The boy dropped his backside at her command.

Her hands balled into fists at her hips, ready for a fight. "That boy is unwell and he needs the fire. Find. Another. Seat. One that isn't occupied by anyone else's arse."

Davey elbowed Jake's admirers aside in his haste to get to

Meg. "I've had quite enough of you, harpy! Is this what you've been doing all day?" He gestured wildly toward the Christmas decorations. "Spending my money when you ought to be earning it on your back?"

Jake left her side and stalked toward the end of the bar, looking ready to throw himself between them if necessary.

"Your money?" she repeated, blood rapidly reaching boiling point. "You've drunk three casks of claret in a week! If you want to earn that back, why don't we put you in a bloody skirt and set you loose on the docks, hey?"

"You--"

His retort was cut off by Jake's hands around his neck. He wasn't trying to kill him, but he had him pinned to the wall and from the look on Davey's face, was threatening him very quietly. She strained to listen.

"--has done a lot of good work and she deserves your respect. You will not speak to her thus. Not in front of the customers, not in private, and not in front of me if you value your life. Do you understand me?"

Jake had his lovely big hands wrapped around her least favorite relative's throat and he was threatening him on her behalf.

Meg couldn't remember being more aroused in her life.

She fanned herself with her hand weakly, her face gone rather hot.

When Jake let him go, Davey gasped for air though she knew Jake hadn't damaged his airways.

Nausea rose in her belly and her blood cooled as she recalled Tom had done something similar to her just that afternoon.

Bloody boxers. All she needed was another lunatic in her bed. If she was clever she'd steer clear of boxers altogether, find herself a clerk or a footman or something.

She laughed out loud at the absurdity of the thought, but no one seemed to notice.

Davey pointed an accusatory finger at her. "I've had enough of the two of you and this cesspit of a town! I'll sell this heap and then you can torment somebody else. Damn the lot of you!"

Davey charged into the street as if he meant to find a buyer at that hour. Her sense of dread at the prospect of his selling the inn out from under her was tempered with the idea that the new owner could hardly be worse than him, and just the tiniest bit of hope she might be able to purchase it herself.

Or that he'd be murdered by brigands for his buttons while he was out. That would be fine, too.

Jake straightened his shirt and returned to his post behind the bar as though nothing had happened. He ran a hand through the gorgeous black mess of his hair and accepted the glass of wine Meg offered him. He raised it to her.

Not only were Anne and Kitty still there, but they looked more affected by his display than she was.

"You're so strong," Anne mooned.

Kitty sighed. "I wish I had a man to defend my honor in just such a way…"

"Go find your own," Meg snapped.

The girls straightened immediately. "He said he didn't have a girl," Kitty protested.

Jake's eyebrows shot up, but he didn't say a word as he watched for her response. She was going to have to talk herself out of this one.

Meg softened her tone. It wasn't the girl's fault Meg was mad. "You shouldn't go chasing after men old enough to be your father."

"He doesn't look like my father." Anne grinned.

Meg couldn't argue with that. She threw up her hands and marched into the kitchen.

♥

The fire had long since gone out when Meg sighed in defeat.

It felt as though hours had passed since she'd gotten into bed, but sleep would not come. She stared at the cracks in the ceiling, wondering how much it would set her back to have them fixed. Idly playing with her hair, she listed the things she had to do the next day over and over again, thinking of everything that could go wrong with each one.

They were out of lye, the grocer needed paying, and Tommy needed new shoes.

She bunched the pillow beneath her head and rolled to face the wall. The sharp quill of a feather pricked her cheek and she yanked it out. She could not for the life of her get comfortable. The bed was cold and the linens were coarse against her legs. Her back hurt so badly that she could feel each day of her advanced years quite distinctly, a patchwork of old bruises and sprains knotting beneath her skin. As for her neck, the less said about that the better. Quite aside from Tom's assault, it was hard as a rock. She couldn't turn her head to the left today and if she didn't get a good night's sleep, she wouldn't be able to turn it right tomorrow.

Determined to sleep, she closed her eyes and took a long breath. It worked until her jaw clenched as though someone turned it with a key. Awake and angrier than before, she punched the pillow with a nasty little jab.

A creak came from Jake's room. She'd heard many such creaks since his arrival. There always seemed to be candles burning next door, even hours after he'd retired. It was less the light keeping her awake than the wondering who was in there with him.

It seemed the reason he wasn't bothered about her was because he already had someone else to hold his interest.

Whoever it was, they were bloody quiet. She'd never heard a woman--not that she had been listening--but more than once, she had heard the accelerated sound of his breath with just the merest hint of a moan.

She put her palm against the flimsy wall that separated their rooms. His bed was on the other side, no more than a few inches away. They were practically in bed together as it was.

His coverlet rustled and she pictured it dragging over his chest. Some men slept in long shirts, but she had a feeling he'd wear nothing at all.

Wishful thinking, perhaps.

A sigh reached her through the crack in the wall. His bed creaked beneath his weight and she heard the soft rush of skin on skin. Innocent, or anything but?

The crack glowed with a lovely warm light and she wanted so badly to see what he was doing. She knew herself too well. Either he'd catch her looking and she'd have to make up an excuse for spying on him, or she'd see him with someone else and her heart would shatter, for surely, any woman he took to his bed would be superior in every way. Younger, sweeter, fewer scars and stretch marks. It didn't matter who she was, but that he wanted her, and that in itself was enough to keep Meg from looking.

She didn't want to know what he liked, because she knew she wasn't it.

Meg drew her knees to her chest, squirming with frustrated want. How ludicrous to ache for someone occupied with someone else. How pathetic! She was *Meg Henshawe* and if she wanted a man in her bed, there was no shortage to choose from.

They were shorter than she was, of course. They were colored in shades of flax and sour milk while she had a terrible thirst for coffee. None of them smelled of cloves and good soap, and she'd defy any one of them to try to lift her. No one else had a smile she wanted to look at, let alone a smile she wanted to cause.

Not a single one of them was Jake Cohen.

Determined to put herself off of him, she tried to imagine what he was doing and who he was with.

The trouble was, without spying on him, she couldn't think of him with anyone else but *her*.

With her eyes closed, it was too easy to imagine he was in her bed. The flutter of sheets became a caress, his hands slipping into her shift to cup her breasts. An exhale became whispered words. Dutch curses, Hebrew blessings, her list of things she had to do--she didn't give a good goddamn as long as it was his voice in her ear.

She stifled a gasp as she dipped her fingertips into the heat between her legs. The firm flesh leapt at the touch, biting her fingers and flooding with need. Her body tingled from her knees to the taut tips of her breasts. Thinking of the way Jake had looked at her when she patched his hands, she bit her lip and increased her pace.

He'd kiss her, he'd take her, he'd pull her hair. He'd pin her down and then he'd whisper--

Whore.

It wasn't Jake's voice she heard in her head, but Tom's. She withdrew her hand and curled up on her side, all desire leaving her.

It wasn't the worst thing Tom had called her, but it was true.

"Christ," she muttered, a tear running into her hair.

His voice was so soft she barely heard it. "Meg? Are you awake?"

"Just about." Her back stiffened. How much had he heard? "Are you alone?"

He laughed under his breath. "As a matter of habit, yes. Why do you ask?"

Meg frowned. "Company might take exception to you talking to the wall, is all."

He didn't answer.

"The candles," she explained half-heartedly. "Thought you might be...awake."

"That's not why."

"It's no business of mine."

He took a deep breath. "It's Hanukkah."

Meg turned to face the wall. "I beg your pardon?"

"The reason for the candles. It's Hanukkah, it's a minor holiday. There are only two days left, if the light bothers you."

"It doesn't," she blurted, ashamed at her ignorance. Living in England, he was sure to know all about the traditions of her faith, but she knew next to nothing about his. "Two more *days*, did you say?"

"Two more. Eight altogether."

"Eight?" she repeated. "You burn candles for all of them? They're too bright to be tallow."

"Not tallow. They're beeswax."

"That's an expensive holiday."

"No worse than Christmas. You burn them all at once."

"Not here, we don't." She flung an arm over her face. "Charlie wouldn't have allowed it. He'd spin in his grave if he could see all the trimmings we've put up this year."

"Charlie?" His voice echoed as though he'd turned toward her.

"My father. *Our* father. Charlie Henshawe." She'd been the one to find him that morning. He'd drowned in his own vomit, as far as she could make out. Crumpled on his front, his face had been swollen and indigo with pooled blood. She'd pushed him over onto his back, asked Mark for a coffin, and went straight back to work. "We weren't close."

He didn't reply.

"He sold the bloody inn." This was as much an accusation as statement of fact. "He sold us to keep it open, and then he gives it to Davey, for what? I paid for this hovel ten times over, and by rights, it should be mine. Ten bloody guineas. He should have asked me. I had it."

After a long pause, he asked, "Did you say he sold you?"

"All of us," she confirmed, trying to keep the betrayal she still felt from her voice. "It's the cost of keeping an inn, he said. 'The ale is bad, the food is worse, but it's you they'll come back for, Meggy. You're gonna keep us in business.'"

She flung the coverlet off, suddenly too hot. Her blood raced and the arousal she'd felt had transmuted into a kind of restless energy that would have her looking for a fight, if she didn't head it off. "The ale is better now, and the food is the best for miles, but he was right. It's me keeps 'em coming back. Or was. He said my sisters would starve if I didn't do it. He would have kept food from them just to spite me."

There was ice in his voice. "Didn't what?"

"You think I was born a harlot, Jake?" she laughed to herself, though the truth of it gave her no joy. "I was fifteen when he gave me to the butcher to settle a debt. He told me to be a good girl, make him happy. Said I might even enjoy it. The man was as old as my father. He smelled of filth and he had a tiny prick. How's anyone meant to enjoy that?"

"Meg," he whispered. "I'm sorry."

"Don't be," she sniffed, surprised to find her cheeks wet. "I'll not having you feeling sorry for me, you understand? I just wanted you to know, is all."

"Know what?"

"Why I'm the way I am." The tears flowed freely into her pillow now. "They damn me for selling myself, but they'd damn me for disobeying my father, too. They damn me for you…"

"I'm sorry."

"Don't be. I damn them, too."

He let out a long breath. "Your father was right about one thing. They do come back to see you, but it's not only your beauty or their lust. You are lovely, welcoming, and witty. A man would travel miles for that kind of reception."

Her rage calmed at his kindness, the heat in her cheeks mellowing into a pleasant warmth. "You're a good man, Jake."

"I can't remember the last time someone said so."

"I'm saying so now. It's true." Her toes curled and she pulled the coverlet back over her shoulders, craving physical contact. "Telling the truth is easier in the dark."

"It's light over here."

"Shall I tell you another truth, then?" she asked, no longer in control of her words. It felt as though everything in her mind came out of her mouth without anything in the middle to filter her thoughts. "I think I'm asleep."

He laughed. "You sound like it."

"That wasn't it," she insisted. "I did like it, eventually. I met someone who knew what they were doing, and I liked it. After that, I liked the power it gave me, and I used it. I'm not a good woman, Jake."

"You might just be human, Meg." She heard him scratch his head. "Was that Tom, then?"

She shook her head, Tom's memory blurring as she fell closer to sleep. "It was Mark."

"Do you still love him?" he asked, his voice small.

She opened her eyes to look at him, and found herself staring at the grain of the wall. "I don't. Neither of them, and that is the truth." She sighed. "The two of them together aren't half the man you are. I want you to braid my hair every day."

He laughed and Meg could picture his smile. It was a good one, she could hear it. "Is that the truth?"

"Every damned day."

"I'll do it anytime you ask," he promised.

She smiled, her tension melting. "Why are you so kind to me?"

"Why wouldn't I be?" She could hear the confusion in his voice.

"No one is," she confessed.

"You're a good woman."

The warmth of his voice rolled over her, sending sparks clear down to her toes. She flexed them, needing to prolong the feeling. "What do you mean by that?"

"Just that. You look after a lot of people, whether they see it or not. Myself included."

It took her a long moment to realize he wasn't referring to sex. "Someone's got to."

Chapter 13

Meg waited in the lane by the servant's entrance, her hands in her pockets. It was early morning, and most respectable folk were still in their beds. Most reprobates, as well. All that was left were the servants, the workmen, the merchants, and everyone else obliged to make a living on their feet, bustling about their tasks in the early morning chill.

The sun was up, lurking somewhere behind the heavy clouds that cloaked the city in a pitiless gray. Ice barbed the air and glazed the stones of the smarter streets. Wet patches of muddy snow sat like filthy laundry in the city's gutters, mercifully covering up the rubbish that lurked inside. Meg flexed her fingers, willing them to warm.

The door opened with a soft whine and Sarah peeked out. She looked older than the last time Meg had seen her, almost a woman grown. Meg could no longer remember the face of Sarah's father, a man who'd left like all of the others years before, but she knew Sarah's nose was his. Her eyes she got from her mother. "Mum," she whispered. "What are you doing here?"

Meg rushed toward her, pulling the bottle from her pocket. "I've brought you something for your birthday. I didn't want you to think I'd forgotten."

Sarah took it hesitantly, her reticence tugging at Meg's heart. Why shouldn't she be suspicious? She barely knew her own mother, after all.

"It's a rose tonic, for your complexion." Meg explained. "Your aunt Bess makes it. We all use it, down at the inn."

Sarah slid it into the pocket of her work dress. "You shouldn't have come."

Meg's heart shattered. She shrugged helplessly. "I know, I won't cause any trouble for you. I just wanted to see you, is all. How are you keeping?"

Sarah looked over her shoulder into the recesses of the house. She was fortunate to have found a position in such a fine place. Most girls Meg had grown up with would have given an eye for a job like that. She was proud of her for keeping it. Sarah's standing wouldn't improve if she was seen talking to a strumpet. "I'm well, Mum. How's Tommy?"

"Great. He's getting taller all the time. He asks after you. You should come around, when you can."

Sarah nodded. "I should get back. Thank you for the tonic." With a sad smile, Sarah retreated into the house.

Meg stood there in the cold a long moment, staring at the closed door.

She took a deep breath, filling her lungs to bursting with the brisk December air. She froze silently for a long moment until the broken feeling abated and all she felt was cold.

Thinking of the fire waiting for her at the inn, she walked down the lane toward the main thoroughfare. She almost tripped over her own feet as she spotted the man on the other side of the street. "Jake?"

He headed toward her, a small sack in his hand. "Good morning, Margaret."

She *hated* that name. Why was she smiling?

While she felt chilled to her bones, the cold had only made him handsomer, if possible. He was awake, happy, and fair glowing with health. What could he be doing on a wealthy street at this time of the day? "Visiting a friend?" she asked, sounding cattier than she'd meant to.

"A baker." He held up the sack. "You?"

Meg looked at her feet, wondering how much he'd seen. "My daughter. It's her birthday."

Jake smiled, his eyes lighting up. "Lovely. What's her name?"

"Sarah," she replied, wondering why he cared. While it was no secret she had children, most men either ignored that fact or were openly repulsed by it.

"Good name." He looked past her shoulder toward the house. "Does she live there?"

Meg shook her head. "She works there. She's in service."

Jake nodded, accepting this, and they walked together back toward the river. Meg slogged through the ice and slush, her feet already soaked through her shoes. She heard her teeth chatter before she felt them move.

"Your lips are blue," he noticed, and Meg had to wonder at the worry on his face. It wasn't like men to worry about her. "Come on." He offered her his arm.

She took it, settling her fingers around his firm bicep. That was one way to warm them up. "Where are we going?" she asked, not really caring.

"Coffee."

He led her down another road and around the corner to a bustling market street she'd never seen before. Shops had thrown open their shutters, selling meat, produce, and dark bread. It looked much like Bridge Street on a Friday, only cleaner, and few were speaking English.

Meg glanced up at Jake askance. He gave her a look that was half challenge and led her through a narrow doorway into a warm little bakery.

The ceiling was so low Jake's head nearly touched it. A table and some chairs were set before the fire burning merrily in the hearth. Meg looked around in wonder. The bakery she went to in Southwark only had a shop front, and she'd never been to one she could walk inside. A short bar not unlike her own separated the narrow room from the kitchen beyond, and every surface was covered in strange baked goods. The loaves of bread were much the same, but they came in different shapes and sizes, and some were even topped in what looked like salt. She didn't know what anything was, but the warm smell of yeast and malt was so comforting that she almost forgot her feet were frozen.

Jake pulled out a chair for her beside the fire. She took it without hesitation. A tiny, ancient-looking woman wearing a scarf over her hair emerged from the kitchen as Jake approached the counter. She greeted him with a bright smile and said something to him in a language Meg could not even guess at. The inn was beside a port and she recognized bits of French, German, Dutch, and Spanish, particularly the profanity, but this was different. Jake spoke to her pleasantly, the very picture of easy charm, as the woman peered at Meg with open curiosity.

Wondering how much Jake had paid for her, no doubt.

Meg shifted uneasily in her seat, feeling every inch the aging harlot. She gave the woman a small smile.

The woman grinned in return and said something to Jake with a finger pointed at his chest. Jake laughed and she disappeared into the kitchen.

He sank into the chair beside her with a smile. Opening the sack, he reached into it only to be admonished by the woman as she returned with two mugs. Jake laughed and rattled out something that sounded like an apology. The woman set a mug in front of Meg with a warm smile. "Thank you," Meg said, truly grateful for the hot coffee. She wrapped her hands around the mug, loving the feeling of the steam on her face. "Is that German you're speaking?" she asked when the woman had gone back into the kitchen.

Jake sipped his coffee. "Yiddish. It's somewhere between German and Hebrew."

The smell of the coffee was so divine Meg almost didn't want to drink it. Her stomach won out and she took a sip. It tasted even better. "What did she say to you just now?"

Jake scratched his head, a boyish smile on his handsome face. "She told me off. I was going to offer you some of the bread I bought earlier, but she's got some warm now."

As if he had announced her, the woman returned with two plates. She set one in front of Jake and the other in front of Meg. On Meg's was an odd, wheel-shaped roll slathered in butter. Her stomach growled. She hadn't realized how hungry she was. "Thank you."

Jake noted her plate with a frown. He said something to the woman, but she just shrugged and replied with something that made Jake squirm. He colored slightly. "Ruta, this is Meg. Meg, Ruta."

"Good to meet you." Meg smiled.

The woman nodded again and said, "*Sholem Aleikhem.*"

Jake lowered his voice and said to Meg, "You say, *Aleikhem Sholem.*"

Meg wrinkled her nose, trying not to slaughter the language with her broad accent. "Ah-LIKE'm Shohl-um?"

Ruta grinned and said something else to Jake, looking Meg up and down. Meg sat utterly still under her inspection. She wasn't one who was afraid to offend, but the woman *had* just brought her coffee and bread on a miserable morning. Perhaps it wouldn't be kind to bite her head off.

Jake replied under his breath and Ruta laughed, disappearing again into the kitchen.

Meg picked up the bread and looked at it curiously. "What did she say?"

Jake cringed. "Do you really want to know?"

"Why not?"

He didn't look at her. "She said we'd have beautiful children."

Meg choked on her coffee. "Lord, I don't think anyone's ever accused me of being a suitable mother. Bit soon for that, don't you think?"

"It's the beigel." He nodded toward the roll on her plate. "Where Ruta's from, they give those to women who are with child. I think she was hoping you were."

Meg's hand drifted to her belly in horror. She had never been particularly slender, but surely she wasn't *that* heavy. "Do I look like I'm with child?"

His gaze softened and drifted over her breasts to her waist, mercifully constrained in her stays, and back again. He had been so frightfully good about keeping his eyes on her face, she felt a smug satisfaction that he was finally taking in her best assets.

"Not in the slightest." He shifted uncomfortably and looked away. "You don't think you're a suitable mother?"

She clamped her jaw shut, regretting saying anything at all. "I do what I can. Isn't always enough, is all."

"You see Sarah often?"

Meg shook her head. "I barely know her, really. My father wouldn't let me keep them in the house, my lot. Couldn't bear the talk. I was good enough to sell, but heaven forbid I raise my own children."

"What happened to them?"

"Same as happens to anybody's. I paid someone else to raise them, didn't I? Always thought I'd marry one day and I'd get them back, but that never happened. By the time my father went to his reward, Sarah and Michael were grown and living their own lives. No use for a mother like me."

His eyes softened with something that looked a bit too much like sympathy. "Michael's your son?"

"He is." Meg sighed. "Last I heard, he was press-ganged onto a ship somewhere. I haven't seen him in three years."

"I'm sorry," he said, his voice a caress.

"Don't be," she dismissed, needing to change the subject. "They're alive. That's more than some can say. I got to keep Tommy, at least."

"He's a good lad."

Meg began to warm. She was glad Jake had noticed. "Yes, he is." Unable to resist, she took a bite of the bread. Unlike the hard, crumbly bread she was accustomed to, it was chewy with an almost crisp outer crust. She moaned. "God, this is good."

Jake brightened. "Ruta's the only baker in London who makes them, as far as I can make out."

Meg closed her eyes as she chewed. The butter was fresh and the bread was still warm. Bliss. She inspected the roll in her hand, wondering what made it taste so much better than common bread. "There are bubbles under the crust."

"They're boiled before they're baked. You like it?"

Meg nodded even as she took another big bite. "Does anyone ever get in the family way just to eat these?"

Jake grinned. "That good?"

"Better." Meg rolled her eyes heavenward. "Did you come up here for these?"

He shook his head. "I come up here for challah sometimes." He opened the sack to show her a golden, braided crust. "I often fancy it on Fridays."

Meg sipped her coffee. "This is a Jewish street, isn't it?"

"It is."

"Is everyone Dutch like you? We've got loads more Dutch in Southwark over the past few years, but most of them are Protestant."

"Not many Dutch. Most come through Amsterdam, but that's not where they're from. Ruta's family is Polish, and most everyone else is from Spain or Portugal."

"Spain? They've come a long ways."

He raised his eyebrows. "They had a good reason for leaving."

Meg waited for him to elaborate, but he didn't. "I thought I heard some Spanish on the street. Does everyone speak Yiddish as well?"

He shook his head. "No, only me and Ruta's family. We're Ashkenazic, and most everyone else is Sephardic."

Meg looked down at her coffee, ashamed of her ignorance. "What's the difference?"

"Apart from language, customs, food, and where we're from?" He laughed good-naturedly. "A lot of the Sephardim are scholars, and they look down on us a bit."

She frowned. It was difficult to imagine anyone looking down at a man like Jake. "Why's that, then?"

He shrugged. "We tend to work with our hands more. Shoemakers, tailors, goldsmiths like me. At least in Amsterdam."

Meg pursed her lips knowingly. "Sounds like the gentry turning up their noses at anyone who's not useless."

"There's a bit of snobbery in it. They're brilliant, though. Not at all useless."

"No one's as useless as the gentry." Meg rolled her eyes. "Is it like English and Scots, then? In the same boat, more or less, but different?"

"I suppose." He puzzled over her question. "I couldn't really say."

"We sort of hate each other," Meg explained. "A little, but not really. But we do."

Jake laughed. "They're good people, but we're different."

Her gaze fell to his hands, folded around his coffee cup. She'd seen those very hands knock a dozen men out. They dwarfed the coffee cup, the uneven patchwork of his long fingers cradling it as though it was made from glass. It was all so civilized, absurd. He looked as out of place as a giant at the little table, but still completely at ease with himself and his surroundings. He was at home here.

Meg warmed, flattered he'd allowed her to see this part of himself. She knew it for the honor it was. She couldn't remember a time she'd enjoyed breakfast so much. She couldn't even remember a time a man had stuck around long enough to have breakfast with her. She smiled at Jake's profile as he relaxed in front of the fire. He really was stunning. He hadn't shaved in a few days and a short beard shadowed his jaw. He looked dashing and more than a little disheveled. "Thought you might come by last night," she said with some regret.

His eyes widened before he turned toward her. "Was I invited?"

He was always invited. She'd take a hammer to his hearth herself if it meant he'd spend more nights in her room. Meg shrugged. "Don't want you catching cold, is all."

He raised his eyebrows and turned back toward the fire. "I'll survive."

Rebuffed, Meg fought the urge to pout. He might survive, but she wasn't sure she would, knowing he was on the other side of that crack. Her toes curled at the memory of his hands in her hair.

Looking for a distraction, she let her gaze travel through the bakery. "I like it here."

"Good. Ruta's lovely, she'll set you to rights."

The moment he mentioned her, Ruta toddled out of the kitchen with a little sack in her hand. She thrust it at Meg with a mischievous grin.

Meg hesitated before she took the bag. "Thank you, Ruta."

Ruta scrunched up her nose at Meg in apparent mirth, then turned to Jake and said something in Yiddish. Jake replied with his hands spread and she pointed a finger at him, telling him off affectionately. Some things were the same in any language. When she left, Meg opened the bag to find it filled with flaky biscuits that smelled of fruit and spices.

"Good lord," Meg muttered to herself. She didn't know what they were, but they looked delicious. She looked up at Jake. "What did she say just now?"

He raised his eyebrows. "She said you look like a nice woman."

Meg snorted. She wasn't, and she'd bet everything in her purse that wasn't all Ruta had said.

After a long moment of awkward silence, Meg turned to him, feeling cheeky. "She's right, you know."

He looked up at her over his mug.

"We'd have gorgeous children," she kidded, though the idea was not at all repellant.

Jake opened and closed his mouth. Meg laughed, pleased she'd said something he didn't have an easy answer to. He finished his coffee and set down his mug, "Only if they look like you," he countered. "Let's get back, shall we?"

Chapter 14

By the time they left Ruta's bakery, much of the remaining snow had turned to dirty brown slush. Jake led Meg through a narrow lane to Bishopgate Street, a busy thoroughfare that would lead them all the way back toward the river, or near enough. Clutching his bag in one hand, he offered her his arm.

She took it again without hesitation, her long fingers settling between his bicep and his elbow. He was almost ashamed he was tempted to flex. There had to be some benefit to putting himself through the rigors to keep in fighting form.

Meg seemed to be as unaware of his dilemma as she was of the fact she was touching him. She looked at the passing buildings and shops with open curiosity as they passed.

"You want to stop anywhere?" he asked.

She sidestepped a particularly nasty-looking slush puddle before she looked up at him with something like wonder on her face. "Never been up this way before. I usually take Broadstreet up to Long Alley."

"You go behind Bedlam? I try to avoid it."

She shrugged as though creeping behind an insane asylum in the small hours was nothing. "I found the way years ago. Not so many take it, so it's faster."

Jake closed his hand over her fingers at the thought, nearly dropping the bag in the process. "The screams don't bother you?"

Her fingers fluttered under his hand and he flexed his arm in response.

Involuntarily, of course.

"I've heard worse in Southwark." She looked at him an odd little smile on her face, appearing to take his measure. It was the first time he'd seen her properly in daylight and he couldn't tear his eyes away. Lovely as she was in the firelight of the bar, by day she was something else entirely. Her even complexion was the color of fresh cream and pink roses. A few dozen pale golden freckles were scattered across her nose, and her eyes were clear and bright as green glass. She held his gaze until he stubbed his toe on the wheel of a cart.

"*Godverdomme*," he cursed under his breath.

She slowed her pace. "You hurt yourself?"

He shook his head though his toes were still throbbing. "I'm fine."

They continued down the street, and Jake tried to direct his focus to the road and any obstructions in his path.

She bit her lip to hide a creeping smile and he nearly tripped over his feet. "Was that Yiddish, too?"

"Dutch. It was a rude word." He let go of her hand with some reluctance. His mother had always cautioned him against using profanity in the presence of ladies, but then again, she never would have imagined him keeping company with the likes of Meg Henshawe.

Meg pressed her lips together and raised an eyebrow. "I gathered. How many languages do you speak?"

"English, Yiddish, Hebrew, a little German. I grew up speaking Dutch, and I tend to curse in my first language."

She responded with a cheeky smile, her lips red as apples in the cold. "You are rather useful to have around, aren't you? If I don't watch it I'll have to raise your wages."

If she kept smiling at him like that, she wouldn't have to pay him anything at all.

Meg looked back at the passing buildings. "Long way to go for bread. We're nearly in Whitechapel. Why don't you live up here?"

He shifted uneasily, his coat feeling suddenly tight. "I suppose I don't know many in these parts anymore. Come up here for bread sometimes, and there's a synagogue over there on Cree Church Lane." He nodded toward the other side of the road as they crossed Leaden Hall Street. "Haven't been in years."

"Really?" She glanced up at him in surprise. "Why's that, then?"

He shrugged. "The fights were always Friday nights. Fell away over time, I suppose. Never felt right to go back. Don't really fit anywhere these days." He sounded pitiful even to himself. Ruta's well-intentioned encouragement had left him feeling reflective, and he didn't like the direction his thoughts were going.

He was nearing forty and had nothing to show for his years. No home, no wife, no family, no community he belonged to anymore. All he had was what little money he'd been able to save, a limp, and a pair of broken hands. His family was dead. The Sephardim looked down on him, and the English never seemed to know what to do with him, short of putting him in the pit. They liked him there well enough.

Where could he go now, a useless old fighter with no family or practical skills to speak of? Even if his heritage could be overlooked--and he didn't want it to be--what woman would have a man who could not provide for her properly?

Ruta had told him in no uncertain terms that what he needed to set his heart at ease was a *zaftig* Englishwoman and couple of babies. He wanted a family of his own, but the older he got, the less likely he was to have one. He had spent years coming to terms with the fact his chance at that had run off with Rachel.

As they neared the river, he noticed people staring at Meg. Even covered up, she was outrageously beautiful, but it was not polite admiration she was receiving. Men leered or licked their lips as she passed, while women rolled their eyes or snarled. One of them even muttered, "Whore."

The only indication Meg gave that she had heard it was the subtle straightening of her spine and the upward tilt of her jaw. Here she was recognized, lusted over, or reviled. She was more than a woman, she was a *legend*. Everyone knew her and had their own opinions about her private life, and perhaps some had even been part of it.

A group of sailors saw them coming and began to cheer. Meg smiled at them before she noticed the cheers were not compliments but off-color suggestions complete with graphic hand gestures. She tried to hold her smile as though it didn't bother her, but the flush of her cheeks belied her embarrassment.

His temper flared and he shot daggers at them with his eyes, employing a dark expression he'd been told was particularly fearsome. *Beastly* was a word that had been used. *Brutish. Chilling. Grim.* Words he'd more than earned building a reputation he wasn't afraid to use when it was needed.

Once they noticed the hulking shadow she held was glaring at them, the sailors returned to their work fast enough. One looked ready to piss himself.

Jake almost smiled. At least his face was good for something.

Once they had passed the worst of the onlookers and turned onto the bridge, Meg let out a breath.

He cleared his throat. "Does that happen to you often, when you're alone?"

"Every time I leave the house." Her voice sounded weary. "Church is the worst."

"Church?"

She nodded. "Always judging me, every one of them. Pitying my son. You should hear the things they say about me. Some of them are true, I admit." She shrugged. "I don't much like going myself. Last week was bad. Don't know that I'll go back."

He raised his eyebrows, surprised at her vehemence.

She turned to him, her eyes sparkling with anger. "Tell me, what kind of a god creates a world where you've got to sin to survive and then damns you for living in it?"

He didn't have an answer. "Don't let them scare you off."

"I'm not scared of bloody anything. Hell itself can hardly be worse than Southwark on a Saturday night." She tossed her braid over her shoulder, rage clouding her beautiful face. Even as she looked able to shoot bullets with her mind, another pair of young men gave her the eye from a shop window.

A man leading a sheep whistled. "Go on, love, show us your tits!"

"Piss off," she snarled, but the man just laughed. Jake threw him a dark look and he stopped laughing.

Everywhere he looked, people gaped at her. He knew she was aware of it, she was as tense as if she'd been fighting. No wonder she had a reputation for rage. If he'd had to deal with all of that every time he left the house, he'd never stop swinging.

Meg's shoulders relaxed as they reached the other side of the river. The men were animals in Southwark, too, but they were animals she knew. "They were much better behaved today," she conceded.

"Really?" He struggled to imagine it. "What is it normally like?"

She glanced up at him, her anger melting into an expression that was almost vulnerable. "Usually get groped more."

His hands formed into fists instinctively. "Perhaps you shouldn't go out on your own."

She balked. "It's my fault, is it?""

He shook his head. "Absolutely not. If they don't know how to behave, perhaps I ought to come with you and show them."

Her face turned a rather remarkable shade of pink. "I can handle myself."

"You shouldn't have to."

She didn't respond. After a long moment, her fingers crept down his arm and slipped into his hand.

He looked at her askance, caught off guard. She kept her eyes on the path ahead, as though she hadn't noticed her hand had landed in his.

Palm to palm, he grasped it gently, her skin smooth and cool against his ragged fingertips. Her touch was a gift she'd given freely, and he wished he could keep it with him always, a balm for his weary soul. "You know, we don't really believe in hell. Not like you do, at least."

"No hell? Perhaps I ought to go to your church." She laughed. "That's a lovely idea, Jake, but hell is real and we're living in it."

He could understand why she thought so. Southwark was easily the roughest place he'd been, full of criminals, drunkards, lepers, and families too big to feed stacked on top of one another in rotting tenements between the refuse pits, gaols, and tanneries reeking of piss. Her father had sold her and forbidden her to keep her children, and now she worked every day in a place where men saw her as a commodity. A life lived in such a place, surrounded by poverty, cruelty, and disease would be enough to drive anyone to madness.

Anyone but Meg. She was stronger than all of it, stronger than him, even. She ran her inn, looked after her family, and lived a life of her choosing. More than that, she *reigned.* If her neighbors consoled themselves for their weakness by throwing stones in her direction, let them. They couldn't touch her.

Some men liked their women weak, subservient.

Jake wasn't one of them.

He glanced down at her marching beside him and was overtaken by a sense of pride he had no business feeling. She wasn't his. She didn't belong to anyone. Knowing this, some part of him ached to belong to her.

"I don't know, Margaret," he said as he squeezed her hand. "Hell doesn't look so bad from here."

Chapter 15

Meg's heart was pounding by the time they got back to Southwark. The worst morning she'd had in ages was turning into the best. She squeezed Jake's hand back, savoring the few moments of stolen intimacy they'd have left before they reached the inn to begin the day's work.

As they reached Love Lane, people were openly staring. It wasn't like her to be in the company of a man in the daylight hours, not since Mark. She was a guilty pleasure, an indulgence to be ashamed of, but Jake didn't appear to be aware of this. Tall and proud, he walked down the street in no particular haste, though she knew his pace likely had more to do with his injury than anything else. Still, he was respected around these parts, and being at his side made her stand a little straighter, too.

People had already heard the worst. Seeing them holding hands--in the morning, no less--would only confirm their suspicions.

Meg grinned.

The feeling fled the moment they got back.

Davey loitered behind the bar with a face like a smacked arse. His lip curled as he noticed them coming in together. "So good of you to join us at last. I see you've forgotten my warning, Mr.

Cohen? I'll just take that--" he gestured toward their joined hands, "--out of your wages. How much more, I wonder?"

Jake's expression darkened but Meg responded first. "No one could forget you're a knob, Davey. He'll not pay you if I give it to him freely."

"You've no right to give anything to anyone. You're my ward--"

"I'm thirty-fucking-five and I'll shag who I damned well please. What are you doing back there? I thought your idea of work was eating my kippers in bed."

"We're out of beer," he accused. "What kind of inn runs out of beer?"

"It helps if you don't drink it all," she snapped. "It's due this afternoon. We'll serve ale until then."

♥

Hours later, they were almost out of ale as well.

Meg paced behind the bar like a caged lion, tensing further every time someone tried to order beer. One by one, even their most loyal punters left, setting out for any of the hundred other taverns and alehouses within short distance. Meg smacked the counter in frustration. "He'd better be dead."

Jake cracked a smile. "It's not as bad as all that. At least you get a night off."

"I can't afford to have a night off," she insisted. "This is the only inn on this street that doesn't sell girls anymore. If there's no beer, we've got nothing."

The bar was rather empty. When it had become clear the supper rush would be more of a trickle, Bess and Judith had busied themselves brewing beauty potions in the kitchen before leaving for the night. Now there were two buckets of hand salve setting in the larder and the whole bar smelled of burnt roses. Every breath was rapture, extravagantly lush and sickly sweet with just a hint of decay. He couldn't tell if it was pleasant or foul, it just *was.*

It went some way toward explaining the way Meg smelled, though. The smell of roses in her hair was like charred petals in a chafing dish, an offering to some ancient goddess. The prayers of the lonely carried through the centuries in smoke. Did she hear their prayers at night, when the bar was quiet?

Had she heard his?

Jake closed his eyes and said another one, failing to articulate the pain in his heart with something as mundane as words. He felt it, though. Perhaps she'd feel it, too.

"It's about bloody time!"

Meg's vehemence yanked him out of his reverie. He opened his eyes to see a rangy fellow stroll through the door with a barrel. He was in no particular hurry and dropped the barrel in front of the bar grudgingly. "There you are."

Meg's hands were firmly planted on her hips, her eyes bright with rage. "What do you mean, 'there you are'? We've got half a dozen coming today. Where's the rest?"

He eyed Jake with open resentment. "You don't need me to bring them anymore, do you?"

"It's what I pay you for, isn't it?"

"You pay for the beer because it's the best around," he bragged. "You want it, you can come get it."

"Don't be getting ideas, Gilbert. I only buy off you because you're cheaper than Bernard. I could sell horse piss and no one could tell yours apart."

His pout emphasized the hollows in his cheeks where teeth had been. "You'll have to, won't you? I'm not selling to you no more."

Meg's face turned the most enchanting shade of violet. "What about my order? I've paid you already."

"You'll have to come get it yourself."

"How do you expect me to do that? I haven't got a horse or cart."

The villain had the affront to look satisfied at this. "That isn't my concern. Come get it or you won't have it. I'll not be coming down to these parts again."

Throughout the exchange, Jake had stood at Meg's side like a particularly menacing shadow. He didn't know what they'd worked out, so he couldn't argue with the man. Still, he'd taken his measure. The brewer was a resentful arse of a man who liked to throw his weight around to feel powerful. His mouth had gotten him into a fight or two, judging by the missing teeth, crooked nose, and lazy eye. He was slight and lean with the overdeveloped forearms of a man in his trade. Jake would bet a sovereign the brewer fought dirty, but one judicious blow and he'd drop like a sack of shit.

Meg flung up her hands, exasperated. "We haven't given you enough business?"

"I don't need your sort of business." He looked at Jake as he said the last, and his meaning was clear.

Meg didn't miss it, either. "Piss off, then!"

He did.

"You want me to have a word with him?" Jake offered while he was still within sight of the door.

Meg shook her head. "Don't bother. It's time we learned to brew ourselves."

Jake loaded the barrel into the empty shelf with a heavy sigh. He knew he'd cost Meg some of her business already, but now her supplier, as well? How many setbacks would she put up with for the sake of a man she barely knew?

"I should leave," he said. "I've caused you enough trouble."

Meg blinked, aghast. "You? Gilbert's been a twat for years. That has nothing to do with you. Damn his eyes!"

In spite of her fighting words, Meg sank slowly to the floor and screamed her frustration into her knees.

Jake sat on the floor beside her. He pulled her into his arms out of instinct, knowing too well the unique helplessness that haunted that kind of anger. She went without protesting, limp as a ragdoll against his chest.

He took a deep breath, inhaling that smoke in her hair. After years without a lover, he was amazed by how quickly he was growing accustomed to touching her. It was easy, natural. Addictive. He held her with no expectation or hope other than to give her comfort.

"What are you doing?" she asked, her voice small.

"Looking after you."

She pulled away from him, her defenses once again in place. She stood, shaking out her skirt as though nothing had happened. "I don't need looking after."

"Yes, you do," he said before he thought better of it. He climbed to his feet, his bad leg shaking. "You need looking after in the worst possible way."

Her eyes seemed to light up the gloom of the bar and a cheeky smile curved across her lips. "Do I? I suppose you're going to give it to me?"

Temptress. He'd only meant he wanted to help her, but if she wanted to tease him, two could play at that game. He let his gaze drift over her lush curves. When it returned to her eyes, she looked as warm as he felt. Perhaps she wouldn't want to keep him, but the hunger in her eyes suggested she at least wanted him.

He smiled to himself. *Good.*

He licked his lips. "I'm going to give it to you, all right. I'm going to see to you properly and you'll make sounds you've never made before. I'll have to teach you whole new words to express the way I make you feel."

Her lips dropped open and she blinked, stunned by his promise.

It wasn't an empty one.

Before she could say a word, he lifted her onto the bar. He left her there while he grabbed a stool and brought it back, setting it between her legs. She leaned back on her hands, breathless. "What on earth are you doing?"

He sat on the stool and pulled off her shoes, dropping them onto the floor. "I'm giving you what you need, Margaret. Don't argue."

For once, she didn't.

His hands trailed up her curvy calves and over her knees beneath her long skirt. He lingered on the warm, bare flesh at the top of her woolen stockings. Some women wore underclothes to protect their most intimate parts from the elements and wandering fingers. He still wondered if Meg was among them.

He glanced up at her, his hands on her knees. Her startled gaze gave nothing away.

Determined to make good on his promise, he rolled her stockings all the way down her long, long legs and took them off her feet, dropping them in his lap. He left one leg dangling off the side of the bar as he took the other bare foot in both his hands. Even her feet were beautiful. He'd bet money no one had ever done this before.

He pressed one thumb into her arch and she gasped.

He followed this caress with another, sliding his thumbs into all the sore places of her feet one firm stroke at a time. Her toes contracted and her throaty moan was more seductive than any other sound he'd ever elicited from a woman. He wanted to hear it again.

Increasing the pressure, he worked over her heel and the ball of her foot, gently tugging on her toes. Her eyes closed and her face contorted with pleasure. "God preserve me."

Jake pushed both his thumbs up the arch at once and she cried out.

He smiled.

By the time he reached her other foot, she was insensible. He took his time working over the tense muscles and tendons, doing what he could to ease the twenty years of toil she held in her feet. His ached after a week at The Rose, he couldn't imagine how hers felt. He caressed them out of compassion, gratitude, and no little lust. He touched her for the pure joy of touching her, his pride swelling with every delicious little sound she made.

Pride, as well as another part of his anatomy.

"More," she gasped.

He smiled as he dug his thumbs into her arch. "*Verder*," he translated.

She groaned. "God, yes!"

He was inclined to agree. He carefully rotated her slender ankle and pressed into her heel. "*God, ja.*"

Her eyes shot open and her face was flushed. She held his gaze steadily. "I'm going to come if you keep that up."

He swallowed, the translation lost in the frankness of this statement. Would she really? He increased his pressure, willing to find out.

She bit her lip and whimpered.

Jake looked up at the squeal of a hinge, just in time to see Davey before he hid behind the door. The bastard was trying to catch them out again.

Meg sat up straighter. She had heard him, too. From the door, all he'd be able to see was Meg on the bar with a man's face between her legs. With a saucy look, she threw her head back and moaned as if she was on stage. "Oh, God...oh, God...yes...God, Jake!"

He knew she was screaming his name to aggravate her cousin, but that didn't keep him from enjoying it. He wanted to hear her say it in pleasure, wanted to push her over the edge. Had she been toying with him when she had said she was close? On the off-chance she spoke the truth, he redoubled his efforts.

Just let the little twat try to charge him for touching her.

"Mother of God," she rasped, and this time it sounded real.

Feeling more than a little cocky, he returned to her other foot and resumed rubbing.

Her eyebrows drew together, her lips fell open, and she said his name with a shudder and a sigh in what had to be the best imitation of a climax he'd ever had the pleasure of seeing. He was perilously close to one himself.

Again, Davey's door slammed as he returned to his room upstairs, presumably dismayed to find Meg in a compromising position with the hired help. If that's what it took to get the man to leave, he'd make Meg scream every night.

Selflessly, of course.

Meg sat up, looking bewildered and perhaps a little embarrassed. "I told you, didn't I?"

He kissed the ball of her foot without a word.

She hopped down off the bar and collected her shoes from the floor. He handed her the stockings back and she took them, patting his cheek like a puppy as she passed. "Good night, Jake."

He watched her hobble to the stairs, unsure if his attentions had affected her at all, or if all of that had been for Davey's sake. Had he imagined the desire in her eyes?

"Good night, Margaret," he said to the empty bar.

Chapter 16

Meg was hanging the last of the holly when Davey's voice slithered into her ear. "Haven't you finished all of this yet?"

She gritted her teeth and glared at him from on top of the bar. "It's Christmas, innit? Folks like a bit of frippery."

Jake offered his hand and helped her down. He shot her a meaningful look as she landed on her feet, clearly more than a little sick of Davey himself. Meg straightened her skirt and swept the pine needles off of the bar with her hand.

"We can't afford all this," he protested even as he poured himself a deep glass of their most expensive wine for his breakfast. "Pine here, ribbons there. Is this an alehouse or a bloody forest?"

Meg clenched her fist around the pine needles and winced as they bit into her palm. They were remarkably sharp. If she smacked him hard enough, perhaps they'd go straight into his brain. "Not that it's any concern of yours, but we paid for half of it months ago. The rest Judith pinched from rubbish boxes. Christmas is our busiest day of the year."

Davey sniffed like a petulant child. "Not in my inn." He carried his glass to the table beside the hearth and slumped into Joe Ledford's favorite chair with a snort. "Decorating with rubbish. I never! Best leave the day to day of things to the menfolk. You and your sisters would spend everything on ribbons and face cream." He smiled to himself as though he had uttered a gem of pure wit.

"Ribbons and face cream," she muttered, attacking the floor with the broom. "I'll give you ribbons and face cream, you worthless sack of horseshit."

Davey barely looked up. "What was that, dearest?"

Meg stopped sweeping and put her fist to her hip. "I said, you miserable old bastard, I'm not certain whether I would prefer to string you up with the ribbons or drown you in face cream."

He scoffed, affronted by her bile. "A man cannot drown in face cream."

"You feel like putting money on that, *dearest*?"

He stared at her blankly and Meg held his gaze, sizing him up. He was shorter than she was and likely heavier. His balance might be better, but he was green as a new leaf while Meg had grown up in the busiest inn in the dodgiest bit of Southwark. Given half a chance, she'd tear his head off.

He broke eye contact first. "You know you're beginning to look a little worn around the edges, cousin. I ought to marry you off while there's any chance of compensation. You'll not command a farthing once the year is out."

Meg clenched her teeth so hard her jaw hurt. She felt a big, warm hand close over her arm and turned to see Jake all but holding her back.

Davey noticed. He addressed Jake. "What would you give me for her, Jew? You've had her. What do you reckon she's worth?"

It was Meg's turn to hold him back once she saw the murder in his eyes.

He looked down at her, the severity in his expression calming as he met her gaze. Her fingers closed around his bicep. The contact was little more than a cheeky grope, but it was enough to distract her from the buffoon who thought he had a say over how she lived her life.

He wanted to marry her off, did he? Just let him try.

Jake's gaze fell to her lips as she smiled. "What?" he whispered.

Meg shook her head, her smile spreading. Any man fool enough to marry her would have to put up with her acid tongue and penchant for handsome boxers. Jake could turn her insides to mush with a look, not to mention the wicked things he had done to her feet in the name of "looking after her." He had some curious ideas about how to best see to her welfare, but he wouldn't hear a word of protest out of her.

"Disgusting," Davey muttered. "Don't you have any shame? It's bad enough you have to play the whore for the miscreants around these parts, but for this one? It's unnatural." He gave a melodramatic shudder.

Meg crossed her arms and glared at Davey. "Better a Dutchman than a swine."

"He's Dutch?" Davey sneered. "Lord, that's even worse. Bring me another glass of this. I find myself in need of fortification."

Meg pulled a fresh glass from the shelf, silently spit into the bottom of it and topped it up with the bottom of the barrel of the cheapest red swill they had. She shuffled past Jake and slapped it into Davey's table, spilling a few droplets over the side.

He caught her wrist. "You ought to be kinder to me, Meggy. I'll need a wife to run this ruin before long."

Seizing her hand from his grasp, she summoned all of the derision she had for him and forced it into one prick-withering glare. "I'd prefer a swine."

Beyond the bar, Bess popped her amber-colored head around the corner. "Breakfast," she blurted, disappearing back into the kitchen as quickly as she had appeared.

Grateful for the interruption, Meg marched toward the kitchen and Jake followed her there.

"Have Judith bring me mine," Davey commanded.

♥

No sooner had they made it into the kitchen than Meg kicked the wall in frustration. "Lecherous, flatulent knob! I'll strangle him with my bare hands before the week is out."

Judith returned from delivering his breakfast with a look a disgust on her face. "He tried to touch my bum."

"Here." Meg opened her hand to reveal a fistful of pine needles. "Put these in his bed when you're cleaning his room."

Judith slipped them into the pocket of her apron with a sweet little smile.

"Don't let him get to you," Bess said as she poured four cups of coffee. "He can't harm us."

"He can't harm *you*. You're a kept woman. You could march out of here any day you like." Meg pointed out, and Jake thought he heard a tinge of jealousy in her voice.

Bess set down her coffee and moved toward the door. "That's right. I can't believe I never thought of that. Thank you for reminding me, dear sister."

"Sit down," Meg protested. "You wouldn't leave us."

Bess laughed. "I wouldn't dream of it. But if he thinks for a moment to marry me off, I'll be out of here, make no mistake."

She offered him a coffee and he accepted it with a smile. He'd only been there a few days, and already the sisters had accepted him as one of them, almost. Though he'd certainly received a speculative glance or two over the first day or so, he'd become as much a part of the inn as the furniture. Totally at ease in his presence, they chatted over breakfast as though he was one of them.

He sat at the end of one bench beside the long narrow table in the kitchen and helped himself to a wedge of good brown bread. "You have a man, do you?" he asked Bess. It was the first he'd heard it mentioned.

Bess laughed. "More or less. My Sue is better than a man, and she knows how to treat a lady."

"Or whatever it is you are." Meg rolled her eyes and Bess threw a chunk of bread at her.

Judith carefully unwrapped her baby from her sling as she began to fuss. She carried her around as she cleaned in the mornings, swaddled and bound securely to her back. Nonplussed by his presence, she loosed her top and began to feed the infant at the breakfast table. Far from offended, Jake was touched that they were so comfortable around him. It had been a dozen years since he'd had any family to speak of, and he hadn't realized how lonely he had been until the Henshawes threw his solitude into stark relief with their affection and noise.

He buttered his bread. "You're kept by a woman, then?"

Bess sipped her coffee. "More common than you think, Jake."

Meg nodded in agreement. "She passes as a man, at least. She wears trousers and none's the wiser. Something to be said for a lover who knows the territory, but you can't beat the feeling of a good hard cock between your legs." She glanced at Jake as though she had just realized he was there. "Not that you'd know. Or, I suppose you would…" She flushed a brilliant scarlet.

Jake laughed in spite of himself. "Why, Margaret. You're embarrassed."

"I am not," she sputtered, and her sisters giggled.

"Has that ever happened before?" he asked them, genuinely curious.

Judith shook her head, grinning.

"Once," Bess announced. "When we were children. That was it."

"You're thinking of Bel," Meg corrected her.

"Oh, right." Bess scratched her head.

Jake made short work of the bread and took some more with a thick slice of hard cheese. "I haven't met Bel."

"She lives in the City," Judith supplied. "She's kept by a

lawyer."

Jake raised his eyebrows. He supposed the best girls of their class could hope for was to be kept by someone wealthy. With his wages, he'd be fortunate to keep a roof over his head, let alone support a wife and family. If Meg married him, she'd likely have to keep her job.

If Meg married him. Where had that come from?

A scuffle of footsteps distracted him from his thoughts and he looked up to see Tommy running into the kitchen with a smile on his face. He barely slowed to kiss Meg's cheek. "Good morning, Mum."

"Good morning, darling." She smiled at him indulgently. "What are you so excited about, then?"

"Chris is coming over again." Tommy grabbed a piece of cheese and plopped down on the bench beside Jake. "I've never had a friend before."

"There are precious few of those in the world." Meg sipped her coffee. "Take care not to annoy him."

Tommy nodded solemnly. "Yes, Mum."

Jake smiled to himself, enjoying the peculiar intimacy of the shared breakfast. Meg probably wouldn't have given it a second thought, but he was touched beyond words to be included.

"We've still got to pick up the rest of the beer today." He reminded Meg. "If you tell me where Gilbert lives, I can go get it."

"It's on the other side of the bridge down an alley in the City. You'll never find it if I don't show you where it is."

He nodded. "This afternoon?"

"Have to be later. I'm expecting the grocer and won't be able to cook supper until after he arrives. I'll see if he's got a wagon we can borrow."

Bess' eyes widened. "It's Wednesday night. They'll riot if we run out again."

"It's Davey's inn now, or so he keeps reminding me." Meg smirked. "Let him handle it."

♥

By the time Tommy had finished his breakfast, Davey was gone.

He'd left his plate, though. He always left his plate. Every morning when he helped Judith clean, Tommy had to clear out wine-stained glasses, greasy plates, and chicken bones. Where had the bastard found chicken, anyway? Tommy hadn't had any, and his mum certainly hadn't roasted any lately.

Tommy stared at the plate, fish oil staining the hunk of good bread Davey had left behind. His mum would throw a fit if she saw he'd wasted it. Tommy had a mind to leave it there; Davey could clean it himself when he returned.

If he returned. Davey stayed out longer and longer every day. For someone who wanted the inn so badly, he spent a lot of time away from it. He didn't want to work there. He only wanted to drink their wine.

Tommy had seen him duck into The Unicorne once or twice. Was he drinking their wine, too?

"Morning, Tommy lad." Joe Ledford slumped into the bar on his spindly legs, looking older than ever. He flashed a toothless grin and slid into the chair Davey had left. "Still warm." He laughed, snatching the bread from Davey's plate. "Is your mother in?"

Tommy scratched his head. "She's helping Aunt Bess make the lye while the kitchen's quiet."

"Can't eat lye, can I?" Joe asked with a twinkle in his eye. The way he said it made Tommy wonder if he ever had.

"There's bread left. Want some?"

"Much obliged."

Tommy took Davey's plate with him back into the kitchen and dropped it into the wash bucket. "Joe's here."

His mum glanced over her shoulder, red from the heat of the ashes boiling over the fire. He'd seen lye in shops, but his mother always insisted on making their own, even though it took days to set before they could use it. "Give him some bread and cheese, and see if we've got any kippers left."

"Yes, mum."

Jake handed him the clean plate he'd been drying. "I'll bring coffee out in a moment."

Tommy loaded up the plate with the heel of the loaf and the last of the cheese. "Joe doesn't drink coffee."

Jake shrugged. "It's kind to ask, nevertheless."

Tommy took the plate out to Joe, mulling Jake's words.

Joe lit up as he saw his breakfast. "There we are. You must thank your mother for this feast."

Tommy paused before doing just that. "Would you like coffee, Joe?"

Joe pursed his lips, surprised as Tommy that he'd asked. "Yes, I think I would."

As soon as he said as much, Jake stepped out of the kitchen with two cups hot enough Tommy could see the steam rising from them in the chill of the bar. "All right, Joe?" Jake greeted, setting a mug in front of him.

"Cheers." He raised his cup in salute and took a sip. "Why's your coffee so much better than Meg's, then?"

"Don't say that to her," he kidded. "I use less powder and I don't boil it as long. I thought you said you didn't drink it. When's the last time you had hers?"

"Years ago." Joe shuddered. "That was enough."

Overcome with curiosity, Tommy asked, "Is it really better?"

Jake offered his mug to Tommy. "Try it."

Tommy hesitated. His father had never offered him anything unless it was some kind of test. If he took it, he'd get a slap. If he didn't, he'd be goaded until he did, and then he'd get a slap.

Expecting a trick, Tommy reached out and took it.

Jake didn't hit him.

Encouraged, Tommy sniffed it. It smelled like the coffee they always made, as far as he could make out. He took a sip.

Jake didn't hit him. He nodded encouragingly, awaiting Tommy's judgment. "What do you think?"

"I-It's sweeter, I think. It's easier to drink."

Jake smiled. "Good. You can have that one if you like. I'll get another."

Tommy curled his cold fingers around the heat of the cup. "Really?"

"Yeah," he replied with a chuckle, as though it was obvious.

It wasn't. Tommy sat down across from Joe with his coffee as Jake went back to the kitchen. Few men were all that kind to him. His father slapped him plenty. When he wasn't around, the others tried to make up for his absence. Strangers had boxed his ears, told him to stand up straight. Not in front of his mother, of course. On the few times she'd caught them, they'd been lucky to leave alive.

They said a boy ought not grow up surrounded by only women.

Tommy *wished* he could grow up with only women. His mum and his aunts were kind. Men, as a rule, were not.

Mark Virtue seemed like a good sort. His mum hated him, though.

Jake returned from the kitchen with a cup of coffee and a glass full of clear liquid. "Is that gin?" Tommy blurted before he thought better of it.

"Vinegar and lemon, for the bar." Jake pulled a face. "We'll try not to confuse them, shall we?"

Tommy ventured a small smile. He still wasn't sure what to make of Jake. He had been there all of a week, which had to be the longest anyone had stayed. He worked all day and didn't do the things other men did. He didn't gamble or drink or put his hands all over his mum and his aunts. He'd met some who didn't do one or another, but never all three at once.

Tommy looked up at the sound of the door to see Chris working his way into the bar. He darted up and held the door open for him.

"Cheers, Tommy." Chris smiled, already looking healthier than the night before.

"Jake made coffee. Do you want some?" he asked, remembering it was the kind thing to do.

"Yes, thanks." Chris smiled, looking as happy to be there as Tommy was he arrived.

"Morning, Chris," Jake greeted. "How's your leg feeling today?"

"Stiff." Chris shook his head and shrugged out of his coat. "It aches something terrible."

Jake gave a solemn nod. "That's how you know it's working. Come here, I'll show you another stretch."

Chris walked to the bar as quickly as he could manage and Tommy followed, curious. "What are you doing?"

"Jake is helping me with my leg."

Tommy frowned. Chris's left leg was badly crippled. What could help that? "How?"

"We're making it stronger," Jake explained as he stepped easily around the front of the bar to join them. "My leg was hurt, too, so I'm trying to help Chris with his if I can."

Chris nodded, unable to contain his excitement. "Same leg, the left one."

Tommy looked at Jake's legs. He hadn't noticed anything different about them. "You hurt yours?"

"I did," Jake confirmed. "Many years ago. Not as badly as Chris. It still gets bad if I don't move it, though. Here, try this." He put his hands on his hips and lowered himself toward the floor like he was about to sit on a chair, but then stood up again. "Can you do that? Go slowly, now."

Tommy did several without thinking about it. "That's easy."

Chris struggled with a single one. Jake held his arm to steady him when he lost his balance. "It's a little more difficult for Chris," Jake said. "Why don't you help him practice these every day, and then next week I'll show you another?"

Tommy nodded, honored to be trusted with such an important task. "Of course."

When his mum finally came out of the kitchen fanning herself with her hand, she frowned with puzzlement to find the three of them attempting to sit on invisible chairs. “What…?”

“We’re fixing Chris’ leg,” he told her.

She watched them a moment with that look on her face she sometimes got when she was trying not to laugh. “Don’t let me stop you.”

Jake stood, losing his balance as he smiled at her.

She didn’t tell him off for being ridiculous or wasting time. She smiled back.

Jake was *definitely* different.

Chapter 17

It was quiet for a Wednesday, the cold and snow had driven the crowds indoors in search of warmer pursuits. The sudden dip in temperature had caused the half-melted to snow to freeze again, and Meg crunched through it like smashing up a sugar cake. Her breath clouded like smoke from the mouth of a dragon. She wasn't cold, she was *breathing fire.* After their brief exchange with the brewer, she certainly felt as though she could.

The snow cushioned the wagon's wheels, preventing any creaking that might alert lurking thieves. It was nice for something to work in her favor for once. "Do you want me to take that for a bit?"

Jake shook his head, dragging the wagon behind him as though it was nothing. "It's fine."

"I'm stronger than I look," she insisted.

He shot an appreciative glance her way and his smile warmed her to her toes. "I know."

She would have struggled to manage on her own, if she'd had to. Not least because Gilbert had made it clear he had no intention of honoring her order until he'd noticed Jake looming behind her like a particularly ill-tempered shadow. The man hadn't said a word and still Gilbert had loaded them down with the five barrels owed plus an extra for good measure.

Then again, that might have something to do with Meg's violent reaction to the name Gilbert had called her. She rubbed the sore spot on her forehead. That would hurt later.

"I've got to be good for something," Jake muttered to himself.

"You are," she blurted. "You're good for more than that."

He held her gaze long enough to make her self-conscious. She tucked her hair behind her ear. On any other man, a look like that would be an invitation. She still didn't know where she stood with Jake. He looked at her as though he wanted her, but he hadn't made any attempt to take her. That kind of restraint wasn't something she'd ever come across before. It was unnerving.

She let out a long, steadying breath. "It's time we started brewing, ourselves. Perhaps you could give us a hand with that?"

His nod was almost cocky. She'd never seen anyone with so much natural swagger, and he was loaded down with a bloody cart. "What does that entail?"

"Setting up equipment, finding the time to do it, licensing. We could store it in the cellar." Meg rambled off what she knew of brewing, which was fuck all. If it was that or destitution, she'd bloody figure it out.

"Ale or beer?"

She shrugged. "Either, both. You know anything about brewing?"

"Not a damned thing." His laugh was a puff of smoke in the night. For all he presented the appearance of calm stability, she reckoned he could breathe fire, too. "We'll learn."

Meg's smile was so wide at first she didn't recognize the feeling on her face. Why didn't she smile more? "Planning to stay awhile, are you?"

"Better had, hadn't I? You haven't got a horse." He smirked.

His joke was innocent, but Meg's thoughts were anything but. Her cheeks flooded with heat and she refocused her attention on the street ahead. "You going to give me rides into town, as well?"

"I'll give you rides anywhere you like."

Meg bit her lip to stifle the whimper that seemed to spring directly from the base of her belly. She looked at him, hoping he was resuming his flirtation from the night before.

He stopped walking. "Jump on," he dared her, dark eyes bright with amusement.

"I beg your pardon?"

He turned his back to her, patting his shoulder. "Jump on."

"I can't!" Her laugh sounded hysterical even to her, like a little girl giggling with the first boy she fancied. "We'd never make it back home with the cart."

"We can. It's not far."

She shook her head. She was sorely tempted to try--how often did one get an offer like that?--but she was deathly afraid she'd crush him. For all her famous proportions, she was heavy as hell. She didn't want to scare the poor man off. "I'd kill you."

He appraised her figure with a look of disbelief. "If you say so." He shrugged and kept on walking.

It felt good to laugh. Unnatural, but good. Most of the times she'd laughed had been out of bitterness or spite. There were few enough opportunities for anything else.

She smiled at him, struck by how rare it was to have a conversation with a man that wasn't a transaction. Perhaps they could talk about the weather next. The clouds hung low over the city in a swathe of hyacinth velvet, illuminating the night with reflected light. The steam from the dye-houses only added to it, insulating the street from the worst of the cold. The wind off the river smelled of ice. Meg shivered. "Looks like more snow," she said, testing the subject.

He looked up at the sky. "I suppose it does. Not likely to get caught in it. We'll be home soon."

Home. The word sounded strange to her, coming from him. She had never known a man to use it in connection to her. Home was always something they had to return to, the reason they couldn't stay. Home was somewhere she was never welcome, and something she had never shared.

Meg glanced at him in the poor light as they walked between the shuttered shops that lined the bridge. He was more fearsome in the dark. Though he wore his strength lightly, it was apparent in the set of his shoulders and the way he moved with steady, deliberate steps through the snow. If his leg was hurting him, he didn't let it show. He wouldn't invite attack, though nothing about him made him look like an easy target. Shadows deepened the hollows of his face, so even his pleasant expression looked more akin to a glower. He'd look fearsome to anyone passing on the street. Kindness could rarely be observed from a distance.

Well and good. His kindness could be her secret. She'd keep it close to her heart with his quiet humor and his wide, wonky smile.

"This is the longest I've been away from the bar at night in twenty years," she confided. "It's almost a night off."

His eyebrows drew together as he regarded her, as though he was searching for signs of a jest. Finding none, he replied, "I'm honored."

"Not over yet, I suppose. Probably still have to work for an hour or two when we get back. Pots to wash, fights to break up."

"I'll take the pots, you take the fights." He cracked a wry smirk and she stopped feeling the snow.

Meg licked her lips, instantly regretting it as they began to burn in the cold. "As you wish, sir. Don't take it easy on me because I'm a woman, now."

His face transformed when he chuckled. "Wouldn't dream of it."

Meg found herself smiling back. He had the most remarkable face. Jake would never be pretty, but he was something more than that.

The hardships he'd weathered, he wore on his face. The

breaks in his nose were the most obvious, perhaps, but he had the beginnings of lines around his eyes and even his mouth, and those lines had not come from joy. His jaw was strong, his cheekbones prominent, and his ears were larger than most. Life had built that face, and no one else could have worn it so well.

Twenty-six or thirty-eight, Meg had never seen him as anything other than beautiful. Any woman would be lucky to have him. "Why aren't you married?"

His eyebrows shot up at her question. "I don't know if you've noticed, Margaret, but women don't much like me."

She snorted. "Nonsense. We've had more women in the bar this week than in the last two months combined. Every time you change a barrel, I have to mop the floor."

His grin split his face. "What a vulgar thing to say."

"I only speak the truth," she insisted, savoring that grin. "They'd be all over you, except they know I'd give them a slap."

"Would you?"

"Too right." Though she was grateful for the increase in female customers, it wasn't easy to control her jealousy. He'd seemed indifferent to their advances so far, but one of these nights he'd take one of them to bed, and Meg would have to listen to it. Alone. "We're busy enough without you getting distracted."

"There's more than enough to hold my attention behind the bar." He glanced at her, his expression softening.

The way he was looking at her, she could almost believe he meant her. She tucked a piece of hair behind her ear and looked away. It wouldn't do any good to start thinking like that. Only the night before he'd reduced her to a babbling mess with his talk of giving her a good looking after. When those big hands closed over her thighs, she had thought for one breathless second that he meant to take her over the bar. Her surprise at the massage was only dwarfed by her shock at her reaction to it. She had almost melted into the wood.

While many of the noises she'd made had been fake, her

climax was real enough.

He really *was* good with his hands.

Still, if he could sit between her legs and keep his hands on her feet, that was proof enough for her he didn't want her. She had never known a man not to take when given half a chance.

"Why aren't *you* married?"

Meg snorted at the question. "You're having a laugh."

He shook his head. "I'm sure you've had offers."

"Not one."

He gaped at her. "Rubbish."

She smiled as though it didn't bother her. "I'm an aging strumpet with three children, a filthy mouth, and a bad temper. Who'd take on all of that when they can see the best parts for a sovereign?"

"Anyone with his wits about him." He stopped to catch his breath. "You're fearless, quick-witted, and more than capable of running an inn and raising a family. Aging or not, you are easily the most beautiful woman in London."

She met his gaze, startled by his words. No one had ever said half so many kind things to her face. It was one thing to be regarded as a beauty, and quite another to hear him say he thought she was beautiful. Caught off guard, she felt herself swaying toward the warmth in his eyes. "Am I, now?"

His gaze fell to her lips. "It is common knowledge."

When she spoke, her voice sounded husky to her ears. "That I am, or that you think so?"

He didn't answer. His look was heated and more than a little helpless. It was not so far removed from the look he'd given her the night before when he'd just touched her feet. She'd give her only pair of shoes to know what he was thinking.

She licked her lips and they stung in the cold. His face was mere inches away. Just one tilt of her chin and she'd be kissing him. She turned more fully into his reach, brushing her breasts against his chest. They were covered by her coat, but he wouldn't be able to mistake the invitation.

Just one kiss, she prayed to anyone listening. *Just one and I'll live off of it for years.*

If he noticed what was on offer, he didn't want it. His gaze strayed between her eyes and her lips, but his hands remained firmly on the wagon. Her heart sank beneath the weight of her disappointment.

She was acutely aware of his every movement throughout the day. When he changed the barrels, she was right there with the local girls, salivating with every stretch. She wanted him, and badly, but he did not seem to be particularly aware she was a woman.

She was sick of embarrassing herself. In spite of everything, she had *some* pride left. It was time she found it.

Meg sighed as she resumed walking. Jake cleared his throat and followed, catching up to her easily in the snow. She could see the lights of the inn up ahead and heard the distant hum of the voices inside. Thankfully, it did not appear to be on fire.

Anxious to get back inside and check on Tommy, she increased her pace. Jake sped up, but could not match her speed over the long distance. She slowed down until they were side by side again. "I don't want to marry," she said, and she almost believed it. "I could never subject myself to the whim of some man. There's protection in marriage, but that's not enough for me anymore. If I want protection, I'll hire myself a boxer."

He smiled. "I could recommend one."

"A husband or a boxer?"

He shrugged.

"You're all the man I need," she said, her brusque tone offsetting what would have otherwise sounded like an overture. "I'll live my life according to my own whims. You just keep looking pretty behind that bar."

He laughed and opened the door for her as they arrived.

♥

They arrived as Bess drained the last remaining barrel. "Thank heavens," she cried as she saw them, and they were greeted by a round of grateful shouts from the bar. In spite of the beer shortage, the bar was full once again.

Jake unloaded the wagon he'd dragged all the way from the city, glad to be rid of it. "They seem happy enough. Did you find more beer somewhere?"

Bess shook her head. "We've been selling that awful gin at a steep discount to get rid of it. No one's asked for beer for hours, but the gin is gone with most of the wine."

Meg shrugged out of her cloak, her face still rosy from the cold. "No wonder they're in a good mood. They drank all of that gin?"

"All of it," Bess replied cheerfully. "May need to help some of them home by the end of tonight, the way things are going."

"I'll say." Meg rested against the bar with a long sigh, her gaze following the movement of Jake's arms as he put the barrels away. She blushed as he caught her looking and immediately focused her attention on her sister. Jake smirked to himself, glad his years in the pit had been good for something.

It was late and everyone was deep in their cups. Jake fell into what had become his new evening routine, pouring drinks, changing money, and keeping the bar clean with a wash of rosemary and salt. After she'd checked on the children, Meg made the rounds, talking to everyone as though she hadn't seen them in weeks. She was in her element, happy in spite of the day's setbacks. This was Meg at her best; friendly, funny, hospitable. If the inn was hers free and clear, she could do anything with it.

The blanket fluttered over the broken window, letting in a gust of freezing air. Jake left his place behind the bar to fix it, pushing the nails through the coarse fabric and back into their holes. They'd need to have the window repaired before they bankrupted the place buying coal to heat it.

Hearing someone knock on the bar for service, he turned too quickly and bumped into Meg. She lost her balance and he caught her automatically, holding her up as she steadied herself.

Someone whistled.

Jake ignored it until another followed, then a third. He looked around the bar in confusion, while Meg turned scarlet in his grasp.

"Bastard mistletoe." She muttered, looking anywhere but at him.

Bess cackled as she passed them, an empty tray lolling on her hip.

Mistletoe. Jake frowned at the spiny leaves hanging from the ceiling. He was meant to kiss her, wasn't he?

It wasn't his tradition, but the punters thought he was odd and foreign enough already without him drawing attention to it. He wouldn't embarrass Meg by refusing. Wasn't it meant to be bad luck if you didn't?

These and a dozen other reasons flew through his mind to justify the fact that he wanted to. He wanted to kiss her very, very badly.

Davey would no doubt try to charge him for it. Fortunately, the little rat was nowhere to be seen.

"What are they waiting for?" someone whispered behind him.

"Kiss her!" Joe Ledford bellowed, covering his encouragement up with a series of contrived coughs.

Finally, Meg looked up at him with an unfamiliar light shining in her eyes.

It was fear.

Was she afraid of him? His heart ached. He knew from experience he didn't have to do anything to inspire fear in women, but he thought he and Meg had grown close, or something like it. He had thought they were friends, though her very presence drove him to distraction and he'd spent long hours talking himself out of visiting her room again. She was different, he knew it. Why was she afraid?

He spread his hands in a gesture of surrender. He wouldn't kiss her if she didn't want him to.

Meg's eyes flickered as her expression changed to one of steely determination. "Bugger it," she muttered and stepped fully into his arms. Standing on her toes, she slid her arms around his neck. He caught her waist automatically, welcoming the feeling of her soft curves pressed up against him. She smelled of rosewater and tobacco, an intoxicating combination at once earthy and sweet. Her eyelashes dropped, and she hesitantly touched her lips to his.

It was not the quick peck he had expected. Her kiss was slow and deep. She tentatively moved her lips against his, testing the way they fit together. He held her flush against his hips, helpless. His hair stood on end as she ran the edge of her tongue along his bottom lip, nipping at it softly with her teeth.

He sighed against her lips, his hands drifting up her back. Seized with wickedness, he wound her thick braid around his wrist. She'd seemed to like it when he'd pulled it before. He tugged it gently and her mouth opened with a low, throaty moan. He could barely hear it, but he could taste it. His tongue delved into the sweet heat of her mouth, savoring the crush of her lips, the caress of her tongue, and a taste that was all her own.

The bar was so quiet he could hear his own heartbeat. Everything seemed to disappear around them except for the crackle of the fire in the hearth and the distant smell of ale, receding behind the delicious scent of the goddess in his arms. She tightened her grasp around his neck and kissed him harder.

Someone cleared their throat. He ignored them.

"So that's that, then," someone muttered.

The odd finality of this comment seemed to reach Meg through the haze and she broke off the kiss too quickly, her hands sliding slowly down his chest. She rested them there a moment and held his gaze with huge eyes bright and green as leaves in the sun; luminous and tinged with gold.

He saw it then. There was desire there, obvious and painful as his own. A measure of confusion, perhaps, but it wasn't as dire as he'd suspected.

Meg Henshawe was *not* afraid of anything.

He swallowed.

Meg smiled and stepped out of his arms. She made a show of straightening her hair and shrugged it off. "Pay attention lads, you might learn a thing or two."

Her comment was greeted with laughter and no few lewd suggestions. Without a backward glance, he excused himself and headed outside.

A sharp gust of wind off the river hit him fierce as a knockout punch. He crossed his arms against the cold. His sleeves were rolled up to his elbows and in his haste to leave, he hadn't thought to retrieve his coat. Borrowed light from the inn pooled out into the street to illuminate a dingy looking puddle and the hindquarters of a rat as it scurried away. Outside of that glow, the night was dark as any he'd seen. The houses looked vacant, though he knew better. If not for the sound of punters carousing inside, he could have imagined himself completely alone.

He needed the quiet to collect his thoughts.

That kiss…

He shivered with unease more than the cold as a sense of fate settled into his bones. She'd been playing with him, he was sure of it. It didn't matter. His life would never be the same again. He knew it as he knew his own name. He ran a hand over his face, trying to pull himself together.

Meg wasn't the first woman he'd kissed, but the experience was so unique, he wondered if he'd imagined the others. A brush here, a peck there. A bit of contact in the night. Nothing came remotely close. Even the more memorable experiences dropped out of his mind in defeat, until there was nothing left but her.

She didn't mean it. She liked to put on a show, that's all. He wasn't inexperienced with women, but in the end, it was a meaningless gesture that had brought him down. He tried to remind himself she gave her kisses freely, but his heart protested, already wrapped up in all the ways she was different from the others. Minor details like the freckles on her nose, the sound of her laugh, and the tilt of her chin wove together like a net around his heart and he hung suspended, waiting for her to put him out of his misery.

He emitted a bitter laugh at the joke he had become.

"Evening, Jake."

He looked up to see Mark Virtue leaning against the wall perhaps a yard away, smoking a pipe. "You're quiet."

Mark shrugged. "Habit. Are you well?" He glanced at Jake's thin shirt, hardly protection enough for December.

"Great, mate." Jake ran a hand through his hair. "Never better."

Mark nodded, his lips pursed around his pipe in a smug half smile. His posture was casual, but Jake felt as though he was sizing him up. He plucked the pipe from his mouth and exhaled. "How long has that been going on, then?"

Jake didn't have to ask what he meant. He bristled. "That's your concern, is it?"

Mark raised his hands in a gesture of surrender. "Do me a favor, eh? I've got money riding on it."

Jake laughed. There was nothing else to do. "What's the bet?"

"You can probably guess." He took a draw off of his pipe. "It's a penny for each day, winner take all. You want in? I won't tell the lads." He winked.

Jake felt his lip twitch into the beginning of a sneer. "How much money you got riding on it?"

Mark chuckled to himself, and Jake got the impression that he really did think something was funny. He just wished he knew what it was. "You're all right, aren't you?"

"Am I?" Jake angled his shoulder toward Mark defensively as

though gearing up for a fight. The gesture had been subconscious, but once he realized he'd done it, it felt like the appropriate thing to do. Mark probably didn't mean him any harm, but Jake wasn't at all certain he liked Mark. He tried to force himself to relax. It wasn't easy in the cold. "Nothing is going on. That was it." He confided, but he wasn't sure why.

"You're having a laugh."

Jake shook his head.

"Truly?" Mark raised his eyebrows. "I just lost some money."

Jake almost smiled at that. "What day did you bet on?"

"Night you got here." Mark tucked his pipe into his coat. "You're not married, are you?"

"Don't have to be." Jake let out a long breath. "Meg doesn't go to bed with everyone she meets, you know."

"Only boxers she's fancied for ages," Mark muttered.

"Beg your pardon?"

"Didn't say a word, me." Mark shrugged. "You know she used to watch you. Years ago, when she was drifting between me and Tom. I'd take her to the fights. She liked going. She'd watch matches all night, but whenever you used to come on, she'd sit forward in her seat. Thought I didn't notice, but there's not a lot I miss. Could say anything to her you liked and she wouldn't hear it until you'd finished. I thought she was going to strangle a woman once for having the misfortune to block her view." He laughed at the memory.

Jake blinked. "You didn't mind?"

Mark snorted. "It was never like that with us. She was like my sister, really."

"Your sister you almost married?" Jake shot him a look.

"Yeah. That sort." Mark thrust his hands into his pockets.

Meg was right, there was something about the darkness that lent itself to honesty. The conversation was odd, at best, but it was easier having it without a clear view of each other. Tomorrow morning he'd wake up, thinking he'd dreamt it all. If it was a dream, he'd better take advantage of it. "Why didn't you marry her?"

"Didn't suit. Besides, I could never hold her interest longer than an hour at a time."

He didn't like the implication that Meg was fickle. From what he'd seen of her, he didn't think that was the case. "She's a good woman."

Mark laughed aloud. "Meg Henshawe is an inferno inside a nice figure and she eats men alive."

"Rather more than nice, isn't it?" He raised his eyes toward the stars. "You two still…?"

Mark balked. "God no, not in years. You *have* seen my wife?"

Jake nodded. "Pretty little thing."

"Rather more than pretty, isn't she?" He scoffed. "No, we're not. Not since Jane. Then she went back to Tom for a time."

"He still comes around." Jake looked at Mark, wondering how much a part of Meg's life he'd remained.

The color drained from Mark's face and his eyes took on a rather frightening glint. "I haven't seen him in years. When does he come?"

Jake frowned, wondering why Mark would care. "Came around the other morning when the inn was quiet."

"Can't imagine he's happy you're here."

"I couldn't possibly say."

Mark emitted a joyless chuckle. "How many of his teeth you reckon you've knocked out?"

"Two. Perhaps three." Jake shrugged.

Mark gave him a warm pat on the back. "Good man. You might have occasion to knock out a few more before long."

Jake frowned. He suspected Mark was right. "What do you make of all this with Davey? Has he been around before?"

"First I've met him." Mark shrugged. "Bide your time, keep Meg from choking him. Man like that won't last a fortnight around here without getting his head caved in, mark my words. He'll go or he'll be forced out."

At this ominous statement, Jake looked at Mark. "What's wrong with him?"

"What isn't?" Mark exhaled a cloud of smoke into the cold winter air. "He's a knob, and there are some who don't take kindly to knobs, especially those upsetting our favorite barmaid. She has friends more loyal to her than she knows."

Jake let out a long breath, beginning to feel the cold. He would believe it.

Mark smiled. "I'd best be off home. You look after her, yeah?"

"Yeah." Jake frowned. As if he needed Mark Virtue telling him to do such a thing. "Give my best to your wife."

Mark shook his hand and headed down the street.

Jake took a long breath, mulling the conversation over in his mind.

A curvaceous shadow fell over him and he glanced up to see Meg standing in the doorway. He remembered what Mark had said about her watching his fights, and felt oddly bashful.

She tucked a long piece of hair behind her ear and frowned at his shirtsleeves. "What are you doing out here?" Her voice was almost lost beneath the sounds of the bar.

"Needed some air, is all." His smile was effortless, a twitch that happened whenever she was near.

Her gaze softened and she hesitated, as though she wanted to come outside but thought better of it. "Is there someone out here with you?"

He shook his head. "Mark's just gone home. Spoke for a moment."

She rolled her eyes hard. "Mark bloody Virtue."

He was inclined to agree.

"Are you coming back in?" she asked, a hint of a smile on her lips. He thought again of what she'd said at the bakery about not wanting him to catch cold in his room alone. It had sounded like an invitation then, and he was tempted to take her up on it now. Still, there were any number of men in the inn intent on talking her into their beds, and he would not be one of them. Meg deserved better than to be treated like a whore. She'd made it clear she'd never been treated as anything else.

"Coming now, love."

She smiled at him over her shoulder as she turned and he followed her back into the inn.

♥

Hours later, a hundred punters had come and gone, but Meg was still playing the kiss over in her head. Chris had gone home and Tommy was in bed, and there was no one left in the bar except her, Jake, and Joe Ledford snoring softly beneath the window.

Jake swept up the last of the dank rushes from the floor as though nothing had happened at all.

Perhaps he was used to kisses like that, but she wasn't. Never had she lost her senses so completely. His arms, his heat, his taste—*oh, God his taste*—it was all so damnably *right.* She'd never been so drawn to anyone before. It ached in the pit of her belly, a relentless driving need to take or be taken.

Her hands shook as she put away the last of the glasses, and they rattled together as she shoved them up on the shelf. She was a *mess.*

Jake was fine. He finished sweeping and went to lock the door.

It was likely too late for Joe to leave, and they both knew he didn't really have anywhere to go. He'd wake up at that table in the morning, and Meg would bring him his breakfast.

Joe's snore rose and fell above the crackling of the hearth. Meg leaned against the front of the bar, warming her hands near the fire. She had been moving for hours and she didn't need the heat, if she was honest, but she had to do something with her hands. It was either that or drink. Anything to keep her hands off of Jake.

He joined her at the bar, a broom in his hand. "Long night."

Meg nodded.

He regarded her carefully. "You feeling better? From earlier?"

She turned to him, unsure of what he was referring to. "You'll hear no complaint out of me," she said, thinking he meant the kiss.

"How long was he your brewer?"

Meg blinked dumbly. "Oh, Gilbert." She snorted. "Since the last one passed. Ten years or more. Good riddance."

"And your head?"

"Oh, that. I'm fine, really. Not the first twat I've had to head-butt."

He grinned and laughed under his breath. "You're an expert. Wish I'd had you at my back in the pit, I can tell you."

Meg shifted under his praise. "What, like fighting together?"

He shrugged. "It's been done."

She looked away, feeling oddly shy. "I'm nothing like you, though. You're…" She hesitated before she met his gaze, looking for the word to describe the perfection that was Jake Cohen. It was the wrong thing to do. She looked at him and all words escaped her.

He blinked first, his eyes drifting to her lips.

She had kissed him before. They were both adults, and free as free could be. She'd been careless with her kisses in the past, why couldn't she summon that recklessness now?

"I'm different." He said the words almost to himself, sounding unhappy about it.

"I was going to say perfect," she confessed. "I've never seen anyone fight like you. Do you miss it?"

He shook his head. "No."

There was something he wasn't saying. Meg had found wine an excellent way to gain the confidence of others, but she didn't much feel like drinking, and she was loathe to leave his side. Inches away from her, she could feel the heat and latent energy of his arm beside hers.

It wasn't enough that he was beautiful or that he appeared to be chiseled from solid rock, but there was a remarkable presence to the man, a pull that was both comforting and terrifying. He'd never been anything but gentle with her, but she'd seen him fight and work and she knew his staggering physical strength. She wanted so badly to get close to him, but the idea struck her as ridiculous as trying to tame a fire by smiling at it. She was going to get burned.

"How'd you become a fighter, Jake?" she asked, hoping it was the right question.

He swallowed. It was. "It was the Fire. We were a few doors down from where it started. Never stood a chance. Before the smoke cleared, folks were looking for someone to blame. I was an easy mark. My family was dead, my girl left me, and I was sleeping under the bridge with dozens of other homeless families. I had an accent. Well, more of an accent. I learned to fight."

Meg frowned. "But your leg…?"

He nodded, staring into the fire burning in the hearth. "Injured. I was desperate to survive, and angry enough to do it. I fought anyone who came near me, and by the time I'd finished, my hands were broken and my leg torn to shreds. There was no one left to work for, and my hands were useless. I stayed at Ruta's until I could walk again. She saved my life. After that, I just kept fighting."

Meg nodded in understanding. She knew a thing or two about all-consuming anger. She had fallen into prostitution in much the same way; by accident, then out of necessity. "You have a girl, then?"

He nodded. "*Had.* Rachel. We almost married. My parents were in favor. You know the story of Jakob and Rachel?"

Meg shook her head. "Is it a love story?"

Jake snorted. "A bad one, perhaps. Jakob falls in love with Rachel, and her father makes him work for seven years to earn her. He does it, and the man gives him her sister, instead. He has to work fourteen years before he finally gets to marry her, then she dies in childbirth."

"Just like Romeo and Juliet."

He smiled. "Isn't it just? At any rate, Rachel's family survived, but they lost a lot. I lost more. They married her to a friend of the family who hadn't lost anything."

"She left you? Just like that? With your busted leg and God knows how many out for your blood?" Meg seethed. "Where is she now?"

"Spitalfields, like as not. I haven't heard from her since." He shrugged. She wondered if it still pained him.

Meg had never had a man of her own, but if she did, she couldn't imagine leaving him to the elements as Rachel had. "Bloody fool," she cursed under her breath. "She had to know she was leaving you to your death."

"I survived," he dismissed. "It's not important. It was a long time ago."

Meg tried to imagine him twelve years before, alone in a strange country at twenty-six, surrounded by people who didn't trust him or, at worst, wanted to kill him. That he had survived had been a miracle. "Jake, can I ask you something?"

He turned to her and gave her a small, sad smile. "Anything."

"This is going to sound ridiculous, and I mean no offence," she prefaced, and she knew it had to be the first time she'd ever said such a thing. "How do people know you're Jewish? I only know because I've been told, but you look like anyone else to me. It's not like you run about showing people your cock."

Jake laughed aloud and Meg began to relax. "You don't think there's anything different about me?"

Meg looked him up and down, her gaze dragging over his delicious form. "Well, you're bigger than most, and darker. You're gorgeous, obviously, but I haven't met a lot of Dutchmen, either. You're clearly a boxer…" she trailed off as she noticed him staring at her. "I've put my foot in it again, haven't I?"

He swallowed. "You think I'm...*gorgeous*?"

Meg blushed. Lord, had she said that out loud? "You *have* seen yourself? You make the blokes down here look like milk maids, that's why they hate you."

His cheek began to twitch and Meg felt herself warming. She was alone--well, *almost*--with an incredibly desirable man. If she'd been surer of herself, she would have pounced on him by now. Why hadn't she?

He let out a long breath, his gaze falling again to her lips. "They're not good enough for you. Any of them."

Meg's heart hammered at his words. That was a new one. She was more accustomed to being the one who was never worthy. "I'm not a young girl anymore," she argued half-heartedly.

His hand drifted toward her cheek, his long fingers tucking a piece of errant hair behind the shell of her ear with a delicacy at odds with his obvious strength. She didn't move. She could barely breathe. She closed her eyes against the pleasure of his rough fingertips at her jaw.

"You're better. You're a woman." His voice was soft as smoke, and just as dangerous.

A fact she was acutely aware of standing next to him. His hand lingered gently beneath her ear. When she opened her eyes and caught the pain in his, she knew.

He wanted her.

Embarrassed, he dropped his hand and looked away. He was inches away from her, so close she could feel his heat and smell the cloves in his soap. His pulse leapt in his throat, a steady beat that mirrored hers. She wondered what it would feel like under her lips.

"I'm Protestant," she blurted. "A bad one, but there it is. Do you care?"

"Not in the slightest." He raised his eyebrows as though he'd surprised himself with his answer. "You may have heard I'm not…"

She laughed under her breath. Her punters wouldn't let her forget. "I am aware."

"Do you care?" He looked vulnerable as he asked. A trick of the light, perhaps.

"It's a part of who you are. I care about that." She shook her head. "But no, I don't mind."

It may have been the dying fire in the dim bar, but his eyes appeared darker still as he met her gaze. Before she could think better of it, she lifted her hand to touch him. It climbed his chest of its own accord, resting on the warm muscle that covered his heart. It pounded under her palm, the pace quickening as he focused on her lips.

He did not rebuke her for her forward gesture, but made no move to touch her in return. The only outward hint he had even noticed the contact was his breath, shallow, fast, and nearly silent. He was affected. He had to be.

She *had* to kiss him.

She needed to do it to prove she could, to silence the voice in her head that demanded it of her every day they were together. She needed to know if she had imagined the intensity of their last kiss, and if there really was something there. She wouldn't waste one more night dreaming of him when he could be in her bed keeping her awake.

Her desire for him pained her more than her fear of rejection. It would not stand.

Meg wasn't afraid of *anything.*

She stood on her tiptoes and touched her lips to his.

He did not resist, but stood still, allowing her to do what she would.

It was not the reaction she had hoped for, but it was something. She ran the tip of her tongue along the bow of her lip and deepened the kiss. His eyes closed and his eyebrows drew together in an expression not so far removed from pain. When he opened his lips and let her into the heat of his mouth, she sighed in relief.

She heard a far off crash she realized was the broom dropping. His hands closed around her waist, sliding up her sides in a slow caress. His kiss was better than exceptional, it was a bloody miracle. He smelled of man and smoke and spice, and his taste was all his own with a sinful richness that made her think of mulled wine.

There was no one watching now. He was kissing her because he wanted to.

Meg smiled against his lips. There were so very many things she wanted to do to him, she hardly knew where to start. She dragged her thumb along his stubbled jaw and opened her mouth to admit his tongue.

He groaned low in his throat, a desperate, hungry sound if she'd ever heard one. Her heart swelled even as her blood rushed downward.

He wanted her. She wouldn't deny him for a moment.

Instinctively, she reached for the ties of his trousers.

He broke the kiss, and she almost stepped backward at the ferocity in his eyes. "Don't tease me, Margaret."

She tightened her grasp and pulled him to her hips by his laces. "Who's teasing?"

Jake wasn't. He sunk a hand into her hair beneath her braid and took her mouth again, with more certainty this time. She arched beneath his touch, her breasts stiffening against his chest. She didn't wonder if he cared for her, and she didn't dwell on her rather confusing attachment to him. All she was sure of was how he made her feel, and right now, she felt as though she was burning from the inside out.

He took his time. His free hand palmed her breast so gently she could have screamed in frustration. He was an enormous, beautiful *brute.* She didn't want to be handled like porcelain doll. She pulled away from his kiss with reluctance and met his gaze. There was fire there, and more than she was getting. "Don't hold back."

That was all he needed. His eyes narrowed at the challenge and he reclaimed her mouth as though he meant to eat her. Without warning, he seized her hips and sat her on the edge of the bar, knocking a cluster of empty bottles to the floor with a crash. Her laugh was as dirty as she felt. She'd sweep that up later with a smile on her face.

She wrapped her legs around his waist as he stepped between them. He pulled her hips flush against his and pushed her skirt up her thighs, running his rough fingers along the bare flesh at the top of one wool stocking. Holding her gaze, his free hand slid down the length of her braid before he wound it around his wrist in slow circles to the base of her neck. The insistent throbbing of her sex increased with the firm tugging on her hair. She closed her eyes at the pleasure of it and the bastard pulled it harder, sending a tremor of pure ecstasy to her core.

Taking advantage of her position, he put his lips to her exposed throat, kisses smoldering like coals from her ear to the space between her collarbones, then lower toward her breasts. She surrendered to the exquisite pleasure of it all, leaning into her hands on the bar.

His fingers bit into the soft flesh of her thigh, rolling her stocking toward her knee. She pulled his hips closer with her heels on the small of his back and immediately felt the evidence of his arousal pressing like a battering ram into her pelvis. His kisses reached the top of one breast and she shifted to allow one hand to sink into his thick, black hair. "Jake."

The door closed.

Jake leapt off of her at the sound while she sat up in confusion.

The bar was empty. Joe Ledford had just left.

Very much aware he had likely caught an eyeful, Meg couldn't contain her laughter. It bubbled up out of her with such mad joy she nearly fell off the bar. Jake's grin was more than a little self-conscious and she could tell he was embarrassed. "We woke him up," he observed with some wonder.

"Wonders never cease." Her gaze drifted to the considerable bulge in his loose trousers. She licked her lips. "Get back here."

Meg giggled in delight as his gaze darkened. Moving with a speed she hadn't seen outside Bear Gardens, he locked the door and pulled the curtains. Meg didn't budge, but took the opportunity to look her fill. He was more than gorgeous, more a man than the finest she'd had the good fortune to meet. She could watch him do the most mundane, repetitive tasks without tiring of the sight.

He returned to his place before her and she wrapped her limbs around him, needing him closer. Even in her fantasies of taking him to bed, she hadn't imagined it would be like this. It was almost as though he'd thought about it, too. She slipped her hands beneath his shirt and ran them over the taut muscles of his back. He dipped his head to kiss her throat and the scrape of his stubble against her collarbone was almost too much. She felt as though she was sinking into him, no longer a woman at all, but a flame desperate to catch.

His hands took their time climbing her legs beneath her skirt, one fingertip at a time until they reached the sensitive groove in the joint of her hips. "No knickers," he murmured, and she felt his smile against the swell of her breast.

The wind rattled the door, and for a moment it sounded as though someone was trying to get in. He lifted his head from her breast with a frown. "Davey might yet return. Upstairs?"

Meg attempted her sauciest smile. "Afraid he'll charge you?"

He shook his head sharply. His chest was flushed beneath his open collar and his hair was a mess. "I'd give an arm to have you."

That makes two of us. She gave a bawdy laugh. "Don't tell him that. He'd take it. Cupboard?"

She didn't have to ask him twice. He slid his hands under her arse and gathered her to him and all she could do was hang on. Squealing as she felt the bar go behind her, she clung to him for dear life. He carried her easily behind the bar and into the open store cupboard. Though she shouldn't have been surprised he could, it was a new feeling for her. She was stronger than she looked, and heavier as well. While most men would have struggled, he held her wrapped around his waist as though she weighed nothing at all.

She jerked the door after them and it hung open an inch, casting a column of fading light off center over his distinctive features. A black eyebrow, a bottomless dark eye, the hollow that dipped beneath a defined cheekbone, the edge of generous lips, parted and panting. He was more than a man, he was lust incarnate.

Bugger fighting it. She just wanted to be taken.

"Don't hold back," she repeated, and even she could hear a hint of begging in her voice. "I won't break."

He didn't.

He pinned her against the shelves with his body and one impossibly strong arm as he freed his cock from his trousers. She gasped as she felt it part her sex. Without hesitation, he drove into her, filling her so completely it was almost uncomfortable.

Once he was seated firmly inside her, his arm snaked around her back and pulled her closer to him, his other hand still gripping her bare arse. Desperate and hungry, he hammered into her, all but flattening her with the force of his want. His breath in her ear was loud as a gale, and the sounds of his ardor increased hers.

The shelves shook and a bag fell and exploded on the floor in a puff of coarse ground flour. Meg ignored it. It wasn't her inn anymore, was it? As far as she was concerned, they could break everything in it.

As soon as she had the notion, a pair of glasses rolled off

another shelf and shattered at Jake's feet. He ignored it and took her harder. Meg tossed her head back with a moan, hitting her head on the shelf as she did. She had never felt less comfort or more pleasure, and the uneasy mix of ecstasy and pain only intensified the experience. Blinded with want, he tore at her neckline with his teeth and bit one stiff nipple.

It was too much. "Jake," she rasped, breathless. It felt as though he was splitting her in half from the hips up, but still she tightened around him--her arms, her legs, her sex--needing him deeper still. The want was intense, nameless and primal. She surrendered to the feeling and let it carry her steadily closer toward her peak.

She felt his lips on her neck, then his breath in her ear. "Do you want me to finish inside you?"

Though merely considerate, the question struck her as absurdly erotic. "God, yes." She couldn't think of a single thing she wanted more at that moment, apart from perhaps an eternity in the cupboard with Jake, fucking each other blind.

He increased his pace and she felt his shaft tighten further, his bollocks slapping her arse. She felt herself open wider for him in anticipation. The world outside ceased to exist, and there was no sound but his breath, no feeling but his flesh, no desire at all outside of her hunger for him. There was nothing gentle or artful about it. It was fucking at its most basic level, desperate, instinctive, and brutal on both sides, and she'd never enjoyed anything as much in her life.

He muttered something into her hair as he came, burying himself so deeply inside her it felt as though he'd made it clear into her belly. She shuddered as she felt the first rush of seed, her every nerve alive and screaming. Her climax tore through her with such intensity she feared for her life. Surely she couldn't walk away from that with all her limbs intact.

Holding her until the tremors subsided, he kissed her neck and stroked her braid. When she came to, she looked at him as though seeing him for the first time. She opened her mouth dumbly, struggling to find words.

He met her gaze, and his slow smile struck her as oddly self-conscious given that he was still inside her.

She kissed him.

He returned her kiss thoroughly, and as slow as if he had an eternity to do it. He'd had his pleasure, but he was in no hurry to leave.

That was new.

She opened her eyes when at last he pulled away and drank in the sight of him, a collection of shadows in the dark of the cupboard. Had that really happened? She had wanted it for so long and it was even better than she had imagined. He had been right before--if there were words to describe the way he made her feel, they didn't exist in English.

She settled for one she knew. "Upstairs?"

He grinned. Shifting her weight onto the long-suffering shelf, he turned away from her, pulled his trousers up, grabbed her legs, and hoisted her onto his back.

Shrieking in surprise, she wrapped her arms around his shoulders and laughed like a lunatic as he carried her up the stairs.

Chapter 18

As Jake began to wake up, he fought it, clinging to a sweet image that hugged the periphery of his dreams. There had been no plot to them that night, only a woman who seemed to be composed of pure sunlight, and the accompanying warmth of her love. She called to him from the deepest reaches of his mind, beckoning to him to return to the comfort of her embrace.

He dimly became aware of the sounds of the inn's residents shuffling about as another day began. Ignoring them, he clung to the woman, nuzzling his face between her neck and shoulder, enveloped by a cloud of sweet-smelling hair. The baby cried upstairs and Judith cooed to her. Alongside the sounds of the outside world, he could hear the woman breathing in his dreams, deep and even as though she, too, were asleep.

Straddling the edge of consciousness, Jake could feel the rough sheets of the bed as well as the flesh of the woman in the dream, smooth, firm, and deliciously bare. He dragged his hand up her back slowly, and her skin was soft as silk beneath his rough fingertips. He didn't want to wake up.

The contented sigh that followed was alarmingly real for a dream. He opened his eyes with reluctance and blinked against the morning light. The first thing he saw when his eyes adjusted was gold.

She looked up at him with a pair of rather sleepy-looking green eyes and his breath caught on her name. "Margaret."

Curled against his chest, she wore nothing but her yard of golden hair. They were tangled together in her narrow bed under a scrap of a blanket. There wasn't nearly enough room for the two of them. He held her as close as was humanly possible, and they were still against the wall with his feet and ankles hanging off the end.

"Jake," she greeted in a whisper, and he treasured his name on her lips. It made it more real somehow. He kissed her with the reverence she deserved. As he slid his hand back down, he let it travel over the inward curve of her waist and the outrageous flare of her hip, his fingers only pausing where her arse met her thigh. She returned his kiss with simple, unaffected joy.

His heart ached with the thrill of it. Any more and it would burst.

She traced her fingertips over his back in a long, languid caress. Her lips still tasted of wine. Breaking this kiss, she asked, "Coffee?"

He shook his head. "Later. I want to look at you."

Meg pulled away with a saucy laugh. She reclined on her side, her head propped lazily on one hand. Seeing her undressed in daylight for the first time, he let his gaze pour over her from the freckles on her nose down her long, graceful neck to the high, firm globes of her perfect breasts. When he reached her belly, she attempted to cover it with her free arm.

He walked his fingers over her hip. "What is it?"

Meg's smile didn't falter, but something like embarrassment had cooled the ardor in her eyes. "Had a baby, is all. Or three."

He frowned in mock seriousness. "Have you, now? That will not do. Only maidens for me."

Her mouth dropped open and he could tell she was looking for truth in his words. Assurances would never work unless he put some action behind them. He gently pushed her over onto her back and inched his way down her lush body, trailing kisses as he went. He kissed the hollow at the base of her throat, the inner curve of one breast and the taut nipple of the other.

"What are you doing?" she asked on a sigh, though she gave no resistance.

He didn't answer. She would know soon enough. He kissed the slight groove down the center of her belly to her navel, kissed the faint white marks at the base of her belly. "You're beautiful," he murmured against her skin. "Every last inch of you. Shall I kiss your feet?"

She giggled. "My feet are still good, really."

"Oh?" Once he reached the edge of the bed, he knelt on the floor before her and placed a solemn kiss on each foot. From his place at her feet, his view was unparalleled. Soft curves, messy hair, and a cheeky smile, the cleft of her sex just visible between long, shapely legs. She raised an eyebrow in challenge. He grabbed her ankles and pulled her down the length of the bed.

She squealed in surprise, but indulged his impulse. He sank back on his heels, drinking in the goddess before him. He couldn't remember ever feeling so compelled to worship.

Settling his hands on her bare thighs, he eased them apart, exposing her to his greedy view. She was swollen and red as her kiss-crushed lips, clearly aroused as he was. Her scent was heady and sweet, and it awoke something inside him, an ageless instinct buried somewhere beneath obsession and insatiable need.

There was nothing he could do but surrender.

He kissed her sex, tentatively at first. She gasped as he rolled his tongue around the bud at the top and through her slick red petals. God, she tasted good. She tasted of woman, roses, and desire itself. A hint of him still lingered from the night before. His cock throbbed as he tasted it, urging him to fill her again.

She opened for him like a flower to the sun, threading her fingers through his hair. The noises she made were hardly human. That foot massage had nothing on this.

She didn't need the damp of his tongue, she was so wet she was dripping. Unable to help himself, he returned his lips to her bud and slid two fingers into the molten heat of her. She quaked around him and he redoubled his efforts with his tongue and his teeth, needing to hear her say his name again.

Her hips bucked as she reached her peak, her legs trembling erratically around his shoulders. She tugged at his hair, insistent. "Take me. Please."

He needed no convincing. Rising above her prone, beautiful body, he replaced his fingers with his cock, sliding into her even as she contracted around him with her climax. Inside her, he felt a tremendous sense of peace and singularity of purpose.

This was what he'd been searching for. This was what he needed. This was the meaning of bloody life.

Blind to everything but pleasure, he clasped her in his arms, sunk a hand into the hair at the base of her head, and drove into her, a little closer to God with every thrust. Meg held onto him for dear life, her short nails digging into his back. She was screaming, he realized, but she didn't sound at all distressed. In fact, there was only one word he could make out.

"Jake!"

He came so hard he could have turned inside out, if not for Meg holding onto him. Catching his breath, he lifted his head to look at her, and found her looking more than a little dazed.

As she met his gaze, a delirious laugh bubbled out of her.

He smiled at the sound. "Did you enjoy that?"

She laughed harder.

Satisfied, he squeezed into bed beside her and pulled her into his arms. "I hope we weren't too noisy."

Meg tossed a languid arm over her head. "We slept late. Tommy will be at school, and everyone else has heard worse around here. I dread to think what Davey will try to charge you if he's back."

He kissed her ear. "I'll give him everything I have. He can

have the clothes off my back."

She took his jaw in her hand and gave him a quick, hard kiss. "Lord knows you won't be needing them anymore. How about that coffee?"

Chapter 19

Mark Virtue brought the cold with him as he arrived the next morning, a gale of frigid wind announcing him with the smell of soot and impending snow. A little girl strolled in ahead of him with an unnervingly similar stride, his hat sitting crooked on a halo of golden curls. Enjoying his first nap of the day, Joe didn't so much as stir as they passed, the hitch in his protracted snore more likely related to dreams of old ships than any detection of movement in the outside world.

Jake greeted them with a nod. "'Morning."

"'Morning," the little girl replied, looking up at him with a pair of rather curious gray eyes.

"This is Lily," Mark introduced his daughter. "Lily, this is Jake. He's the only bloke in these parts quicker than your old man, yeah? We have to watch ourselves or he'll sort us right out."

Lily pursed her lips and shot Mark a dirty look more suited to an orange seller than a child of perhaps six.

Mark laughed, beaming with pride. "Reckon she's mine?"

Jake raised his eyebrows. "Got to be. Get you some coffee?"

"Cheers."

"You two are out early this morning."

"Davey asked me to come by." Mark scratched his head. "Reckon he means to sell the inn."

Jake's eyebrows shot up. *Sell it, so soon?*

At the sound of voices from the bar, Davey emerged from the kitchen, licking his oily lips. Jake knew he had finished off the kippers before he smelled them, clinging to the man in a haze of brine. "Mister Virtue. So good of you to come." He ambled past Jake to grasp Mark's hand.

To his credit, Mark didn't flinch. His grin betrayed nothing as he replied, "Pleased to be of service, though I'm afraid I'm unlikely to tell you anything you want to hear."

"Your assessment is all I require." His alarm was plain as he noticed Lily at Mark's hip. "You have brought a child."

Mark nodded in her direction. "She's my apprentice, ain't she? Knows the business better than I do, and all. Isn't that right, Lily V?"

"Yes, Daddy."

"Too right." Mark knocked the hat askew on her head and she straightened it with an irritated pout. "Shall we have a look around?"

"By all means. You--" Jake assumed Davey was addressing him, "Coffee."

Mark met Jake's eyes at Davey's disrespectful tone. Though he did nothing else to acknowledge it, Jake knew he'd noticed. "Right, off we go." Mark charged through the bar with Lily on his heels, Davey lagging behind. Though Davey claimed ownership, Jake knew Mark had spent years in that bar and likely knew how it was put together better than anyone.

He likely knew the women in it better than anyone, as well.

"You see this beam here?" Mark gestured toward the ceiling for Davey to look. "Used to hang people from it if they misbehaved. It's cracked now and needs replacing. That and the others. You see those cracks spreading there? You'll need to reinforce the ceiling this year or it'll cave in on your punters. Joe wouldn't notice, would you, Joe?"

Joe snored.

"That's not the half of it. Wait until you see this."

Leaving them to it, Jake retreated into the kitchen. Judith stirred the fresh pot of coffee hanging over the fire while Tommy fed the baby thin porridge at the table. Judith's shoulders relaxed as she saw him. "Thank God it's you. I thought he'd never leave me in peace. What are they doing out there?"

Jake pulled three mugs down from the shelf. "Davey has a mind to sell the place. Mark's here to tell him how much it's worth."

"He's going to sell it?" Judith let out a long breath. "Meg won't like that. She'll be down any moment. Lord, what will become of us?"

"How do you mean? New owner would keep you on, like as not."

Judith took the mugs from him and filled them with coffee one at a time. "We'll still be his wards, every one of us. Imagine he'll drag us back to Suffolk with him."

Jake frowned. He did not like the sound of that. "We'll see."

Coffee finished, Judith sat beside her mug at the table and pulled the baby into her lap, trying to coax her into eating a little more porridge. Relieved of his duties and bursting with apprehension, Tommy followed Jake back to the bar and perched on the edge of a stool, trying to pretend he wasn't straining to listen to Mark's list of problems with his family's inn.

As Mark, Davey, and Lily circled back, Jake set two mugs of coffee in front of them, his already half gone. Mark accepted one and passed Davey's to Lily. She took it and drank it without flinching. Davey sputtered at the slight, but said nothing.

"I don't know what to tell you, mate." Mark sipped his coffee. "What do you reckon, Lily V?"

"It's fucked," she said gravely, the coarse language at odds with her tiny voice.

Mark nodded, accepting his daughter's judgment. "The lady is correct. It's a disaster. A travesty, mate. We are fortunate it's not falling down around us now, and I'm not being funny, but I'd as soon as get Lily out of here before it does. My missus would kill me if she came to harm, you understand?"

Davey's face was ruddy with disappointment. "How much could I sell it for?"

Mark shook his head. "You're not hearing me. I'm saying you can't sell it. No one with their wits about them would buy it for scrap."

A vein twitched above Davey's eye. "You can't be serious."

"Afraid so. You keep it, it's only a matter of time before you're standing in splinters. Not to mention the new ordinances, of course."

Davey loosed his collar. "What ordinances?"

"Since the Fire." Mark let out a dry laugh tinged with torment. "Can't build these anymore. Galleys are banned and everything's being replaced with brick, like the houses by the bridge. City will tear this place down, if it doesn't cave in first."

"B-but it must have some assets as a business…"

Mark shot Jake a look. "Run into the ground. Meg can't keep a book to save her life--"

"I beg your bloody pardon?" Meg shot into the bar from the stairwell like a fireball of red skirts, burning cheeks, and golden hair. "My books are immaculate! What do you know of it, at any rate?"

"Meg." Mark warned.

"This inn would not be standing today if it wasn't for me--"

"Meg."

"I haven't made an error in the books in fifteen bloody years-
-"

"MEG!"

"Don't *Meg* me, you miserable piece of--"

Clearly at a loss, Mark pinched her arse.

Meg slapped him hard, but she stopped talking.

"Lily," he said gently. "Go sit by Tommy for a bit."

Lily nodded and climbed onto the stool next to Tommy.

"Jake, why don't you show Mister Henshawe the books while I have a word with Meg?" Not waiting for an answer, he grabbed Meg's arm and dragged her off into the courtyard.

The whole bar seemed to buzz as they left it. Jake knew Mark was only trying to help, but still he felt the unwelcome weight of envy settle into his bones. Their history was as dangerous as that crack in the ceiling. It could be nothing, or it could bring down the inn and everyone in it.

Lily sipped her coffee, oblivious to the argument taking place outside. Tommy reached over the bar to grab what was left of his bag of boiled sweets. He popped one into his mouth and offered the bag to Lily. She smiled brightly and took one.

Focusing on the task at hand, Jake opened a book of Meg's meticulous ledgers and set it in front of Davey. They didn't make a lot of sense to Jake. He spoke English better than he could read it, and as the ledgers were not in Hebrew, he couldn't tell bills from a grocery list.

Davey took the book from him, frowning over Meg's even lines of numbers. "Twelve shillings six on ale? Leave it to Meg to run this place into the ground." He slammed his fist on the bar, ignoring the children. "Hellfire and damnation! I'll sell her up and down the country to make back my money!"

On his bench, Tommy was quietly turning purple. Jake's heart leapt into his throat as he at first assumed the boy was choking. His breath was even, if shallow, his eyes bright and shoulders rigid. The boy looked enough like Tom Callaghan as it was, but enraged, they could have been twins. If he didn't diffuse the situation, Davey would have his face torn off by a ten-year-old.

"Not worth it, mate," Jake said to Davey, immediately receiving a look of betrayal from Tommy. "Meg's tougher than she looks. Listen, Virtue's right. Sell this place for what you can get and go home. It's more trouble than it's worth."

Davey ran a hand through his thin, greasy hair. "Where will I find someone stupid enough to buy it? Christmas is days away. I'll be stuck here for months."

Jake shuddered. "Nobody wants that."

When Meg walked back in she was subdued and pale as a sheet. Jake didn't want to think of what Mark had told her to calm her down. Without a word, she rushed past them and into the kitchen.

Davey laughed. "Man certainly knows how to handle that one. Perhaps I should let him keep her."

Jake cracked his knuckles. *Pop.*

Mark reentered the bar, tucking his pipe into his coat. "How's it looking?"

"Dire," Jake replied.

Davey spread his hands. "Perhaps we can come to terms, you and I. You are a carpenter. Let me sell you the place for the materials."

Mark's mouth dropped open. At the look Jake shot him, he replied, "I haven't got enough spare with six children and all, but we'll find you a buyer."

"I'll buy it," Jake said, too quickly.

Davey recoiled as if he'd been slapped. "You? You can't own property, you're a Jew."

Jake shrugged. "Put it in Meg's name."

Davey snorted. "More fool you. She'll keep it when she tosses you out."

"That's my concern. I'll give you three guineas for it now." It was all he had on him.

"Three guineas?" Davey spat. "Cheating heathen! What do you take me for?"

"Three *guineas*?" Mark repeated, clearly surprised the sum was quite so small. He recovered himself. "Only fair. More than fair. You'll not do better than that, sir."

"Nonsense!" Davey protested. "I'll piss on it for the pleasure of it before I sell it to a Jew for *three guineas?*"

Jake crossed his arms to keep from striking the man. "Ten. You'll get back what you paid for it."

Davey screwed up his face and for a moment, Jake thought he meant to hold his breath like a child in a fit of pique. "Twenty."

"Twelve."

"Eighteen."

"Fifteen and I keep the girls." Might as well have been fifty. Jake didn't have it and he didn't know how he'd get it.

"You can have the old ones, but I'm taking the young one with me. Keep the brat."

Jake felt his temperature rising. He wanted Judith but he'd separate her from her child? "Fifteen guineas, and I take over wardship of all four unmarried sisters and their children."

Davey stared at him, taking his measure. Jake met his assessment with an unflinching glare. Jake had never willingly shown vulnerability before, and he wasn't about to now.

Davey smiled as his courage faltered. "You want to open a brothel, do you?"

Jake didn't blink. "Do you care?"

"No," Davey replied, his voice flat. "I'll consider it." He rose and headed for the bar, seizing his coat from the peg. "Damn you and the rest of them." He left, slamming the door.

Joe woke at the noise. Seeing only Jake, Mark, and two children at the bar, he went back to sleep.

"Fifteen guineas?" Mark said incredulously. "You're fortunate that man is a fool."

Only as Jake felt himself relax did he realize how tense he had been. "Yes, I am."

"I was telling the truth," Mark warned, real concern on his face. "It'll take more money than anyone has got to save this place."

"I know." He crossed his arms over his chest. Whether or not it fell down, at least the Henshawes would have jobs and a place to live.

Tommy had gone rather pale at the end of the bar. "You want to buy the inn?"

As serious as he was, it was easy to forget Tommy was still a child. Jake wanted to comfort him, but he wouldn't make promises he couldn't keep. "I'm going to try. I don't know if it'll work, but I won't let you and your mother be homeless, you understand?"

Tommy nodded gravely. "And Aunt Judith? And the baby?"

Looking into Tommy's sad green eyes, Jake felt the weight of the world on his shoulders. Somehow, he'd inherited a whole family. He couldn't have Meg without taking them all.

Rather than crumpling beneath the weight, he welcomed it. He'd always wanted a family.

"Yeah," Jake answered, meaning it. "One way or another, I'll take care of the lot of you."

Mark's breath whistled through his teeth. He gave Jake a resigned pat on the back. "You're braver than I thought. Good luck to you, mate."

♥

Meg scoured the burned blackness from the bottom of the pot until her hands were raw, Mark's voice still ringing in her mind.

Keep quiet for once. I'm doing you a favor.

"Some favor," she muttered, perspiration gathering beneath her arms. She'd scrubbed the same damned spot until her arm felt ready to tear itself from her body, but the dark blotch still clung to the base of the pot to spite her. The salt and vinegar in the scrub strung her dry skin. She groaned in frustration. Any harder and she'd wear a hole right through it.

She heard Jake's uneven step on the stones before she felt his hands on her waist. "Meg," he soothed, and his breath on her ear sent a shiver down her spine so violent she dropped the pot into the basin. Hands dripping, she gripped the edge, her knuckles cracked and red as burning coals.

He touched his lips to the base of her neck, relieving some of the tension that stabbed between her shoulders like a dagger to her spine.

"Mark might have convinced Davey to sell the place."

"What good does that do me? I can't buy it." She turned, drying her hands on her skirt. "You heard him. It's a hovel *I've* run into the ground!"

Jake pulled her into his arms, heedless of her sodden apron. Her cheek found its natural home in the valley between his chest and shoulder, his heart pounding in her ear. How many times had she longed for a man to hold her in just such a way?

"We can buy it off him," he said into her hair. "You, me, and the girls."

Meg huffed. "I can't buy my son shoes. You think I can buy a bloody inn? An inn that's mine by right?" Prying herself from his chest was no easy task. The kitchen was a good deal grimmer when she couldn't smell the spice in his skin.

She had woken up smelling it, woken up with his hands tangled in her hair. How was she meant to go back to her life after *that?*

"I won't whore for him," she said, more to herself than anyone. "If he thinks I can't keep books, what good am I? He'll cast me out."

"I won't let him," he pledged, setting his jaw as if walking into a fight. He was so sure of himself she almost believed him. "What all did Mark say to you?"

She shrugged. "Nothing useful. Told me to keep my mouth shut. He'd like that, wouldn't he? Says he's looking out for me. Fat lot of good that's done me. I'm not good enough to marry but I can wait on his wife. Now he'll see me on the bloody street!"

The lines around his mouth deepened as he frowned. "I thought you were on better terms now."

"Better terms? He plagues me!" Her fingers contracted into

claws and she gripped her skirt to keep from tearing her hair in frustration. "Ten years of my life I gave to that man and for what? My youth gone, my looks gone, my children--" her voice cracked but she did not cry. She *would not* cry. "I fed him. I looked after him. I let him run around on me for years and he leaves me for a useless chit with a pretty face? That's gratitude for you!"

Jake's face was ashen. "Do you love him?"

"I never loved him!" She shouted, pacing to rein herself in. "I never loved him," she insisted, quieter. "He was my friend. My only friend. We had an understanding…I needed him. His house, rather. My father wouldn't let me keep my children here. I paid for their care, knowing I'd get them back when I married. *If* I married." She gave an ugly laugh. "When I lost him, I lost them, too. They grew up. Now Sarah's ashamed of me and Michael's *gone...*" Her throat closed under the force of the sobs she held in. Her eyes throbbed with it, the room spinning around her faster and faster until she fell.

Jake caught her, holding her upright through the maelstrom of her grief. He was something to cling to, straight and solid as a mast. She'd hang onto him until it passed, her arms around his waist all that kept her from drowning. She'd listen to his pulse, feel his breath on her face, and she'd let herself believe—just for a moment—he'd stay.

He kissed her forehead. "Did he know what it meant to you?"

"He should have. If he did, he didn't care." Her breath shook. "I never got to be their mother." She closed her eyes, the naïve dreams of her youth coming back to her in fractured images like the reflection in a broken mirror. She'd wanted a home of her own, a family, a cat or two to keep the mice away. She imagined walking Sarah and Michael to the petty school in the morning and cooking for them when they came home. She'd wanted clothes without holes in them and a good man to keep her warm at night.

She'd wanted Jake.

He had seemed strange to her, the first time she'd seen him.

Different, forbidden. People had been even more suspicious of him then than they were now, but still she sat at the edge of her seat every time he came on, breathless.

How different her life would have been if she'd gone for him instead of Tom. If she'd left Mark before he had a chance to leave her.

"It's too late, isn't it?" she said to herself, her breath muffled against his shirt.

"You're hardly old, love," he consoled, misunderstanding her. "You have Tommy."

Meg sighed. "I do. He's been the light of my bloody life." She smiled. "I'll not let Davey turn him out."

Chapter 20

It didn't take long to find Davey.

Tommy followed the smell of kippers down the lane toward the river. Davey was slow, half-drunk, and predictable; Tommy guessed he'd wind up at the Hanging Sword sooner or later. Sure enough, as he peeked through the window, he saw Davey's distorted image on the other side of the filthy glass. There wasn't a dodgy deal in Southwark that didn't go down at the Hanging Sword. Buying, selling, or settling scores, the worst of the worst could be found there at all hours. The fact Davey was so comfortable there was Tommy's first clue he wasn't as virtuous as he made himself out to be.

He darted inside, narrowly missing a stream of brown spit from an old man. Weaving between two sailors, he took the long way around the bar to get to the other side of Davey's table. No one paid him any mind. He was big for his age and anyway, the whole place was so dark it was easy to keep to the shadows.

Tommy reached the table behind Davey's high-backed bench just as a couple of thieves were leaving. Seizing his moment, he dove into the rushes beneath the bench as quietly as he could and tried to make himself small. The rushes were damp and stunk like a tannery, all piss and meaty grime. He was glad he couldn't see what he was lying in. Immediately, his skin began to crawl.

Resisting the urge to scratch, he closed his eyes and listened.

Davey was muttering to himself. He only stopped to drink his ale, swallowing hard and sighing. Before long, Tommy heard the scrape of a stool being dragged across the floor as Davey was joined by someone. Tommy couldn't see him without giving away his hiding place, but he could hear the clunk of metal in his pocket as he sat down.

The barmaid brought the man a drink and topped up Davey's from a pitcher. One of the men slapped her arse as she left. She didn't complain, but Tommy heard a faint groan high in her throat.

"What's the damage?"

"Not as bad as I feared," Davey lied, a tremor in his voice. "Cosmetic, mainly. I'll let you have it for fifty guineas."

The man laughed. "My eye. That heaps' not worth ten."

"Ten? Be reasonable. I couldn't part with it for less than forty."

"I'll give you ten and you'll be lucky to get it. What else will you give me?"

"What else? It's a thriving business. What else could you want?"

"All five sisters."

Davey sputtered. "There are only four."

"You'd best find me another one, hadn't you?"

Davey took a long breath. "See here, the one is married and another has a protector. Neither's been seen in sometime. You can have the other three."

The man spat. "Three guineas."

"Three guineas?"

"Three girls, three guineas."

"You're having a laugh." Davey laughed, but he sounded more afraid than amused. "Meg alone is worth ten. Every day I get blokes looking for her. She's famous, like. I had one from bleeding Bavaria yesterday."

"Meg Henshawe isn't worth shit."

Tommy held his breath. Hearing people trying to put a price on his mother made his blood boil. He rather feared they were about to say something disparaging about her, and he wasn't sure he could hear it without making a scene.

When Davey spoke, his voice was small. "What makes you say that?"

"She hasn't had a trick in weeks and everyone knows it. You can't control that one. Now she's got goddamn Jake Cohen in her corner, you think anyone'll get near her? You think anyone wants to?"

"He'll move along soon enough."

"Don't signify if he does. She's soiled, ain't she?"

Davey's laugh was genuine this time. "Twenty years of whoring and it takes a heathen to soil her?"

"Dead serious, mate."

"Don't be ridiculous. Hebrew is hardly catching, is it? At any rate, she knows more than one way to please a man."

"Knows, aye, but she's as likely to light your knob on fire as she is to suck it. I wouldn't touch that one with a barge pole."

Good. Come near my mother and you'll wish only your knob had been burnt off when I get through with you.

Tommy's thoughts of murder were interrupted by a toe between his ribs. He rolled over to find a barmaid around his aunt's age crouching to peer at him beneath the bench. "You want a drink?" she whispered.

He shook his head, startled anyone knew he was there.

With a shrug, she straightened and carried on.

Tommy swatted something crawling over the back of his neck. If the barmaid had seen him, it was only a matter of time before someone else did. Davey's negotiations didn't seem to be going well, regardless. With any luck, this man would turn him down and Davey would let Jake buy it instead.

As quietly as he could, Tommy crept out from underneath the bench. No one noticed but a second barmaid, and she didn't so much as blink. God only knew what they saw in there every day. Tommy kept his head down and walked away from Davey, sneaking as quickly as he dared toward the door. He paused as he reached the threshold, and stole a look toward the man looking to buy the inn.

Gilbert the brewer?

Twice a week that man restocked their ale! Tommy had known him his whole life but here he was, haggling over the price for his mother and aunts like they were cattle!

Horrified, Tommy tore down the street toward the inn as fast as he could. Narrowly dodging a flock of Christmas geese, he leapt over a crate and slid through the slush, landing hard on his arse in the mud.

He looked up at the sound of laughter. Looming over him was Nathaniel Porter and two of his nasty mates, all boys he'd gone to school with until they'd reached twelve and dropped out to follow in their fathers' footsteps of drinking and thieving. Now they were older still, taller than before but no kinder.

"Look, it's the whore's boy. Did you fall on your arse, whoreson?"

Tommy stood, blood pounding in his ears. "Don't you say a word against my mother!"

Nathaniel laughed, a deceptively jolly belly laugh that drew the attention of people passing by. "It's the truth, isn't it? Your mother is a whore. Everyone's had her once or twice. My brother said she's a fire ship!"

Tommy had no idea what that meant, but it couldn't be good. "You shut your mouth! I'm warning you, Nathaniel!"

The boy laughed in his face. "You going to cry to your father? If only you knew who he was!"

Tommy's vision turned red. All thought masked by blind rage, he flung himself at the boy, knocking him to the ground. He pummeled his face, over and over again until his stupid smug smile broke into a grimace of fear.

"Don't talk about my mother! Don't talk about my mother!" Tommy shouted as he struck the boy as hard as he could, blood spattering the snowy street.

"He's mad! Pull him off, for God's sake!"

Hands hooked around his arms and he struggled as they pulled him away. He kicked, bellowing like a baited bear. They thought him harmless because he was just a boy, but he'd prove them all wrong.

The moment he was upright, he was knocked to the ground again. Fists rained down on him, boot toes hooking into his ribs. He curled into a ball to protect himself from the blows as Nathaniel and both of his friends tried to beat the piss out of him. It wasn't the first beating he'd suffered from the boys at school. It wasn't even the first that week, but it hurt the most. The three of them were so much bigger than he was, being a good four years older. They could kill him if he didn't get up. He could die right here on Bridge Street before his eleventh birthday.

"Stop it!"

A little relief, as one boy was knocked to the side.

"You better run! His dad's coming!"

The boys stopped cold and Tommy opened his eyes. Through the blood, he could just make out Chris Cooper limping toward them with a stick in his hand. What he thought he was going to do with that, Tommy couldn't guess.

"He hasn't got one." Nathaniel spat red into the snow.

Chris wielded the stick with uncertainty, his eyes bright with fear. "You know very well his dad's Tom Callaghan and he'll give you the thrashing of your life. I just saw him round the bend. Run while you still can."

The boys looked at each other for a long moment. Apparently beating Tommy to death wasn't worth risking the wrath of Tom Callaghan, and they did indeed run, splitting off into different directions.

Once they were gone, Chris hobbled to Tommy and offered

his hand.

Tommy took it, but didn't put too much weight on his friend. As he stood, he became aware of how wet he was, drenched in blood and melting snow. His clothes were filthy and every inch of his body ached but his feet and his scalp, and those itched something terrible. "They could have killed you."

Chris leaned on his stick and Tommy realized it was the one he used to walk. "I'm getting stronger."

Tommy looked down the street toward The Hanging Sword, emptier now than it had been. "My father isn't coming, is he?"

Chris looked at his feet. "No, sorry. I didn't know what to say to make them stop."

Of course his father wasn't coming. He never was. "It's fine. It worked."

He set off toward home, Chris slumping beside him on his stick. It hurt to breathe, and the cold air seemed to burn his chest. Tommy stumbled and Chris offered his arm. Tommy took it gratefully, and the two of them helped each other back to the inn.

Tommy had never known his brother. He hoped he'd be like Chris, if he ever met him.

He tripped over the threshold as he reached the inn, the first sign he was hurt worse than he'd thought.

The second sign was the look on Jake's face when he saw him.

"*Godverdomme*," Jake muttered, a strange word in a strange language that wasn't English. Was that why everyone seemed to hate him so much? His face was so white it was almost blue. It made his eyebrows look even darker. It was an odd thought to have as the room started to swirl around him.

Jake was there to catch him as he fell. "What happened to him?"

"He got into a fight with some older boys. Three of them."

"Fuck," Jake cursed, and that was a word Tommy understood.

"Chris chased them off," Tommy said, the taste of blood in his mouth.

"Thank you, Chris," Jake whispered, real gratitude in his voice. "Meg's just gone to the baker, she'll be back any moment. Will you watch for her?"

Tommy didn't hear an answer. Next thing he knew, he was lying on the kitchen table. He felt a light, methodical prodding over his chest and grimaced at a sharp pain to his ribs.

"That might be a break."

He opened his eyes to see Jake standing over him, his face drawn as he assessed the damage. He looked so serious and frightened. The only other person who'd ever looked at him like that was his mother.

"Is that the only one?" Tommy asked.

Jake doused a cloth in clean water and wrung it out in the basin. "That and your right hand. Your finger's broken. Don't look at it."

Tommy looked at it. His hand was cut up and rapidly turning black, the third finger swollen and bent. "Will it mend?"

"Mine did." Jake held up his hands, showing Tommy the backs. He'd never noticed them before, but they were thick as gloves and patched like trousers.

"What happened to them?" Tommy asked him.

"Never mind that. What happened to you?" He carefully sponged the blood from Tommy's face. "Is that straw?"

"Followed Davey to The Hanging Sword," Tommy admitted, fully expecting Jake to shout at him. "I hid under a bench."

Jake was calm, the only indication he'd heard the lift of his eyebrows. "You'll need a bath as well. You got into a fight at the Hanging Sword?"

Tommy shook his head, wincing at the pain in his cheek. "On the way home. I saw Gilbert the brewer and ran, and Nathaniel called Mum names and said I was a bastard."

Jake frowned over Tommy's broken hand. "You got into a fight with the brewer?"

Tommy yelped as Jake bandaged his broken finger. "No, I fought Nathaniel and his stupid friends. Gilbert was trying to buy the inn."

"The brewer?" Jake shook his head. "Makes sense."

"Not just the inn. Mum, too. And Aunt Judith and Aunt Bess. Davey told him Alice got married so he lowered the price."

Jake's eyes darkened. "You don't say."

Tommy sat up, took the cloth, and wiped at the back of his neck. "He won't buy it. I think he's afraid of you. Mum, too."

Jake cracked a smile. "He should be. What did he say?"

Tommy grimaced. "Which part? Davey said Hebrew's not catching, whatever that means, and then Gilbert said Mum's as likely to set a man's knob on fire as...do anything else to it."

Jake blinked, horrified. "You *are* ten?"

"You asked." Tommy shrugged.

Chris popped his head around the corner and Jake waved him in. "I brought you clean clothes."

How had he done that? He could barely walk upstairs. "Thank you," Tommy said, appreciating the effort it must have taken for Chris to climb to the top of the inn and come back down. He was a true friend.

"You'd better change before your mother comes back and sees you like this," Jake advised. "I'll give you some privacy. Take care with that rib."

Tommy nodded, reaching for the clean shirt with some difficulty.

"And Tommy?" Jake grabbed it and handed it to him. "If anyone speaks badly about your mother or tries to hurt you or her in any way, you tell me, you understand?"

Tommy nodded, feeling better already. "Even my father?"

Jake's face fell. "*A gift from an old lover*," he muttered to himself with a faraway look. Suddenly, his expression hardened, his eyes sharp. “Especially your father.”

Chapter 21

Jake stopped mid-lunge as he heard Meg close her door. His leg shook as he stood, his concentration broken.

They'd spent last night together, but neither one of them had mentioned it. They barely spoke at all after Mark left, except to look after Tommy.

Meg had been distraught when she came home to see her son bruised and covered in bandages. Not surprised, he noticed. Apparently Tommy had made a habit of defending his mother's honor. She had said his fuse was shorter than Tom's and twice as bright. Jake believed it. The boy had barely flinched when he'd set his broken finger.

In spite of the terror Jake had felt seeing Tommy in such a state, life resumed as usual once Meg had him tucked up in bed.

He watched her flit from table to table all evening, wondering what he could say. They hadn't spoken privately since falling into bed together--or leaping, rather--and Jake was at a loss. Asking if she enjoyed herself or if she'd like to see him again seemed trivial, given the circumstances.

I'm sorry your child nearly died today. I'm sorry your cousin's trying to sell the inn to the brewer. I'm sorry Mark Virtue ruined your life…

Except he wasn't all that sorry about the last one.

He was sorry she hadn't gotten to raise her children, but he couldn't be sorry she'd avoided a marriage of convenience with the carpenter. People married without love every day, but he'd never wanted to. What could be worse than a loveless marriage?

Then again, maybe she *had* loved him. She'd fought for him, hadn't she?

She said she didn't care for Mark, but for all her protestations, she must have once. That kind of anger could never burn from indifference. Seven years on and it still ate her up. What but love could do that?

Having nursed a broken heart for a dozen years, Jake might have been the only person on earth who could sympathize. Who was he to be jealous of Mark Virtue when he still thought of Rachel most days?

Come to think of it, he hadn't thought of Rachel since last week. Meg brought such a light into the room with her, she could banish any ghosts that lingered there.

She hadn't invited him back.

Perhaps she wouldn't.

Resolved not to trouble her, he resumed his nightly routine at the dressing table. He lathered his good soap between his hands—his only real indulgence—and washed his face and body with the fresh rosewater she'd left him. He never saw her do it, but it was there every night. There was something about her scent of roses mixing with his soap that struck him as extravagantly erotic and again, he thought of tapping at her door.

Just last week he'd chased a boy away for doing that very thing, and now he *was* that boy.

The crack stood out like a livid gash in the wall, the light from Meg's fire red in the gloom of his bedroom. Drawn to it—to her—he climbed into bed and sat against the wall.

"Are you awake?"

He grinned to himself as he heard her voice. "I'm awake."

She hesitated before she asked, "Are you cold?"

He wasn't. "I could be warmer."

Jake waited for an invitation, but it didn't come.

"Do you…need me to light your fire for you?" He asked, knowing full well it was already burning.

She laughed under her breath. "Bit late for that, don't you think?"

He smiled. "If that's what you want to call it."

"Call it anything you like. You say *fire*, I say *take me roughly in the cupboard…*"

His breath caught. Here he was talking around the issue, and Meg just blurted it out. "…and after that?"

A long pause. "After that?"

"What happened then? I want to hear you say it." Certain parts of his anatomy wanted to hear her say it more than others. He closed his eyes and remembered.

"What, the part where you tore my door off the hinges?"

"Just one hinge. It still locks." He reminded her, leaning into the wall.

She let out a long, shaking breath. "You mean when you cracked my bed?"

"It's far too small for two people." He pushed the heel of hand down the rigid length of his cock.

"It is when one of them's the size of a bloody great big ox," she teased.

"Do you mind?"

"Do I hell." Her laugh was half-whisper, another secret in the dark.

"The candles are out." He turned his face toward the crack, needing to be closer to her. "Tell me a secret."

"I watched all of your fights." The wood beneath his ear vibrated gently with her voice. "When Lorenzo Valentine broke your nose, I spat in his beer."

Jake laughed. "Which time?"

"*Both* times." A soft moan escaped her throat. Was she doing the same thing he was? "Tell me a secret."

"I knew you were there." He gripped his shaft and pumped once, twice, a jolt of pleasure ricocheting down his legs.

"Everyone did. That's not a very good one." She took a deep breath. "I'm ashamed I was a harlot."

Three, four, five times. "I'm not."

"What do you mean?" Her tone changed, and she sounded more alert than sultry.

"It's not something to be ashamed of. Sex is sacred, it's another path to God. Perhaps loving the lonely is your way to serve Him." No one was lonelier than Jake. Having her had felt like the best kind of charity, better because it was given freely and not out of pity.

It *was*, wasn't it?

"You mean that?"

Jake grimaced. He'd only meant to start another fire, not a theological discussion. "I don't say things I don't mean."

"You would…" her voice faltered as she wrestled with her words. "You wouldn't hold it against me? What I've done?"

"Never."

"You wouldn't behave like a madman when I talk to other blokes?"

She was clearly referring to Tom. "You can talk to anyone you like, but if they try to take liberties, I'll break their fingers."

A sharp intake of breath. She was doing *something* over there. "You'd still want me? Knowing half the town's had me twice over, you'd…be my man?"

How many ways did he have to say it? "Margaret, I've never known another woman like you. I want you like I want my next breath. No matter what you think about your past, I would be proud to be your man." He was a little surprised by his own admission. He'd known it, but it was another thing to hear it aloud, in his own voice. "It's not a secret, but it's the truth."

Her silence troubled him. Meg had something to say about everything. Had he frightened her off? "Meg?"

Her door closed. Confused, he stood and opened his door to find her standing in the hallway, mid-knock.

With her wild eyes and rosy cheeks, he'd have taken her for drunk if he didn't know better. Unsure of what to say, he took a chance and kissed her.

Their noses bumped as he ducked to meet her lips. He wasn't good at this yet. New as they were to each other, they were still figuring out how they fit together. She was so different from the kind of woman he'd imagined himself with, he felt like he'd stolen her. She was too beautiful, too English, too wild. Not at all the kind of woman his mother would have approved of.

Still, she was here and in his arms and he'd love her as long as she let him.

Enthusiasm made up for the initial awkwardness. If Meg had any misgivings about him, it certainly didn't feel like it. She kicked the door shut with her heel and stumbled into him, knocking him off balance. One way or another, they ended up on the floor in a tangle of limbs.

Meg didn't miss a beat. She laughed as she stood, offering him a hand to help him up.

Feeling wicked, he took her hand and pulled her down into his lap.

He'd only meant to hold her there, but she turned to face him, sliding her long, long legs around his hips. He pulled her arse closer, his cock threatening to burst the seams of his breeches to get to the heat of her on the other side.

She didn't say anything at all, didn't maul him like the night before. Folding her legs behind him and wrapping her arms around his shoulders, she clung to him like a lover she'd waited years to find. That's how he felt, at least, holding her there on the floor. She was too much, too perfect to be real.

She's not for you, a voice warned from the corner of his mind. *She'll never accept you.*

He was past reason, past restraint. He swept her hair away

from her eyes and tucked it behind her ear. Nose to nose, he could feel her breath on his lips, her threadbare night rail bunched in his hands.

Her eyes were huge, hopeful, and oddly serious. She looked younger, more vulnerable.

He realized he was seeing her with her guard down for the first time.

She brushed her lips over his, more of a blessing than a kiss.

He cradled her head just behind her ear, his fingers diving into the silk of her hair. He touched his cheek to hers just to feel the contrast of her petal-soft skin against his day's growth of beard. Reverently, he kissed the corner of her mouth where it dimpled when she smiled. Her sigh swept past his ear and straight down his spine.

Without a word, she reached between them to grasp his erection. He gasped as much from pleasure as surprise. Holding his gaze, she fit him to her. Taken by the peculiar intimacy of the moment, he watched her face as he moved inside her, inch by slow inch.

It almost killed him, but it was worth it to see her expression fall from desire through bliss to an ecstasy that almost resembled pain. She quaked around him, slick with want, her eyes darkening as he hit the end of her. There were no words for the way she felt, no feeling he could name. He was beyond the reach of the warnings in his head. All thought was replaced with blazing light and driving need.

The heat of her was a stark contrast to the floor freezing his arse, her lush, myrrh-scented flesh more than enough to fight the winter whistling through the cracks in his window. There in the dark, she told him a secret with her eyes, the truth with her body. She kissed him slowly, working out the way their lips fit together. She ran the tip of her tongue over his teeth, rocked her hips back, and sank down on him again.

She caught his groan with her mouth. She twisted her fingers into his hair as she deepened the kiss. He surrendered to it, palming her breast over her night rail, her nipple hard against the pad of his thumb. She rode him silently, desperately in the dark, drinking his mouth as if she meant to swallow his tongue.

No matter how she felt about past lovers, it was him she wanted now. As he gripped her hips and slammed inside her, she gushed for him, her short nails digging into his back. This was enough, past be damned. She was more than he wanted, more than he probably deserved, and there wasn't anyone else he'd rather have in his arms or his bed.

Or on his floor.

She took the lead as she reached her peak. He fell back onto his elbows to give her more control, and she took advantage of the deeper angle. She came like the springtime, in bursts of life, each more beautiful than the last. She clenched around him like a vise, wrenching his orgasm from him. His voice broke as he moaned, "Margaret."

He'd started the day with that particular prayer, and it looked as though he'd end it the same way.

She unfurled herself along the length of his body, his seed pulsing from her, soaking the edge of his open breeches. With one last kiss, she rolled off him and onto the floor, stretching like a cat.

As his wits returned to him, he remembered their conversation before she had come to his room. Was he her man now? It had felt rather like she'd claimed him.

He opened his mouth to ask her, but she spoke first. "It's freezing in here."

"You want to sleep in your room?" he asked, pulling her into his arms.

She treated him to a wicked smile. "Who said anything about sleep?

Chapter 22

Meg shuffled through the slush with a song in her heart, a wordless melody she'd probably heard butchered by the tanner's boy on his two-stringed guitar. It was nearly tuneless as well, the way she hummed it, but she couldn't help herself. The sun glared at soot-stained houses, drab and well-worn as paupers' coats lining the streets of Cheapside. Even the river glittered like diamonds today, a vast stretch of them thick enough for ships to sail. She filled her lungs to bursting with fresh, freezing air and almost didn't smell the sewer as she skirted it.

Had there ever been a more beautiful day? She couldn't remember being happier, though it could be her wits were addled. For two nights now, she'd had so little sleep she'd been walking into things; tables, chairs, poor Joe Ledford snoring by the fire. He hadn't noticed, bless him. Even Davey had been keeping out of her way since That Night.

That Night--the one when she'd kissed Jake and he'd fucked her senseless for the first, second, and third times--would forever stand out in her mind as the night her life had finally started looking up. She swung her basket over her shoulder and smiled because she had to.

"We've got grain, eggs, a sugar cake, kippers, butter, cabbage, the wine is coming later and the beef will be delivered on the day…" Bess counted off the shopping list on her fingers. "Did we need aught else?"

"One more thing." Meg led her around the corner to Bishopsgate Street.

"The 'change is the other way," Bess pointed out. "Not that you'd notice today."

"What was that?" Meg asked, half-serious. "It's not much further."

Spitalfields was a bit like Southwark, if newer. It was not affluent like the West End or derelict like St. Giles, but overcrowded with people hard at work.

"This is a Jewish street," Bess lowered her voice. "What are we doing here?"

"Got as much right to be here as anybody," Meg said bravely, though she noticed more than one curious glance fired her way. "I've got to pick up something. The shop's 'round here somewhere."

"You ever go this far out of your way for Tom?" Bess asked, her smile in her voice.

Meg sneered over her shoulder. "God, no. I wouldn't cross the street for Tom."

Bess caught up to her, lugging her basket. "He lives up here somewhere, don't he?"

"Down off Newgate street with his wife. Why?"

"I'm trying to use distance to figure out how much you like Jake."

Meg almost stumbled at his name, but recovered herself and slowed her pace. Her hand sought the end of her thick braid like a talisman. For what, she wasn't sure. "I like him."

Bess laughed under her breath. "I daresay he likes you, too. Your hair looks nice this morning."

Meg flushed. "Where is this going?"

"Nowhere." Bess shrugged. "He's different, isn't he?"

Meg frowned. She and Bess hadn't always seen eye to eye on

each other's choice of lovers. Meg had tried to protect Bess from one bad decision after another, but her sister was just as headstrong as she was. She'd have every right to get her own back by dismissing Jake. "You don't like him?"

Bess threw her free hand up in the air. "I like him fine. I like what he's done to you better."

"What's that?" she asked, her mind diving into the gutter. Bess hadn't been there for any of *that.*

"You're happy," Bess replied easily enough. "I'm never seen you so happy, even though Davey's around."

"Who wouldn't be happy looking at him all day?" she kidded.

Bess shrugged. "You'd be surprised. Not everyone thinks he's as handsome as you do."

"Not everyone's got working eyes, have they?"

"Some are saying the same about you, you realize."

"What's wrong with him?" Meg snapped defensively.

"Apart from big ears, a smashed nose, and a hostile expression? He's got lines in his face from scowling, for God's sake."

Meg sighed, knees weakening just thinking about him. "Oh, *I know.*"

Bess laughed at the look on her face. "He won't have that body forever, mind. Will you still fancy him when he's older still and more...scowly?"

"Whose side are you on? You just said you liked him."

Bess threw up her hand in a gesture of surrender. "I do! It's only that you've always preferred prettier boys. It would be out of order if you let him stay only to toss him out when you get bored. He's mad for you."

Meg stared at her sister. "You're afraid I'll tire of him because he isn't 'pretty'?"

"You always tire of them, for one reason or another. You know I love you, Meg, but you have to admit you're a bit fickle."

Fickle. Meg's shoulders sunk. It might look like that from the outside, but being fickle required emotional attachment, however fleeting. She'd gone through more lovers than she could count out of a bottomless sense of loneliness she could never shake. She had sought understanding in their eyes and home in their arms, finding only lust and rejection in the process. In twenty years, not one other encounter had ever involved her heart.

Meg sighed. "You know, when he smiles you can see every one of his teeth? Really smiles. You have to make him laugh."

Bess laughed. "What's it got to do with his teeth?"

"I'm telling you so you'll understand," she said evenly. For all of her honesty, she wasn't often serious. "I like his smile. He's got a voice like smoke and the warmest, kindest brown eyes. I like his big ears and his mashed nose. I like his hands and I even like his limp. He's got a beautiful face, and I'd like nothing more than to sit on it until I die."

Bess cackled loud enough to frighten the birds from a rooftop across the street. "That was almost romantic."

"It was plenty romantic." Meg turned up her nose. "Bugger the lot of them and what they think. If a finer man exists, I haven't met him."

Bess grinned. "I like seeing you happy. It's strange."

Meg snorted. "I wouldn't go that far. Just because I've got a man doesn't mean everything else isn't shit."

She strolled into Ruta's bakery like she owned the place--chin up, shoulders back, and tits like the prow of a galleon. On the rare occasions she was nervous, she cloaked her fear in arrogance. She also took great care with her cosmetics, and when she'd left the inn that morning, she'd looked perfect as a painting come to life. She tried not to think about the toll hours of shopping must have taken on her rouge.

Judging by the look of surprise on the woman behind the counter, it was a mess. "Are you lost?"

"Even harlots got to eat now and then," she snapped before she could stop herself. To her right, Bess covered her face to disguise her amusement. "I beg your pardon," Meg corrected, the words out of place as a bag of marbles in her mouth. "I've come for some bread. Is Ruta in?"

The woman eyed her with obvious suspicion, but called over her shoulder, *"Matka?"*

As she waited for Ruta, Meg scanned the bakery for anything that looked familiar. At least half a dozen types of bread were displayed on shelves behind the permanent counter, all plump, shiny loaves in every shade from golden brown to black. The lighter ones looked like what Jake had bought before, but she didn't want to come all the way up here only to buy him the wrong one.

The bakery smelled of good coffee. She could certainly use a cup, but there was nowhere to sit.

A woman watched her from the only table, the one she'd shared with Jake the first time he'd brought her here. Though dressed like a fashionable widow of means, she was young yet and couldn't have been married for long. She sipped her coffee and pretended to be interested in the bread display all the while sneaking glances at Meg's hair. Hers was mostly covered, but what Meg could see of it framed her heart-shaped face in chestnut-colored curls. She was too obviously pretty to be jealous of Meg, surely. Perhaps she hadn't seen many English women in Spitalfields.

Ruta bustled around the corner and lit up as she saw Meg. "Sholem Aleikhem," she greeted with a smile.

"Aleikhem Sholem," Meg replied, pleased with herself for remembering.

Ruta pointed a finger at her, clearly pleased. "Good!"

Meg grinned. She was fairly certain the only other words she'd picked up were Dutch curses, so she might not get to use those here. Still, the day was young. "I'm looking for the bread Jake bought last week. Do you have any more?"

Ruta nodded and headed back into the kitchen.

Her daughter frowned. "The challah's right here," she muttered to herself. "You want challah? For Shabbos?"

Meg shrugged. "I think so. It's braided? He says he fancies it on Fridays."

The young woman gave a knowing nod and pulled a loaf off of the shelf. "This one?"

It looked right, as far as Meg could make out. "Cheers."

As she wrapped it in paper, the widow by the fire cleared her throat delicately. "I beg your pardon. I couldn't help but notice your hair."

Meg's hand returned to her braid. "What about it?"

"It's beautiful," she said honestly, but there was recognition in her amber eyes. "It's a very unusual pattern you have there. Where did you learn it?"

She hadn't. Jake had done it while she was balancing the ledgers this morning. Well, as she tried to balance the ledgers. She had been so distracted by his hands in her hair she'd had to take a break. Her desk was stronger than her bed, it so happened. Meg stroked her braid with no little pride. "My man did it for me."

The widow's eyes looked like they were about to pop out of her head. "Man?"

"He's very good with his hands." Meg sighed.

Ruta chose that moment to return with a basket of beigels. She held them out to Meg and nodded hopefully.

Meg held up her hands. "I'm not with child."

Ruta shook the basket at her and raised her eyebrows.

Meg laughed. "Go on, then." She took two and handed one to Bess.

Bess accepted it with suspicion.

"Try it," Meg encouraged her. "They're gorgeous. You'll thank me later."

The young woman handed her the challah. "Penny and half." She winced as Ruta elbowed her in the ribs and said something Meg didn't understand but sounded like an admonishment.

Rolling her eyes, she corrected, "Penny. The beigels are a gift."

Meg handed over her penny gladly. "Thank you, Ruta. We'll enjoy these."

Ruta nodded and replied with something that sounded pleasant enough, but firm.

"Matka!" her daughter protested.

Ruta replied to her daughter and gestured at Meg.

"I can't say that!"

Ruta nodded and pointed insistently at Meg.

The young woman groaned. "My mother wants me to tell you that she hopes you're with child the next time you come back."

Meg's laugh punctured the air, so sudden and loud it startled her and everyone in the bakery. Her childbearing days seemed to be over, but she rather liked the idea of one or two more with dark eyes. "Tell her I'm working on it."

"Christ, Meg," Bess muttered.

The young woman turned ten shades of scarlet, but did relay the essence of Meg's message to her mother. Ruta laughed and nodded her approval.

Though Meg couldn't understand a word they said, Ruta's daughter lowered her voice and asked her something, gesturing toward Meg and Bess. Ruta's answer seemed to surprise her, and her voice rose as her words spilled from her mouth. "*Jakob? Jakob Cohen?*"

The widow by the fire choked on her coffee.

The word "English" flew past Meg, along with a lot of other words she rather suspected were not complimentary. Several times Ruta's daughter said *Jakob*, although she pronounced it *Yakov*. Was that how he said it? She couldn't blame him for adopting the English version given Londoners' tendency to shorten names. "Jake" was common and wouldn't give anyone pause; he could hardly shorten it to "Yak."

Bess leaned in and whispered. "We should get back."

"Yes, go!" Ruta's daughter gestured toward the door. "You leave Jakob alone! He's a good man."

Meg's free arm rose to her hip, anticipating a fight. "I won't hold that against him."

Ruta talked over the both of them until her daughter stopped her posturing and listened. Finally the young woman threw up her hands in despair. "Heart? Following his *putz* is more like it," she muttered and stormed into the kitchen.

When she was gone, Ruta shrugged her apology. Meg gave a weak smile. The girl was right. Jake was a good man and she had no business being with him.

"I love him," she told Ruta weakly.

Ruta nodded again, but Meg wasn't sure she had understood.

Chapter 23

Two nights.

Two nights without sleep and Meg was radiant as ever, serving the Friday night crowd with her usual good cheer. He dropped a glass as he watched her, the crunch of it cracking pulling him back to the present. It fell like teeth around his feet, as though the inn itself was ready to eat him. The wine-stained floor was red as a great beast's mouth, the smoke in the air its fetid breath. The inn was a living thing, as much alive as anyone in it. So many felt as though they owned it, but it owned them, didn't it? They belonged to it--the Henshawes, the punters. He was beginning to feel like he belonged to it, too.

Verdomme, he needed some sleep.

And yet…

Meg swept past him with a saucy smile and sideways glance. It was the kind of look that said *I know what you look like when you come.* Much more of that would bring him to his knees.

He immediately started thinking about ways to please her from his knees.

"Take care. There's glass by your feet. Don't move." She grabbed the broom and swept it up in seconds, treating him to a view down her bodice. In normal circumstances he'd look away to be polite, but there was nothing polite about Meg or what they were doing together.

Together.

What were they, exactly? Lovers, certainly. They were living together, but he wasn't sure if that made a difference. He didn't fully understand Christian marriages, let alone marriages among the English poor. He'd had a lengthy engagement with Rachel and he'd made her a ring; the ink was still wet on the ketubah when she'd broken it off. As far as he could make out, marriages in Southwark weren't anywhere near as formal. Still, he'd sound daft if he had to ask, *'Are we married now?'*

Lover, wife, woman, friend.

Mine.

Whatever she was, she was his. He was happy with that.

She turned to take the glass into the kitchen to throw it out, her braid swaying like a pendulum above her arse. He caught it and tugged.

Meg whipped around, her eyes bright and her cheeks warm. She wasn't the only one who could tease.

Her lips parted as though she was about to say something, but no words came out. She was adorable, standing there all flustered.

He didn't think about it too hard. He kissed her.

She kissed him back, glass sliding out of the pan and back onto the floor in a shower of shards.

Mine.

Her kiss was a place of peace in the noisy bar, somewhere to rest and take succor. It was a blessing, a gift, a reminder of joy experienced and a promise of joy to come.

Someone whistled.

Meg murmured his name. The sound of it on her lips shot straight to his cock. He pulled away before he embarrassed himself.

At least *part* of him was awake.

"Leave the bar with the girls for a moment. I have something for you in the kitchen," she whispered with an inviting smile.

He swallowed. Whatever it was, he was fairly certain he wanted it.

She swept up the glass for a second time with a single, masterful swipe and he followed her into the kitchen.

Meg emptied the glass into the rubbish box. "Sit down."

With the evening meal out of the way, the kitchen was quiet. The fire burned low in the hearth beneath a pot warming the last of the day's stew. The bar was only yards away, but the noise seemed to him a distant rumble, no more disturbing than a cart passing in the street. He took a seat at the end of the table, glad for the chance to sit.

Meg stretched to the top shelf on the wall and pulled a parcel from a battered old pot. The moment she put it into his hands, he knew what it was. He unwrapped it slowly, the firelight illuminating the soft ridges of the braided bread. It was the first gift he'd been given in twelve years, and she'd gone to Spitalfields to get it.

He was more touched than he could say. He felt himself grinning. "You hid it?"

"Davey eats anything he finds in the cupboard." Meg filled two small dishes with stew for the both of them. "We hid most of the food for Christmas in Judith's room." She passed him the dish with a spoon as she sat across from him.

He put his hand over hers. "Thank you."

Her smile was sweeter than any he'd seen. She was happy she'd pleased him. "So what's this Friday business, then? Why do you fancy it on Fridays?"

"It's Shabbos. I mentioned it before, it's like Sunday for you. It's a day of rest. It begins Friday at sundown and ends Saturday at sundown. Sharing the challah is part of the Shabbos meal."

Meg paused with her spoon halfway to her mouth. "Sundown was hours ago."

He shrugged. "I haven't celebrated Shabbos properly in

years, but it's nice to be able to share it with someone."

She puzzled over the bread. "How would you do it properly? Celebrate, that is?"

"There's a lot to it." An understatement. "As lady of the house, you would light the candles and say the blessing to welcome the Sabbath. I would say Kiddush with the wine, and then we would wash our hands and say another blessing before we eat."

She dropped her spoon. "I already started eating, sorry."

He laughed. "It's fine, we're just having supper."

"You want wine? That's one thing I can do, at least." She got up before he had a chance to answer and returned with half a bottle of decent claret. She poured two glasses and passed one to him. He accepted gladly.

She took her seat and sipped her wine. "What about the bread?"

"That's the best part." He rose and washed his hands, saying the blessing to himself before he dried them. They might not be celebrating it right, but it still felt wrong to tear the challah without washing first. He grabbed the salt pot before he returned to the table and took the bread in his hands. "Then I salt the bread and pray before we eat. *Barukh atah Adonai, Eloheinu, melekh ha-olam hamotzi lechem min ha'aretz. Amein.*"

Meg pursed her lips. "What does that mean?"

"I've never said it in English before." His laugh was self-conscious. Perhaps he should have by now. He'd been away so long. Too long, really. "It's something like, *blessed are You, Lord, our God, King of Heaven, who brings bread from the earth.* That might not be a good translation."

Meg's eyebrows lifted. "Sounds just like what we say in church."

He shrugged. "Same God."

She smiled. "Amen."

Jake tore the bread, saying a private prayer of thanks in his heart for the woman on the other side of the table. He passed her a large piece and took one for himself. Between Ruta's bread and Meg's claret, it was the closest to home he'd felt in years.

"It's so light," she said between bites, "and a bit sweet, too. Good with the stew. Is the stew all right to eat with it?"

He shrugged. "I haven't kept kosher in years. It's impossible, living down here. I'd never eat a thing. What's in it?"

"Beans, carrots, turnips. A leek or two. A bit of flour and beer."

"It's delicious. That's fine for me. I still don't eat pork or shellfish, but I'm far from perfect. Old habits, I suppose."

"Clever, is what it is." She pointed her spoon at him to make her point. "That fish monger Sam Turner is always selling rotten oysters. I've seen what that can do to a man's guts, and I'll stick with beans. Cheaper, as well." She finished off her stew and immediately went to refill her plate. "You want a bit more?"

"Go on, then."

She gave him another portion and they ate in companionable silence. It was mad, but he enjoyed that almost as much as what they got up to after hours. Having someone to eat with was no small thing.

When he had imagined his *bashert*, never in a million years would he have thought of Meg Henshawe. She was an English woman of middling years with three children, a formidable temper, and a filthy mouth.

She was beautiful, hard-working, and honest to a fault. She was a devoted mother and capable of acts of great kindness and generosity. He liked kissing her. He liked working beside her, and he liked seeing her on the other side of the table. Who could hope for more than that?

What would his parents say if they could see him now? He was three guineas and a temporary job away from abject poverty in a Southwark inn, ready to pledge himself to an English prostitute.

His mother would die of apoplexy. *Die.*

His father had been a bit of an adventurer with a good sense of humor. He'd probably understand.

Possibly.

Perhaps.

He'd get a good laugh out of it, at least.

Meg emptied her glass. "Aren't you meant to take the day off as well?"

He nodded. "Yes, but that hasn't always been possible for me."

She tucked a strand of hair behind her ear. "You can, if you'd like. We'll cover for you," she offered, and he understood it meant a great deal that she had. Meg worked hard and expected the same from everyone she employed.

"Not tonight," he said, taking her hands in his. "This is enough."

Chapter 24

Sunday morning, Meg seized the opportunity to attack the wine stain while everyone else readied themselves for church.

Meg wasn't going. The whole town had long since suspected she was sleeping with Jake; by now they must have known it was true. The two of them had made no great secret of it, taking every chance to smile, touch, or kiss. She had nothing to be ashamed of, but no desire to be rebuked with a thinly veiled sermon about apostasy. Shagging someone's brains out was not the same thing as converting to their religion, but was the curate likely to understand? Was he hell.

One side of town or the other, she'd still be on her knees. May as well scrub her floor as cleanse her soul. Her floor, at least, might still be redeemed.

She was humming to herself when the door slammed.

She glanced up from her scrub brush to see a pair of boots pass her in a flash of leather and grime. A familiar fist twisted her hair; far past pleasurable, she felt nothing but excruciating pain as he dragged her to her feet. "Have you got something to tell me?" His voice was low and deceptively pleasant. It was the same voice he'd used in better times. Same tone, same pitch. She wished to God she had heard the venom sooner.

"Let me go, Tom," she demanded, taking care not to raise

her voice. Though the bar was empty, the inn was stirring and anyone could walk in to find Meg hanging by her hair from Tom Callaghan's fist. "For God's sake, Tom, I can't think straight."

He let her go and she fell to her knees like a sack of bricks, dropping the scrub brush onto the floor she'd been scouring all morning. She made no sound as she landed, dumb with the shock of the pain shooting up her legs. The whole room rang around her and she focused on her breathing, willing the pain to subside enough for her to be able to stand.

Tom cuffed her over the ear. "Where is he, hey?"

Tommy. Oh Lord, Tommy's in the kitchen. "Tommy's out," she lied, hoping the boy would have the presence of mind to hide until his father had left. Tom's wrath was blind when he got going, and she wouldn't let him hurt her son. She grabbed the brush, struggling to stand.

He kicked her in the stomach and she reflexively wretched, crashing to her elbows as she landed. "Stupid whore. *The Jew.* Where's the goddamned Jew?"

Meg raised herself onto her knees, gasping for air. She grabbed the edge of the table and pulled herself up, turning to face Tom. She wouldn't give him the satisfaction of keeping her down. "Is that what this is about? You jealous, Tom?"

He was beyond jealous. He was livid. His face burned violet with rage, a distended vein throbbing in his forehead. He clutched her shoulders and shook her until her teeth rattled. "What were you thinking? You're mine, you filthy bloody trull. I thought I'd come around to remind you since you've clearly forgot."

Jake was still upstairs. If she screamed, she might draw Tommy out from wherever he was hiding and she would not alert Tom to the boy's presence. She'd die before she let any of her punters see Tom get the better of her, so she'd have to keep quiet and hope Jake came downstairs before long.

Unless she could provoke Tom into making enough noise to alert them both.

"I'm not anymore." She spat blood at his feet. "Jake's my man now, or haven't you heard? You can't touch me, unless you want him to give you the beating of your miserable life."

"You're lying to me. No one wants you." He slapped her harder.

"Mum!"

Tommy stood horrified in the doorway of the kitchen, and her heart broke at the look on his face. No point in keeping quiet now. "Run outside, darling. Keep running until you get to Mark's house, do you hear?"

"Let him stay." Tom laughed. "He'll be a man soon. Let him see how to put a bitch in her place."

As Tom was caught off guard, Meg seized the chance to get one in herself. She threw all of her weight behind her fist and forced him sidewise with a blow to his cheek. In the moment it took him to recover, Meg cracked a stool over his hunched form and knocked him to the floor.

Meg spat. "In your place now, *bitch*?"

Tommy seized the opportunity to dash past Meg and Tom and ran upstairs.

Tom swept her feet out from under her and she fell with a thud. He hit her across the face with a neat jab and she cried out involuntarily. "Did you fuck him?" He barked as his hand clamped over her thigh. "Don't lie to me."

Meg licked the blood off of her teeth. "I did, and let me tell you, Tom, the pit is not the only place he's bested you." She brought her free knee up sharply into his chin.

His head snapped back, but he did not loosen his hold on her thigh. "Goddamned whore!"

Barely grasping the scrub brush, she smacked him over the head with the wooden handle.

He pulled the brush out of her hand and threw it across the room. Closing his hands around her neck, he dragged her to her feet and pushed her over the nearest table, forcing her face into the wood. "You're mine, do you hear me? *Mine!*"

She kicked backward wildly, but her feet met only air. The world turned gray and began to sparkle as he choked her. Her ears rang and she struggled for breath but could draw none. He shoved her skirt over her arse and the gray deepened to black. Her last thought as she lost consciousness was *he's really going to kill me this time.* Her legs kept kicking weakly and some part of her mind urged her to fight against the rest of his assault.

It never came.

Meg's hearing came back first to the sound of glass shattering. Her vision returned to a shower of diamonds and rubies raining into the street.

Meg slid off the table and landed heavily on the floor. Tommy threw his arms around her, tears streaming down his ruddy cheeks. They ran like rainwater off the end of his nose and onto her skirt. "Mum! Mum, can you hear me? Mum!"

She blinked slowly and pulled him into her arms as she regained her senses. "Tommy." She kissed his cheeks and smoothed a hand over his hair. Her bloody knuckles looked like raw meat. She looked at them dumbly, wondering how they had gotten that way.

Judith's gasp drew her attention upward. Her sister's gaze was riveted to the street.

Knees screaming with pain, Meg climbed to her feet with Tommy's help and looked outside.

The diamonds she had seen were shards of shattered window. The rubies were the pieces that had scraped Tom on his way through it. Jake had thrown Tom through it with such force even the rotten wooden panes had cracked, leaving splintered posts protruding at odd angles. That was two of them gone now. God only knew how much it would cost her to get *both* fixed.

Meg sat on the table she had almost died on and watched the fight through the hole in the front of her inn.

Bloody but running on rage, Tom fought Jake blindly,

throwing fists every which way. A gash on his scalp poured over his face, adding to that red he turned when he was angry.

As for Jake, she had never seen anything like him.

He had always been so careful in the pits. Measured, capable, devastating.

They were a ways away from Bear Gardens.

Miles past furious, Jake fought like a man possessed. He caught several blows but didn't seem to feel them as he pursued Tom through the street with murder in his eyes. Everyone passing on their way to church got out of the way. They watched with bated breath from windows and alleys, crouching behind carts even as they cheered for either side.

It was like a fight in the pit, but no bets had been placed and no one would stop it once either of them had been knocked down. More than that, it was like watching Tom try to strike an unchained bear intent on tearing his throat out. He didn't stand a chance.

Meg wiped the blood from her lip and looked on as her current lover beat her previous to a pulp in broad daylight.

On a Sunday.

Meg's smile spread into the bruise forming on her cheek. It hurt like the very devil, but she couldn't help herself. Bess offered her a pipe and she accepted it, drawing the smoke as deep as her battered ribs would allow. They were bruised, but they didn't feel broken. He'd broken them before, and that had been much worse.

Bess, Tommy, Joe, Judith, and the baby surrounded her like a protective wall, all of them watching solemnly as Jake thrashed Tom to within an inch of his life. She'd never wanted a man to fight her battles for her, but she had to admit seeing Jake fight the man who'd terrorized her for so long was more than gratifying. She had always enjoyed watching Jake fight, but it was another thing entirely to know he was doing it for her.

He was, wasn't he?

Perhaps it was only their rivalry coming to a head. Whatever the cause, she would allow herself this moment to believe Jake was defending her honor.

Meg chuckled to herself. *Honor.*

Tommy never took his eyes from Jake, his mouth hanging open. Meg closed it for him with a gentle tap beneath his chin.

He looked up at her, his hazel eyes huge with wonder. "I want to be a fighter."

Meg groaned. "Oh, Lord. Another one. You want to be like your father, do you?"

Tommy shook his head. "I want to be like Jake. I won't let anyone hurt you ever again."

Meg blinked back the tears that clouded her eyes and put her arm around her son's shoulders. The world was a brutal place, and she wished she could have shielded him from more of it for longer. "You watch him, then." She said with a sniff. "He's the best there is."

With one final, terrible blow, Jake knocked Tom clean out. Tom collapsed into the gutter in a bloody heap and Jake stood over him, catching his breath. His shirt was torn at the shoulder and covered in blood and filth. Sweat poured down his face and his hair was soaked with it.

Jake dropped the brick he'd been holding--when had he picked that up?--and limped back toward the inn. His steps were uneven. He must have hurt his leg sometime during the fight.

Tommy tugged at her sleeve. "Mum, there's a lady here."

Meg couldn't even see Tom anymore from where she was sitting, but proof of the fight still filled the street. Shattered glass glittered in the sunlight as the poor scavenged the onions and turnips left from the overturned vegetable cart. The vendor dragged it away with a mangled wheel and broken axis, shaking his head and muttering oaths to himself. Blood was splattered across every surface like a cockfight only so much worse; it was a wonder the two of them had any blood left in their bodies. She hoped they did.

She hoped Jake did, at least.

His shirt was torn and his leg was injured; even from fifty paces she could see he'd really been hurt. Not only could she see it, but all of Southwark would be able to, too. He looked toward the inn, his hair a mess and face covered in blood, and increased his pace.

Her heart leapt as though it had been long dormant; after years asleep, it was finally awakening with the first rays of the sun. Meg slid off the table. She'd lost her shoes in Tom's attack but didn't pause to find them. Meg slipped past a woman in brown velvet loitering in the doorway and rushed into the street.

Jake was still some ways away, doggedly closing the distance between them though his poor leg was all but useless. His gaze was intense, purposeful, and filled with enough fire to burn her alive.

She charged headlong into the heat. Shards of glass bit her feet as she went to him, but she barely felt them. It would take more than broken glass to keep her away. She broke into a run, her heart racing with joy.

He caught her willingly, holding her as though they'd been apart for years rather than an hour. He crushed her to his chest and kissed her temple, shaking with something that might have been relief. As she kissed him in the street, he returned it tenfold, claiming her mouth and cradling her face in broad daylight in front of God and Southwark and anyone who cared to look.

Her heart sang and some long-troubled piece of her soul rested at last.

At last.

A distant cough was lost in the noise of passing carts and braying livestock. Laughter and speculative murmurs came from every direction, drowned out by the sound of the blood pounding through her veins. Her euphoria felt much like anger only more intense; she lost all feeling below her knees, her cheeks burned, and her heart sped so high and fast in her breast she felt certain she could fly. The only thing tethering her was Jake; he was the center of the world and the only thing keeping her from orbit. If she lost hold of him, she'd float to the moon.

When at last he broke the kiss--God knew she couldn't--he held her face and examined her for bruises. From the anguish in his eyes, she knew the fingerprints around her throat were dark enough to see. They'd be black in a day. He stopped short of touching a tender spot on her jaw. "I'll kill him," he muttered to himself. "I'll bloody kill him."

The grim threat might have filled another woman with fear, but it only added to Meg's bliss. "You won't have to. He'll never come back now."

"No, he won't," he promised. He kissed her slowly, reverently, and thoroughly until the numbness in her feet spread throughout her body and she felt weightless.

Another cough niggled its way into her hearing, like an insect buzzing as one tried to sleep. She swatted it away in her mind and deepened the kiss.

"Jakob."

She didn't hear his name at first. A foreign pronunciation in a soft, feminine voice, it could have been anything. A particularly insistent breeze, gone and forgotten.

Again, and this time she recognized it.

"Jakob?"

Jake didn't miss it. He stiffened as though he'd been doused with freezing water and all but dropped her. He looked over her shoulder, as pale as if he'd seen a ghost.

"Rachel?"

Chapter 25

Meg fell back to earth hard enough to shatter bone. It felt as though her knees turned to jelly and the rest of her followed, liquefying into a puddle of blood and viscera. They'd have to scrape her off the road if the rain didn't wash her away first.

Rachel.

Jake's reassuring grip on her arms told her somehow, some way she had survived the fall intact and was, in fact, still a woman and not the remains of one. The fire in his eyes was extinguished and in its place was shock.

Rachel, the woman he'd almost married.

Rachel, the woman who'd married his friend, instead.

"Rachel, the one who left you to die in the street?" she asked, hackles rising.

"The same," he whispered.

Standing in the doorway was the widow from Ruta's bakery. Chestnut curls fluttered away from her face in the wind, and she was pale as the snow as she got a good look at Jake. It wasn't worry Meg saw there, but horror. She'd heard Meg tell Ruta she loved him, but she'd come anyway, and now she had the nerve to look at him like he was some kind of *monster*?

Anger jolted her heart back to life and she moved away from Jake, prepared to give the woman a piece of her mind. "Oh, we're going to have words."

"Don't," he warned.

"Why not?"

"It was years ago. It doesn't matter."

Meg frowned, tension tightening her jaw. "Are you protecting her?"

He shook his head, clearly exhausted. "She's not like you and me."

"What does that mean?"

"You'll eat her alive."

"You don't want me to." She gaped. "You don't want me to hurt her."

His eyes softened. "I don't want her to hurt you, either."

Meg snorted.

A flash of a dimple appeared in his cheek as he fought a smile. He offered his arm and she took it, holding her head so high it might have been paraded on a pike, defiantly proud though her heart had just been torn from her chest.

♥

Rachel Moreira was in Southwark.

Twelve years without a word and at last she turned up to see him at his worst, limping and covered in blood after nearly beating his nemesis to death over a woman. He ran a hand through his short hair, bare headed as any Englishman, and wondered that she recognized him at all. He'd come a long way from the boy she'd jilted. The winter chill cut through the tears in his shirt like a knife seeking his vitals, and he felt a twinge of shame at his appearance.

Meg bobbed along beside him, her chin in the air. She was proud as a queen to be on his arm, and he loved her for it.

The thought caught him so off-guard he missed a step, his ankle buckling beneath him. He recovered himself before he stumbled. As he looked down, he noticed an irregularity to Meg's gait.

She was limping, too.

He stopped in his tracks. "What's happened? Are you hurt?"

She looked up in surprise. "It's only my feet. Caught a little glass."

What did *that* mean? He was on his knees before her in an instant, lifting her skirt to her ankles.

Someone whistled.

"Jake," Meg warned, blushing.

To his horror, she was barefoot. Her feet were a dusky shade of blue and bleeding from a network of scratches her could plainly see around her toes. If not for the cold freezing the mud, they'd be covered in filth as well. "*Godverdomme!* Where are your shoes, love?"

She looked down at him speculatively. He wondered what she saw. "I wanted to get to you."

She did? Perhaps he was more than an amusement after all. "We need to get these cleaned and put up. Feet bleed for hours."

His first instinct was to carry her, but his leg was in such a state he knew he couldn't do it. He wrapped his arm around the small of her back. "Put your arm over my shoulder. You can lean on me."

There was uncertainty in her eyes, but she did as he asked. He helped her to walk without putting as much weight on her feet and she, in turn, propped him up. They limped together back to the inn like a cart missing a wheel--broken and wobbling, but still going.

Rachel gave them a wide berth as they passed, fidgeting with her gloves. Jake helped Meg into the kitchen and Judith followed close behind.

Bess looked up from the bottles she was filling. Again, the scent of roses clouded the room. "What happened here?"

Jake set Meg on the edge of the table. "She's cut her feet. We need clean water and bandages."

Judith set off to gather supplies, Pea gurgling from her sling.

Tommy popped his head around the corner. "Jake, there's a lady here to see you."

"She's going to have to wait," he dismissed, examining Meg's feet. He drew in a long breath as he saw the extent of the wounds. "Meg!"

"She just stands by the door," Tommy said. "She doesn't want a drink or anything."

"I'm fine," Meg insisted. "Go see…" she waved a hand, not saying Rachel's name.

Jake frowned. Meg's tone was dismissive, as though she couldn't care less whether he was there or not. He studied her face and she looked away, not meeting his eyes. She was hurting. "I didn't know she was coming," he said softly.

Meg glanced at him, eyes wild as a hare caught in a trap. "It's not my concern," she snapped.

If she wasn't angry, she was certainly withdrawn. She crossed her arms over her midsection like she was guarding herself from a blow. Still, she leaned into his hand as he cupped her face. She met his gaze, softening.

He pressed his lips to hers in reassurance. The kiss was chaste, firm, and charged with devotion. He hoped she felt it, whatever it was he was feeling for her. She gave him strength and he needed it. Before he saw Rachel again, he wanted to remind himself that Meg's kiss could stop time.

Heart racing, he touched his forehead to hers. "I'll see what she wants and send her home. I'll come right back. Will you be all right for a moment?"

She nodded, oddly silent.

"I'll come back," he promised.

♥

The silhouette in the doorway was no longer familiar to him, but he supposed she hadn't changed. She was a small woman with a slender, neat figure in an elegant dress. Her dark hair was swept up in an English style, a tasteful arrangement of her natural curls pinned at the back of her head. Not a hair was out of place, not an inch of skin showing that might be deemed immodest. She was wearing brown, for God's sake, and Rachel still radiated beauty. She waited with her eyes on the street, back stiff and hands trembling. A woman like her didn't belong in Southwark. Why had she come?

"Rachel?"

She turned at the sound of her name, her face almost blue in the cold. She was lovelier, if anything. Age had taken the girlish roundness from her face. She had been pretty at sixteen, but at thirty-odd, she was a great beauty by any standard.

He used to feel dumb when he looked at her. Now he was just confused.

"Why are you here?" he asked. "Is something wrong? Is Ruta well?"

A little furrow appeared between her eyebrows and even that was tasteful. "I came to see you."

The itch of drying blood on his arm reminded him he still needed to wash. He scratched it and put his fingers right through a hole Tom had torn in his shirt. He grimaced. "I'm not much to look at at the moment. Do you mind if I change my clothes?"

She glanced around the bar with obvious distaste. "You would *leave* me here?"

It was late afternoon and the bar was half empty. Most of their regulars were off working or thieving and wouldn't be in for another hour or more. Three men played a card game near the fire, oblivious to the shattered windows. Joe nursed his gin at the bar, pretending not to listen.

"You're safe enough here."

He could tell from her expression she didn't believe him.

"Is someone with you?" Twelve years ago, Rachel wouldn't

have crossed the street without an escort.

She shook her head demurely. "I...I wanted to come alone."

Jake frowned. If anywhere required an escort, it was Southwark. If she had ventured there on her own, she didn't want anyone knowing she'd come. What should he make of that?

"Come away from the door," he said gently. "We'll get you a table and a cup of coffee. You'll be fine."

She pouted, looking as though she wanted to say a hundred things at once. She settled for, "The windows are broken."

"Yeah, that was me."

She raised an eyebrow.

He shrugged, feeling small. "Tom Callaghan thought he'd try to have his way with my missus, so I tossed him through one."

Joe banged his glass on the bar in approval. "Hear, hear!"

Rachel shot Joe a look of disgust.

Jake bit back a laugh. The words had rolled off his tongue easily enough, as though he had just said he was thirsty so he'd had a drink. He had nothing to be ashamed of.

He suspected Rachel disagreed.

"You're *married*?"

He shrugged. Many men referred to their women that way whether they were married or not. Common law was an odd thing in Southwark. As far as he could make out, the legality of it didn't matter so much as how they chose to live and with whom. He doubted most had anything signed at all, let alone something as formal as a ketubah. "No, but I've got somebody."

"That...*woman*," Rachel said, as though woman was the most generous word she could think of. "She's English."

"Yes."

Rachel set her shoulders and stepped carefully over the threshold as though the rushes were filled with snakes. He took exception to her hesitance. He'd only just changed them yesterday.

She stopped after three steps. "Do we have to stay here?"

"I live here."

She didn't argue, but looked distinctly nauseous.

Granted, it was in a bit of a state after the fight, but The Rose was still the best inn south of the river. He wasn't asking her to step into a sewer. Jake glanced toward the kitchen for strength, and grinned as he saw Tommy spying on them from around the corner. Jake motioned to him to come over.

Tommy stepped out of the shadow. He looked guilty at being caught listening, but Jake was so relieved to see a friendly face he could have kissed him.

"Just the man I wanted to see. Tommy, this is Mrs. Moreira. Would you please bring her a coffee and sit with her a moment while I go upstairs?"

Tommy glowered, a dark expression he'd seen on Tom's face once or twice. Come to think of it, the boy *had* seen Jake beat the daylights out of his father that morning. Were they still friends? "Mum won't like it," he protested.

"Ask Judith, then."

"She's wrapping Mum's feet." Tommy regarded Rachel with such hostility one would have thought she'd struck him. "I'll go," he conceded reluctantly and marched back into the kitchen with a noisy sigh.

"You have children?" Rachel asked breathlessly.

He resented her surprise. He hadn't seen her for a dozen years, had she expected him to remain celibate? "Tommy is Meg's son. Do you have children?"

She ignored the question. "She's a widow?"

"No."

Her eyes widened. He wondered if she was regretting taking those three awkward steps into the bar. Tired of fielding her questions, he turned and led her to a table near the back of the bar beneath the last window that wasn't broken. She followed, clutching her cloak at the base of her throat. She examined the bench before she sat down.

Tommy dutifully brought out a mug of coffee and set it in

front of her.

Rachel frowned at it, then looked up at Jake.

He shook his head. "It's coffee. It's fine."

She gave a tight smile but she didn't drink it.

♥

No one gave him any credit for it, but Tommy put up with a lot.

He'd been the one to run and get Jake when his father started hitting his mum. He *hadn't* stabbed his father, which had been his first instinct when he saw him hurting her, and when the lady in the brown dress came in asking for Jake, he *hadn't* pretended not to know him and told her to piss off.

Which is what he should have done, and what he wanted to do now.

Except now she knew Jake lived there, and she was probably going to take him away, which is what ladies in fancy dresses did when they turned up at The Rose looking for men. They'd find them sitting with his mum or one of his aunts and drag them out by their ears, never to be seen again.

Tommy glared at the woman, sitting there like she'd never seen a cup of coffee before. She was pretty, but his mum was prettier, and if she thought she was taking Jake away, she had another think coming.

If Jake left, who would help Chris with his leg? Who would make his mum smile and keep his father away? Who was going to teach him how to fight?

Tommy hadn't asked him to yet, but he was sure Jake would say yes if this woman didn't make him leave first.

She was very small, not much taller than Tommy. She'd have a harder time dragging Jake *anywhere* by his ear.

"Your name is Tommy?" She smiled at him like she was kind, but he saw right through it. Very few people were kind, when it came it down to it. "I have a son around your age. Adam."

Tommy clenched his jaw. "Is Jake his dad?"

The woman gasped and her cheeks flushed a brilliant shade of fuchsia. "Of course not."

Tommy sat back in his chair, his broken rib still aching with every breath. "Where's his dad?"

She pursed her lips, looking like Aunt Bel in a fit of pique. "Where's yours?"

"Jake threw him through the window. I reckon I need a new one."

The woman didn't attempt to disguise her disgust as she looked at him. He was still covered in bruises from his own fight, not that she could see all of them. His eye was swollen, but he could still meet her gaze with a glare of his own.

The lady muttered something he didn't understand that sounded a bit like a prayer. "Will he come back if Jakob leaves, do you think?"

"Yeah, that's the problem." The woman was obviously stupid. He took her coffee in his taped hand and sipped it.

She crossed her arms and looked away. "How long has Jakob lived here?"

He shrugged. "A fortnight."

She narrowed her eyes and looked at him as though she was trying to detect a lie. He held her gaze and didn't so much as flinch.

"How long has he…*known* your mother?"

Tommy shrugged. He couldn't say for certain. His mum had seemed to know him when he moved in that night, but Tommy didn't remember seeing him before. They could have known each other for years for all he knew. "Why do you keep calling him 'Yackoff'?"

"That's how you say it."

"That's not how I say it."

"You're saying it wrong, aren't you?"

Tommy blinked. "That's not how Jake says it, either."

They didn't say another word until Jake returned a few minutes later. The woman looked up with a look of obvious relief not unlike his own. Jake looked much the same--bruised, bloody in places--but he wore a clean shirt and his hair was wet as if he'd washed it. There was no hiding he'd been in a fight, though.

Tommy's heart swelled with pride. Life would be so much easier if Jake could be his dad. He was everything a father ought to be; he was kind to Tommy, he didn't drink too much, he knew how to set a broken bone, and he wouldn't let anybody hurt his mum. That was more than he could say for any other man he'd met. Even Mark Virtue had hit the gin too hard from time to time.

Jake smiled at him. He'd already showed Tommy more kindness in a fortnight than Tom had in ten years.

Tommy stood to give up his chair, and impulsively hugged him around the waist.

Jake caught him hesitantly, but he didn't hit him.

Taking that for a good sign, Tommy finished the woman's coffee and took it back to the kitchen.

♥

Jake stood for a moment, stunned. Tommy had hugged him.

Here he'd been afraid the boy would hate him for thrashing his father, but it would seem that had endeared him to Tommy instead. Perhaps it was that he was still coming down after the fight, but that small gesture of kindness made him feel like weeping. He had always wanted children. Not so long ago, he'd thought Rachel was his only chance at that.

Now here she was.

As he took the seat across from her, the bar was oddly silent. He'd dreamed of this moment for years, but now that she was here, it was nothing at all like he'd anticipated.

She wasn't leaping into his arms. To his surprise, he didn't want her to. All their years apart yawned like a chasm between them; she puzzled over his face as though trying to recognize the stranger on the other side of the table.

He had loved her once, he knew he had. Not a month before, he would have sworn he still did, but she was not the woman he remembered.

Superficially, she had changed very little. She still had a good complexion and those odd colored eyes. He used to smell cinnamon when he looked at them, but now they made him think of jasper, hard and cold. She couldn't hide the subtle downward twitch of her lips as her gaze leapt from scar to scar. His eye was swelling and he was certain he'd broken his nose again. He'd done his best to clean the blood from his face, but there was no hiding the changes to the bones or the lines that had settled around his mouth. When he was younger he used to wear his hair long, in no small part to disguise the size of his ears, but he'd long since grown out of such nonsense. It was easier to wash the blood out of it when it was short.

She let out a little squeak as her gaze rested on the flattened bridge of his nose. "What happened to you?"

He took a breath. "How long have you got?" After she'd left him alone, he'd been beaten and run down by a mob. He'd managed to evade them long enough to make it to Ruta's. She hid him until the madness passed, then allowed him to stay months until his leg had healed enough to walk. He wouldn't tell Rachel that, though. He'd lived through it, he'd earned his pain. He didn't know her well enough anymore to want to share it with her. She didn't deserve it.

She tore her gaze away, as though looking at him was too much to bear. "I heard you were fighting...I never expected…" She let out a breath. "You used to be so handsome."

This statement hit him like a slap. *Used to be.*

"Some don't find me so difficult to look at," he muttered, wounded.

"They'll say anything if you pay them," she snapped, and

seemed to immediately regret it.

He clenched his jaw. "Does Aaron know you're here?"

She paled. "He passed."

"*HaMakom y'nachem etkhem b'tokh sh'ar a'vaylay Tzion v'Y'rushalayim,*" he said automatically. *May God comfort you among the other mourners of Zion and Jerusalem.*

Her expression softened somewhat. "I have missed the sound of your voice," she confessed. "When will you come back to Spitalfields?"

The way she said it, it sounded as though he'd been wandering in the desert for years. "I live here now. I work here."

"You don't have to." Her eyes sought his and again he saw the idealistic girl she had once been. "You always did such lovely work. More shops have opened since you've been away. Anyone would be lucky to have you."

"I can't."

"Of course you can," she soothed.

He shook his head, growing frustrated. "I know you mean well, but I work here now." *They need me here.* "I'm fine."

Her eyebrows drew together. "You can't be serious. Look at this place. Look at yourself." She waved a hand to indicate his general appearance. "We're surrounded by tenements. Do you have any idea how many brothels I passed on my way here? I hardly recognize you. That shirt you're wearing has got to be older than my son and you talk like an Englishman. That nasty little boy could use a firm hand, and that...*woman--*"

Jake felt his temperature rising. "You should go."

She closed her eyes and took a breath to steady herself. When she opened them again, she was calm. "Forgive me, it is only that I am concerned for your welfare. You must know I still care for you."

"Do you?"

"Of course," she insisted. "I want to discuss something with you."

"I'm listening."

"Not here." She shuddered. "Come to my house for tea this week."

As uncomfortable as the conversation was, it was a kind offer and it would be rude to turn her down. Still. "I have to help with Christmas preparations."

"*Christmas*, Jakob?"

"I work here," he repeated defensively. "I haven't converted."

She sniffed. "I am most relieved to hear it. Perhaps not everything has changed."

Chapter 26

Meg shivered as she lit the candle beside her mirror. The night bled long shadows across her room and every hollow of her face until she couldn't see the bruise forming on her temple. She knew it was there, though. When Tom hit someone, they felt it.

She patted a little rose salve over the area. The color had deepened throughout the night, but no one had mentioned it. Everyone knew what had happened.

Her gaze settled on the reflection of her empty bed in the mirror, the linens still scattered asunder. She could almost see Jake in it, and she knew when she climbed into it alone later, she'd still smell the cloves in his soap.

He said he'd only see Rachel home safely, but he'd been gone for hours. Perhaps he wouldn't come back at all.

Who would want a used up moll when they could have a beautiful, wealthy widow? Jake would be warming her bed from now on, no doubt, and Meg would be left alone again until Tom drank too much and shoved his way into her room.

She drank deeply from her mug of wine and rubbed a little more salve onto her lips. They were blue, but whether that was the wine, the cold, or Tom, she couldn't say.

No one else had noticed. Jake would have.

Her heart felt so heavy it was a struggle to stand. No man had ever made her so miserable. Not Tom, not Mark, and not any of the dozens of others. She'd been a fool to let herself get attached.

Still, she peered out the window toward the bridge, longing to see him limping back to her.

"Fat bloody chance," she muttered to herself and blew out the candle.

Moments after she crawled into bed, she heard the heavy rattle of the lock downstairs. She groaned into her pillow. Davey had been out since catching the tail end of the fight. She saw him blanch and head for The Hanging Sword, but she'd been so relieved to see the back of him, she hadn't cared.

Rather than Davey wheezing up the stairs, she heard a familiar uneven step.

He was back.

She sat up in bed. The curtains were still open from when she *hadn't* been watching for his return, and the room was cold. Her hearth had long since burned out, and the room was dark but for a column of bluish light from the full moon. Would he stop by? She needed to know what had happened with Rachel, but she'd be damned if she asked. She was fairly certain she already knew.

He knocked so softly, she almost missed it.

Meg rushed to let him in, her white night rail fluttering like cobwebs around her legs. She jerked the door open to find him leaning against the jamb, his expression pained, caught somewhere between sorrow and want. She opened her arms to him.

He embraced her so quickly she lost her breath. Pushing the door shut with his boot, he took her face in his hands and kissed her.

It came easier now, kissing him. She'd done it so much over the past fortnight, it had become her natural state. The newness of it all had settled into something better; a sweet familiarity comforting as it was addictive. It felt like she was kissing her other half.

In all the years she'd chased just such a feeling, no one else had come close. No one else had taken the time or interest to see who she was, no one had given so much without demanding something in return. For all the injuries he'd sustained—physical or otherwise—he was perfect. She knew his pain as she knew her own.

She knew his heart and it felt like home.

He was in no hurry tonight. He was still so cold. The tip of his nose was ice against her cheek. He traced her face with the pad of his thumb, a whisper of a touch that soothed like a spell. Anyone else would have had her on her back by now, but Jake only held her in the doorway, archiving her features, the weight of her hair, and the texture of her lips.

It felt as though he was trying to commit her to memory. He kissed like it was the last time.

She didn't have to ask what had happened with Rachel.

Meg swallowed the sob wringing her throat. She had only just gotten used to him. Already she had begun to crave his arms, his smell, the sound of his breath. How could someone come and just tear him away?

As he broke the kiss to catch his breath, Meg opened her eyes. The moon outlined him in faintly silver light; beyond that was only darkness, as though he was already fading from her life. She would hold him as long as she could. She would make the most of their last night together, for surely that's what it was.

Meg couldn't compete. She wouldn't try.

She might not be able to give him wealth, status, or security, but there was one thing she was better at than anyone else, and that's what she'd give him tonight.

His hands swept down the sides of her breasts and her nipples stiffened at his proximity. He ran his hands over her ribs and around her waist, spanning the small of her back. She drank in the exquisite heat of his mouth, tasting his tongue and dragging his lip between her teeth. Needing to feel his skin again, she pushed his coat from his shoulders.

He let it drop. He skimmed her night rail over her hips and breasts, only breaking the kiss to pull it off. His gaze roamed her naked body in the moonlight, her legs, her sex, her waist, her famous breasts. He moaned low in his throat and reached for her, his hands mapping the territory his eyes had already devoured.

The feel of his big, rough hands on all of her softest parts was such a delicious contrast she could have purred. Surrounded by his heat, his strength, and his smell, she wanted to lose herself in him, to sate this longing one last time. What were her years of lovers but practice for this one man, this *one moment*?

He put his lips to her throat and she sighed, boneless with pleasure. The night had a texture of its own, that bittersweet beauty of mortality that both makes a kiss and spoils it with the knowledge that this, too, must end. Her nerves burned with it, every minute touch charged with the understanding this would be the last time she'd feel it.

The linen of his shirt was coarse against the tips of her breasts. She tugged at it impatiently and he cast it off almost as an afterthought. By the time he reached his trousers, she had already loosened the laces and pushed them halfway off of his arse. He bent to take off his boots, but she wouldn't wait. She pushed him into her bed on his back, his trousers around his knees and his cock pointing skyward.

He didn't say a word as she took him into her hand. She ran the tip of her tongue up the sensitive underside of his cock and encircled the head, relishing that delicious warm taste of flesh and salt. The noise he made as she took the whole engorged length of him down her throat was hardly human. He tangled his hands in her hair, pulling her closer, and it was all she could do to resist sucking him dry. She loved giving head and she knew she was good at it, but that's not where she wanted him tonight.

In one swift movement she was over him, straddling his hips with her calves. His dark eyes were wide, searching. He looked oddly vulnerable for a man she knew to be unbreakable. *He needs this as much I do*, she realized. She'd give him what he wanted.

She dragged the head of his cock between the waiting folds of her sex. She was more than ready for him, she was aching. She had turned to honey in his arms and it was that honey soaking him now. His answering groan was somewhere between shock and pleasure.

Meg knew he'd only come back for this. This was all she was to them, a sure thing. Cheap entertainment. It wounded her to her soul, but it wouldn't stop her now. She would take him for her own pleasure as much as he wanted her for his.

She sunk onto him slowly, his hard, bare flesh splitting her an inch at a time. It was easy, too easy. He fit like he belonged there, filling her to bursting as he glided home. She took him in until she felt his bollocks on her arse though it hurt to have him so deep.

He let out a long, shaking breath and took her hips in his hands. She rocked a little, adjusting to the sweet pain of being so thoroughly impaled. She sat straight as the rod inside her, though it was almost too much, because she knew the posture displayed her assets to full advantage. She might not get to keep him, but she owned him for now. She would give him something he could dream of, a silver-limned, insatiable goddess with a lush body and a quim hot and hungry as the gates of hell. Our Lady of Perpetual Arousal. Meg almost laughed. *Let him think of* this *when he's in bed with Rachel.*

"Margaret," he begged.

She walked her fingers up his beautiful body from the place where they joined, over the tight bands of muscle that crossed his hips, up the ridges of his flat belly, to the firm, broad plains of his chest, lowering her hands over his shoulders. Her breasts raked his skin and she smiled with wicked pleasure at the scratch of his hair against her nipples.

She kissed his jaw once she could reach it, kissed the broken bridge of his nose and the defiant tilt of his chin. She'd miss those when he was gone. His beard scratched her cheek as she took his earlobe between her teeth. She kissed the bruise forming high on his cheekbone from a blow he'd taken for her. No one had ever stood up for her in such a way, and though she hated he'd suffered, his pain was precious to her.

Anchoring herself on her hands, she began to slide back and forth, giving into the need to feel the friction between them once more. He groaned and rolled his head back into his pillow as he pushed her down his length, guiding the movement of her hips with his big, broken hands. He thought they were useless. Meg almost laughed. She let him set the pace, rolling her hips in deliriously slow waves, as deep and all-consuming as the sea. She kissed his throat, tasting the salt of his skin with the tip of her tongue. His moan reverberated against her lips and she bit him.

Impatient, he increased the pace. She followed his lead, changing her angle with her hands on his chest. She rocked against him, watching the pleasure on his face shift to agony and back again. He was tightening inside her, tense as a bowstring, and she was wetter than she'd ever been. She had wanted him for so long that now she finally had him, she was constantly dripping.

His mouth was open and he was breathing fast. She had never seen him half so bothered in a fight. He was hers now—his body, his pleasure, his pain—and she knew *in her bones* that no matter what he did tomorrow, he would never be able to forget the way she made him feel.

Giving into her own pleasure, she rode him straight to heaven and out the other side. She dug her nails into his chest and rocked backward, wanting more of him, all of him. He hit her in places she hadn't known existed and she couldn't get enough of it. She opened her eyes as she neared her peak to find him watching her face as she had watched his. She wanted to fall into the starless night of his eyes. She gave him a wicked smile before she took his lip in her teeth.

Lost, he pushed her hips downward and buried himself inside

her as deep as she could take him. She quaked at the first pulse of seed. He gave the hair that fell down her back a knowing tug, almost an afterthought, and she clenched around him harder with a moan. She needed it, wanted him inside her with a primordial thirst she didn't fully understand. Briefly losing control of her body, she came harder than she'd ever come in her life, falling to pieces and crashing into his arms.

He gathered her to him, holding her tight as he caught his breath. He smelled her hair and kissed the top of her head.

Meg could have stayed there forever, her face resting on his chest, listening to his heartbeat.

It didn't beat for her.

Sadness settled into her bones though her flesh still tingled from his touch. She climbed off of him and grabbed a rag to mop up the wreckage of her thighs. He sat up behind her and kissed her shoulder like a real lover might. It was too much. She knew what she was.

"Rachel wants you back," Meg heard herself say.

His voice was quiet. "I think so."

"She's beautiful," Meg allowed. "Wealthy." She dropped the rag to the floor.

Jake snorted and pulled her into his arms. "She's not Meg Henshawe."

Meg used to think more of herself, but she'd been knocked down enough times to realize being Meg Henshawe was not a good thing. It was to Rachel's credit she was someone else. Jake had to know that by now.

"When will you see her again?"

He shook his head. "She asked me for tea sometime in the week. I'm not going."

"You should. Her tea is likely better than anything we have around here." Even Meg thought she sounded bitter.

He ran his fingers down the length of her arm. "You want me to go?"

She shrugged. "Wealthy widows don't come around every day. It would hardly be a tragedy to take what's on offer. She's young, pretty. You've been in love with her for ten years…"

"Twelve," he corrected. "Ten was you and Mark."

She sat up, putting distance between them. "See?"

He was irritated now. "I don't want her. I want you." She heard him pull his breeches up.

"I'm nothing."

He pushed himself up to sit beside her and took her face in his hands. The sincerity in his eyes was enough to bring tears to hers. "You are everything to me."

She turned her face away. He thought he wanted her, but what could she give him? A family to feed and a drafty old inn they ought to burn for firewood? She wouldn't even have that much longer. He'd have a better chance at happiness with Rachel. A better chance of not starving to death when Davey kicked the lot of them out.

"It's for the best," she said firmly. Tommy already loved him. The longer Jake hung around, the worse he'd break his heart and hers. "You should go before we get attached."

"You're not?" he asked, betrayal in his voice.

She wouldn't lie to him. "I've learned my lesson, is all. There's no point standing between a good man and a virtuous woman. When Mark left--"

"I'm not bloody Mark," he snapped. "You're heart's still so full of him there's no room for me it. I'm here, Meg. I'm not leaving you."

"You should. Leave while you still have the chance, and never look back."

Clearly hurt, he grabbed his coat and left.

Chapter 27

Just like that, he was gone.

Meg tiptoed down the stairs of the too-quiet inn, feeling like the last woman on earth.

It was early yet, the inn was closed. They hadn't had any guests since the fight. Judith would be at the market with Bess getting the last of what they'd need for Christmas dinner, and Tommy had school.

The threadbare curtain they'd nailed over the shattered windows fluttered in the morning wind, a sad, limp flag for the losing side. Anyone could have climbed through if they'd thought to. Shredded to ribbons, but they could have robbed her blind.

She had nothing of value left to take.

The fire was out, the hearth sooty and cold. She'd grown so accustomed to the smell of coffee in the morning, she felt its absence in her bones. If she were clever, she'd put some on to boil before she balanced the ledgers.

Meg passed the entrance to the kitchen and headed for the gin.

She pulled the cork out and dropped it where she stood, swallowed enough to make her dumb if not blind. As she pushed her hair out of her face, her fingers caught in a knot. Past caring, she pulled the whole tangled mess of it over her shoulder.

She had to make the coffee. Do the books. Light the fire. Make supper. Feed herself. Take another step. Keep breathing. Tommy would need to eat when he came home, and the stew wouldn't cook itself.

The gin swung beside her skirt as she shuffled her way into the kitchen, numb. It was not only that things were less beautiful without him or whatever poetic nonsense the playwrights peddled, but the world seemed grayer to her somehow. Flat, cold. It was as lifeless and desolate as she felt herself, a reflection of perfect misery.

She'd been sad before, but not like this. When she'd left her children with the caretaker she'd wept for weeks, feeling their absence as acutely as though limbs had been severed from her body. Life was colder without them in it, and devoid of that joy she hadn't known before giving birth.

Losing Jake was another beast altogether. He wasn't a limb, but her very heart; he had taken all her hopes and dreams with him. She saw her future unfurl before her in a long, dark road she'd have to travel alone and forgotten, knowing in her soul she'd fucked it up.

He was hers. Almost hers, anyway. Wasn't he?

Perhaps Tom was right. He got what he wanted and off he went, just like everybody else.

Meg took another swig of gin, blood simmering.

"He's left you, has he?"

Meg turned to find Davey rummaging through the pantry for his breakfast.

She had hers in her hand. Her fingers tightened around the bottle.

"It's for the best," he said cheerfully, examining a wedge of cheese. "Coarse blighter, wasn't he? I don't pretend to understand you, cousin mine. Be easier for you to bag a protector without your Jew knocking about, at any rate."

Meg snorted. If she couldn't bag a protector at twenty-five, she wouldn't be able to bag one now. "I'm done with men," she said weakly. If she took another man to her bed, she might forget what Jake felt like there. His soap on her pillow would be replaced with civet and grime.

Davey laughed in apparent disbelief. "I certainly hope not. You haven't got anything else to fall back on, do you?"

Meg sipped the gin. "You may not have noticed since you've been upstairs drinking all of my good wine, but I happen to run this inn."

"Not for much longer, you don't." He smirked. "I've sold it."

Meg's eyebrows crashed together with the promise of a tension megrim. "What do you mean, sold it?"

He laughed as he helped himself to a hunk of stale bread. "Mr. Virtue said it was worthless, but I found a buyer readily enough. You know him. Gilbert the brewer."

"Gilbert." Fear twisted her guts. He wasn't likely to have forgiven her for head-butting him the other night. She may have also called him some choice names, none of them flattering.

Davey took the bread and cheese to the door, pausing at the threshold. "He's coming for the keys tomorrow. You need to be out by then."

"Out?" she repeated, her voice small. "Where will we go?" She was asking herself more than anyone. Try as she might, she'd never seen a future for herself without the inn in it.

"It's only you he wants gone. The others can stay." He took a bite of cheese. "For now, at least."

She didn't scream. She didn't cry.

Davey strolled out the front door without a care in the world. He wasn't bothered by the fact she'd be homeless tomorrow.

She was alone. Finally, truly alone. She always knew she would be someday.

Her heart slammed into her ribs and she gasped. In her shock, she'd stopped breathing altogether. Her arms tingled and her fingers went numb as the blood left them, surging to her head.

Was this what it felt like to faint? She'd never been much of a fainter, but there was a first time for everything.

Face burning, she surveyed the kitchen.

It was clean, cold. There were few traces of the years she'd worked in it. Twenty-five, thirty years? Her earliest memory was of washing dishes in a basin on the floor. Thousands of days, each indistinguishable from the last with a few notable exceptions.

The pot hook was bent from Christmas of '67, when they couldn't afford meat and they'd tried to make enough pottage to feed the street in a single enormous pot. It had fallen into the fire and Meg had scalded her hands trying to pull it out before the whole mess of it burned. The inn stunk for weeks and she'd escaped the smell by sneaking off to Bear Gardens.

That was the first time she saw Jake fight. He was younger then, skinnier, but even more frightening. He was rage incarnate, a desperate outcast with nothing left to lose. When the crowd had recoiled, she leaned forward. *Here*, at last, was someone as angry as she was.

Proof of her anger littered the kitchen, evidence of abuse everywhere she looked. The table still had claw marks on the underside, an uneven set of half-moons she'd put there in '58 when her father had sold her maidenhead. Beside it, another set from another sale.

The bite marks not an arm's length away were hers as well. She'd tried to break things off with Tom and he'd broken her nose. He'd ravished her over the table, pushing her mouth into the wood to stifle her screams. She had scrubbed it for days, but she never could get all the blood out.

She'd lost her youth, her honor, and no little blood in this goddamn kitchen. She'd sold her body for this inn, wasted every chance she'd had at life just to keep it open. When the other girls were in school, she'd been working. When they were chasing boys, she'd been loaned to men. When they married, she'd been abandoned time and time again. When they'd cared for their own children, she'd had to give hers up and return to work.

Every morning. Every night. Every day until she died.

Or so she'd thought.

Her vision darkened around the edges and she recognized the feeling at last.

She wasn't going to faint. She was angry, angrier than she'd been in her life. It robbed her of rational thought and changed the texture of time itself. All that was left was energy surging through her veins. She surrendered to it.

The shelves leapt as she struck them with the bottle, glasses, dishes, and pots raining down around her. They shattered, sputtered, and dented as they struck the stone floor, the noise so loud they could probably hear it at Mark's house down the road. He'd put up the damned shelves and it was a testament to his work that they withstood her blows. When the bottle broke and drenched her with gin, she only paused long enough to grab the largest pot off of the floor. She hefted it over her head and threw it as hard as she could at the wall. All the shelves but the highest splintered and fell. Satisfying, but it wasn't enough.

She wouldn't go without taking the kitchen with her.

The long tables came away from the walls easily and didn't break when she kicked them, so she broke the legs with a chair and piled the pieces in the hearth. She heaved the basins out the back door into the garden, where they smashed with a particularly satisfying sound.

The table--that goddamn table where she'd been used shamefully so many times--would have to go. It was much larger than she was, but she was determined. She jerked it upward by two of the legs. It felt hot in her hands, as though it was alive with all the memories embedded within it. Tom was in there with the butcher and dozens of others. Her father weighing her breasts with his hands like bags of grain for market, watching her first encounters to see that she pleased his friends.

She hurled the table through the window with a bellow

tortured enough to wake the dead. It barreled through into the garden, its legs catching on the windowsill. Her father's stool she dragged outside and lobbed into the open sewer beyond. It sank readily into the muck, a single fat bubble rising in its place.

As she waded through the wreckage on the kitchen floor, the good memories came back to her, too. Baking her first good pie with Bess, kissing Mark when she was sixteen. She'd taught Tommy to count in here with beans for the pot. Jake putting out the fire, holding her on the floor. Pretending not to look as she took off her stockings.

Years of abuse, fleeting joy, and inevitable abandonment.

The hammering of her heart slowed to a horrible twinge. It felt like a wet rag being wrung out.

She was going to weep.

She would not weep.

The kitchen had taken so much from her, she wouldn't give it her tears as well.

Calm as anything, Meg retrieved the good brandy from the bar. She took a deep swig of it, then emptied the rest on the broken furniture on the floor. There was too much of it between her and the hearth for her to start the fire there, so she lit a candle instead and touched the flame to a broken chair. It spread quickly and burned bright, the kitchen filling with smoke. It stopped as it reached the inside of the hearth. She hadn't replaced the rushes yet, so there was nothing to cause it to spread to the other rooms.

She didn't think so, at least.

Of course if she was wrong, she would not only destroy everything her family owned, but all of the houses on the street and likely most of Southwark. The cramped wooden tenements were so close together, they'd catch like kindling.

The city was still recovering from the Great Fire a dozen years later. She wouldn't cause another one.

A great heap of burning furniture stood between her and the well outside. At a loss, she hauled the last barrels of Gilbert's foul beer into the kitchen and tossed them onto the pile. It succeeded in putting out the fire, but filled the room with a stench akin to rotten bread.

Meg's eyes stung so badly from the smoke she could barely see the charred remains of the kitchen. She coughed so violently her stomach wretched. Fighting the urge to vomit, she ran into the street and took great, choking gasps of fresh, cold air.

Grief, anger, fear, and relief fought over what was left of her. Overwhelmed, she fell to her knees and screamed.

Her scream was a terrible, hoarse-sounding bark, and it set her off coughing once more. The streets were all but empty. If anyone heard her, they paid her no mind. A pair of crows eyed her with interest from the roof across the street.

In the distance, a high-pitched scream answered her own.

She listened.

Seconds later, another.

Blood-curdling and agonized, it was the kind of scream one could never forget. She'd be hearing it in her nightmares for years. It sounded like someone was being murdered. A woman.

She stood on shaking legs, moving toward the sound with uncertainty. What was she walking into?

A third scream, louder and more pained than the last. There was a hint of a voice on the end, a sob.

By the time she heard the fourth, she was running. That woman's attacker would wish he'd never been born by the time Meg was through with him. She didn't care who it was, she was angry enough to tear a man's head off with her teeth.

She ran so fast she almost missed the little girl standing in the street wearing Mark's hat.

The child threw her hands up and rushed toward her. "Meg! Meg!"

Meg stopped so fast she slid through the slush. "Lily? What's happened?"

Another scream, closer this time.

Lily's face was white, her eyes wide in terror. "It's Mum! There's something wrong with the baby! Come quick!"

Chapter 28

Jake started the long walk to Spitalfields early in the morning.

He'd barely slept, thinking of Meg through that crack in the wall. She'd told him to leave. He'd told her how he felt and she'd told him to leave. He was angry, he was miserable, and he couldn't pretend to understand her. Though it felt like she'd ripped his heart out and stomped on it, he kept listening through the wall, wondering if she was all right.

That couldn't be *it* for them, could it?

He'd thought they were all but married and he'd been happy about it. In spite of everything it would seem he'd only been an amusement after all.

He couldn't believe that, he wouldn't. She'd shown him such kindness, such passion. She'd gone to Spitalfields to get his bread.

As Ruta's bakery came into view, he found himself stepping inside out of habit. It was early yet, and it couldn't hurt to have a cup of coffee before arriving at Rachel's. She might not even be in at this hour. Either way, his leg was aching and he desperately wanted to sit down.

Ruta's face lit up as she saw him. "Jakob! Back so soon?" she greeted him in Yiddish.

He smiled in spite of his terrible mood. Ruta was the closest thing he had to family, and she always made him feel welcome. "I was nearby and thought I'd stop in for a cup of coffee."

"Yes, yes, of course! Sit down, sweetheart. Did you bring your pretty Englishwoman?"

Jake's heart sank. "Not today, sadly."

"I've just made a fresh batch of rugelach. I'll give you some to take back to her."

"Thanks, Ruta." He smiled sadly as she disappeared into the kitchen.

Ester watched him from the counter with a knowing smile. "Come to your senses, have you?"

He frowned. "What do you mean?"

"I saw you walking with Rachel last night. She's been alone for years. It's about time you two got back together. She's missed you."

Years? He'd been under the impression Aaron had passed recently. "I haven't been hiding. She could have found me any time."

"I don't think she realized it was urgent." Ester laughed to herself as she put out the fresh bread for the morning.

"What are you on about?"

Ester grinned, every inch the cheeky little sister. "Don't play dumb. We saw your new friend last week. That woman? The one with the hair and the--" she mimed enormous breasts. "What must you be thinking?"

Jake set his jaw, irritated beyond measure. "I was thinking I'd finally met a good, honest woman and I was fortunate to have her. You mean to tell me Rachel only came looking for me after she saw Meg?"

Ester shrugged. "What of it?"

"What is she playing at?"

"Trying to keep you from making a horrible mistake, I imagine." She rolled her eyes.

Ruta emerged from the kitchen with a tray of coffee, bread, and smoked fish. "You sound so dramatic out here. What is this horrible mistake?"

He accepted the breakfast gratefully and Ruta sat across from him with a cup of coffee.

Ester's eyes widened. "That woman!"

Ruta waved a hand. "Have you married her yet?"

Ester groaned. "He can't marry her, can he?"

Ruta sipped her coffee, not particularly bothered by this statement. "I don't know how the English do these things. There must some way. Or don't and skip to the good part." She giggled.

"Matka!"

"He's thirty-eight years old, Ester! How much time do you think he has?"

Jake ran a hand over his face. He didn't quite feel at death's door yet. "Thanks, Ruta."

"It doesn't bother you she's a *shiksa*? Either of you?"

Jake frowned. "Hey!"

"Ester, mind your language." Ruta's sigh was a touch exasperated. "Meg seems nice enough. How many unmarried Jewish girls do you think he has to choose from here? Are *you* offering to marry him?"

"You know I'm not." Ester folded her arms across her chest. "What's wrong with Rachel?"

"Nothing is wrong with Rachel," Jake answered. Nothing had ever been wrong with Rachel, exactly, but lack of obvious fault wasn't enough of a reason to marry someone.

Ester nodded, satisfied with his answer. "Remember that. Perhaps it's time you came back."

Ruta pinched the bridge of her nose like she was coming down with a headache. When she looked up, she wore her usual good-natured smile. "Ester, go check on the bread. I can hear it burning."

She cringed. "Matka, you cannot *hear bread burning*."

"I can," she insisted. "It's burning right now. Go save it or we'll have to begin again."

Ester dragged herself into the kitchen with a long-suffering sigh.

Jake looked into his coffee, his heartache returning to him in the silence. "When did Aaron pass?"

"Five years ago. Six, perhaps."

"Did Rachel ever ask about me?" He'd never asked her before, but he needed to know. Too much was at stake for him not to.

Ruta sighed. "If she did, she didn't ask me." Her usually cheerful face held a look of distaste. Subtle, but it was there.

"You don't like her," he observed.

She was taken aback. "I like your Englishwoman just fine!"

Jake laughed. "No, Rachel."

"No, I don't like Rachel." She grimaced. "Ester means well, but she didn't see you after you lost your parents and Rachel left you. I did. You are a son to me, Jakob, and my heart broke for you to see you like that. When you came in here with your Meg, you looked so much better. You were happy again. I want that for you, sweetheart. A man should not be alone." She closed her cool, wrinkled hand over his, the palm worn smooth from decades of hard work.

If only it was a matter of choice at this point. Meg had told him to leave in no uncertain terms. "I don't think she wants me, Ruta. She told me to go back to Rachel."

Ruta snorted in disbelief. "A *mensch* like you? Nonsense. She is devoted to you. Sometimes people do stupid things for the ones they love."

♥

When Lily couldn't keep up with her, Meg tossed the child over her shoulder and ran with her to Mark's house. Lily went with it, apparently accustomed to being carried like a sack of washing. "My house is on the corner!" she shouted.

Meg knew very well where it was. She burst through the front door as another chilling scream rent the air.

Inside, Jane gripped the table in front of the hearth as her daughters--there seemed to be a hundred of them--surrounded her, helpless. Her face was pallid and covered in a sheen of sweat. She looked up as she heard Meg, the hope in her eyes giving way to dread. "Oh, Lord! Not you!"

"Where's Mark?"

"Nick's place. Baby's early." With her jaw clenched and forehead creased in pain, Mark's wife at last looked less than perfect. Rather than satisfying, it was more disturbing than Meg could say. She needed help, but if she died, Meg would be blamed for it and possibly hanged.

Nevertheless, there was no real choice to make.

She turned to Lily. "Lily, I need you to go get Tommy from school, do you hear me? Make him take you to your uncle's house to get help. Tell him I said it's important."

Lily nodded sharply and took off running.

"She's six years old!" Jane protested.

"She'll be fine," Meg dismissed. "Tommy knows what he's doing. Let me get a good look at you."

Jane hesitated, looking at Meg as though she expected her to bite her. She sniffed. "Is that...gin?"

"I spilled it on my skirt," Meg explained it away as she brushed past Jane to the well she knew Mark had outside. She tossed the bucket over the side and heard it break through ice when it hit the bottom.

Jane followed her, one slow step at a time. "You're in your cups."

"I am." Meg hauled the bucket up and took it inside. "But I'm all you've got at the moment, so we'll have to make do. Where's your lye?"

"There--" Jane gestured toward an empty basin in the kitchen before she doubled over in pain. "Christ alive!"

"Sit down," Meg ordered her, scrubbing her hands with the harsh soap in the icy water. Hands dripping, she asked the oldest child, "Clean linen?"

The girl was insensible, a perfect miniature of her mother cowering beside the oven. "Is Mum going to die?"

There was a decent chance of death with any birth, but Meg wouldn't tell her that. She didn't want to lie to her, either. "Linen, child. Where is it?"

"Go find it for Meg, please," Jane asked her patiently though she looked unsure of her chances herself.

The girl scurried away like a rat and had it back in moments. She handed it to Meg, looking up at her with Mark's blue eyes, her face streaked with tears. Meg took it, softening her tone at the despair on the girl's face. "Thank you. Would you be a dear and run to The Rose for some brandy, please?"

Mary nodded. With a last, sorrowful look at her mother, she ran out the door, auburn hair streaming behind her like ribbons.

Jane screamed again, a hand on her distended belly.

"Why aren't you sitting?" Meg snapped.

"I can't!" Jane sobbed. "It's already...it's halfway here!"

Meg dropped to her knees in front of Jane, her hands on her belly. She pressed firmly, feeling for the baby's feet. Jane groaned in pain. Before she could protest, Meg threw up her skirt. "Squat down," she ordered.

Jane looked sick. If there was any blood in her face at all, Meg had no doubt she'd blush. Embarrassed or not, she followed Meg's command. As her legs parted further, Meg could see she was right. If the baby had been the right way around, it would have already been out, but it wasn't the baby's head she was seeing.

"It's too late to turn it." Meg told her. "We're going to have to help it to come out."

"What does that mean?"

"It's fine," Meg assured her with false bravado. "But I'm going to have to get closer to you than you ever wanted me to be.

Keep crouching."

"You--You've done this before?"

"Yeah," she lied. She'd seen it, at least. "Same thing happened to my mum. Leave it to Alice to come out arse-backwards." Meg stared at the baby, searching her memory for what the midwife had said. Its arse was out, but it was on its back and didn't seem to be moving. Either that was very good or very bad.

Jane groaned in agony, her legs shaking.

"Very bad," Meg muttered to herself.

"What was that?" Jane squeaked.

"Nothing," Meg replied. "I'm going to move it. I need you to try to relax."

"Relax?!" Jane spat. "You hate me! How do I know you won't kill me?"

"What are you like? I'm here to help you!" Meg took the baby's arse in her hands.

Jane flinched. "You want my husband!"

"I most certainly do not," she scoffed. "Mark's a git and you're welcome to him. Now relax." Very gently, Meg turned the baby so it was facing down.

Jane shuddered. "That did something. I think it's moving."

Meg let out a genuine sigh of relief. "Good. We're not done yet." The baby was stuck like a cork. She could hardly yank it out, but perhaps she could help it move. Without thinking about it too hard, she dipped two fingers inside to grasp the baby's shin. She knew how fragile infants were when they were that small, and she'd never forgive herself if she hurt it out of carelessness. Thinking of Tommy at that age, she hooked a finger of her other hand behind the knee to support the thigh and very slowly eased the first leg out.

Jane relaxed. "What happened?"

"The first leg's out." Feeling braver, she repeated the maneuver on the other side. "You were right. It's a boy."

Jane punched the air. "I knew it!"

Meg laughed. "We've still got a ways to go. Can you push?"

Jane pushed until her face turned violet, but the baby didn't move. He still seemed to be too wide to come out. Meg turned him to the side to help him out and he came a little further, his elbow appearing. She braced the tiny arm in much the same way she had with his legs and it fell out fairly easily. "We have an arm."

Jane grinned, her color returning little by little. "Yes!"

Meg tried to pull out the second arm, but it was pinned beneath his body. She bit her lip with determination as she turned the baby once more, and was more than gratified when the arm all but popped out. "Second arm."

She could feel its head, maddeningly close to being born. The cord was beside it rather than around it, so that was a blessing. "Push," she ordered as the turned the baby onto its back.

"What are you doing down there?" Jane demanded. "He's not a bloody wheel."

"We've gotten this far, haven't we? Now push!"

She did. Meg didn't want to pull him, but he was so close she almost felt like she could breathe again. As Jane took a deep breath and pushed again, Meg braced his back with her hand and tilted his arse upwards. As if by magic, the baby was out. "Got him."

"Got him?" Jane asked her voice high-pitched enough to break glass. Meg held him up so she could see her son, wriggling and covered in blood and viscera. Jane cried out in relief, tears falling on Meg's hair like rain.

The afterbirth followed without any trouble, and by the time Mary appeared in the doorway with a bottle of spirits, Jane was holding the baby quite happily in a chair in front of the fire. Chris limped along behind her, fear on his face. Mary all but shoved the brandy at Meg in her haste to get to her mother.

Jane caught her with her free arm and kissed her head. "We didn't need the brandy," she said brightly.

"The brandy was for me." Meg yanked the cork out with her teeth and drank.

Chapter 29

Ruta's words stuck with him the rest of the way to Rachel's.

Rachel lived a few streets west of Spitalfields in a house as large as The Rose and so new he could almost smell the wet plaster. She led him into a bright parlor with an unexceptional view of the common ground across the street. A week before, he had met Meg on this street when she had come to see her daughter. The house was certainly big enough to require servants. Rachel had clearly done well for herself.

He paused in the doorway, taking in the elaborate moldings and the few pieces of sumptuous furniture. The cool mint green of the walls only seemed to emphasize the draughty chill of the room. It was so different from what he was used to these days he felt as though he was trespassing.

Rachel perched on the edge of a chair with the practiced grace of a noblewoman. She motioned for him to join her.

He hesitated before he took the upholstered chair opposite her. For all that it had been designed for comfort, the craftsman had not built it for a man with Jake's frame. The chair gave a nauseating creak as he shifted his weight in the seat, and for a moment he held his breath, fully expecting it to break.

Rachel watched him with a sorrowful gaze, her bottom lip trembling as she appeared to bite back words. It was difficult not to stare as, again, he tried to reconcile the woman she had become with the memory he had of her. Though some things had not changed, there were enough differences that she seemed to be only vaguely familiar, a woman who bore a passing resemblance to a girl he used to know.

She had grown into herself in the years they had been apart. Her dress was immaculate, tasteful, and modest. He braced his hands on his knees, feeling more than a little out of place in his scruffy workman's trousers.

Her delicate sniff seemed to echo through the room. She wiped away a tear.

Years before, he would have taken her in his arms at the first sign of distress. The connection between them had long since been severed, and all he felt at her display of emotion was discomfort. "What is it?"

The tears evaporated as soon as they had been spotted. Her stiff posture did not quake. "Your face...I'm sorry, I can't get over how different you look. Your nose…it's worse today. Will it heal, do you think?"

He raised a hand to touch his nose and heard Meg's voice in his ear. *You're gorgeous.*

"It won't be different when it does. This is how it looks now."

"When I saw you fight that man yesterday, I couldn't believe it was you." She looked away as though the sight of him was too much to bear. "Such savagery...I didn't know you had it in you."

There were a lot of things she didn't know about him. "I'm not fighting anymore. I'm an innkeeper these days."

"An innkeeper." She gave a bitter laugh before she met his gaze. "Of all the places I thought you might be, I didn't expect to find you there."

The obvious disapproval in her eyes told him she hadn't expected to find him in the arms of another woman, either. "I've not been hiding. I've fought most weeks for the past twelve years.

You could have come to any of them."

She shook her head in obvious distaste. "You know I couldn't. It wouldn't have been right."

A married woman venturing into some of the most dangerous places around the city to see an old suitor would certainly raise some eyebrows, and Rachel had always treasured her sterling reputation. "You might have written. Or left word with Ruta. I've come up here hundreds of times and I didn't even know you were still in town."

She looked at her hands in her lap. "I was married."

"We could have been friends, if you had been bothered. Aaron was once a friend of mine. Was he looking for me, too?"

She didn't answer, but she was holding back something. He had been spoiled in his weeks with Meg. If there was something she wanted to say, she said it, no matter how ill-advised that might be. He loved her candor, whether she was telling him she wanted him or threatening to pull some punter's bollocks out of his eye sockets. His cheek twitched at the memory and he bit back the smile.

Rachel saw it. "It's good to see you."

He blinked, unsure how to respond. She had left him to die, then hadn't spoken to him in a dozen years though she could have found him at any time. She had been a widow almost half that time, but had waited until he was happy with a good woman to come looking for him. "I'm glad you're well," he allowed.

Satisfied with his answer, she gave a tight smile and rang a little bell on the table at her side. "Tea?"

Jake nodded. He hadn't had tea once in the years since his parents had died, and their modest fortune with them. He drank coffee these days, powdered and boiled, with the rest of London's dissenters and undesirables.

Within minutes, a young maid entered the room and set up the tea service on the table between them. Obviously English, she had pale freckles and her hair was swept up and pinned into a linen cap. From what he could see of it framing her face, it was the exact color of spun gold. There was no mistaking whose daughter she was. "Sarah?"

She jumped at the sound of her name, rattling the tea cup as she set it down. She curtsied, clearly uneasy. "Sir," she greeted briefly then continued her task, pouring two cups of tea from the steaming pot.

He accepted the cup from her with a warm smile. She looked so like her mother. He had never had children, but he felt an instinctive need to protect her. If things had gone the way he wanted them to with Meg, he could have been her father by now.

She curtsied again and left the room, silent as a shadow.

Rachel eyed him with speculation. "You know my maid?"

Jake shook his head. "I know her mother."

"Yes, I am given to understand many people do," she said softly, a hint of venom in her voice. She sipped her tea.

Jake's blood pounded at the slight. He took a deep breath and tried to think of something that would calm his anger. His lack of sleep was not helping his nerves, though the memories of their nights together were sweet and still fresh in his mind. Meg's laugh, her kiss, his name on her lips. Meg's arms around him as they surrendered to sleep at last.

Meg telling him to leave.

"She was the woman from yesterday? The one you were…"

Jake didn't blink. "Defending? Kissing? Carrying?"

She blanched.

"I should go."

"Wait." Rachel set down her tea and reached out to him, ready to physically keep him from leaving. When he did not immediately move, she placed her hands demurely in her lap. "I would like to speak to you about something."

He finished his tea, dreading her next comment. "Yes?"

She examined a loose thread on the edge of her chair. "I'm a widow now, and very wealthy. It has been years since Aaron died, and I am free again."

"No," he answered before she got around to asking.

"My sons need a father. I can set you up with a shop of your own. A man your age ought to be married..."

He shook his head. "No."

She pulled a chain from inside her high neckline and he was startled to see a rather familiar looking ring on the end of it. She took it off and handed it to him.

A flood of memories overwhelmed him as the gold touched his fingertips. Late nights spent working on it after hours, months and months honing something beautiful out of scrap fragments and gold dust he'd melted down and recast, again and again until he had enough.

The heavy, ceremonial betrothal ring was never meant to be worn. They would have had simpler rings for daily use if they had married, but this one he had made as an exercise of skill and devotion. Rachel's Sephardic parents had always looked down on him, but he'd wanted *so badly* to prove he was worthy of her.

The band was thick and covered all over in his own seven-strand braid, embellished with enamel and crowned with a tiny red-roofed house that opened like a locket. He popped it open to see the inscription inside: *mazel tov.*

"Why now?" He pressed the roof closed with the pad of his thumb. The enamel used to feel smooth and cold, but now he couldn't feel it at all. "You've been a widow five years and you can't look at me without cringing."

"I think you know I've always loved you."

Jake ran his thumb over the braid. He could never make something so delicate again, but he'd woven that same pattern into Meg's hair and he liked it better there. For all that he had regretted he could never return to his craft, he preferred the silk of Meg's hair between his fingers.

He couldn't go back, but he didn't want to anymore.

"Did you love me when you left me under that bridge to die?"

he asked coolly. "I lost everything, and you walked away."

"What choice did I have? It wasn't my decision to make."

"You could have stayed. You could have taken me with you. You didn't have to marry me, but you didn't have to leave me there, either."

She dabbed at her eyes with a spotless handkerchief she seemed to pull from thin air. "I was a good girl."

Yes, she was. She had always done precisely what was expected of her.

Perhaps a good girl was not what he needed.

He let out a long sigh. "I forgive you."

"I don't need your forgiveness. I didn't do anything wrong," she insisted. "I want you back. I'm willing to overlook the boxing, your past...*indiscretions*..."

"And my face?" he supplied bitterly.

She winced. "Looks aren't everything."

He stood, straightening his coat. "I think I've stayed long enough."

Rachel stood. "Please don't go. I didn't meant to offend. We were good together once. Think about it, we can have the future we wanted now."

Jake frowned, trying to remember the dreams he'd had as a young man. There was a time he had wanted nothing more than Rachel and a place at his father's shop. He'd wanted a big family, people to love. He still wanted that feeling of belonging, but the family he'd envisioned looked different now. Instead of Rachel's relatives around a dinner table, he saw Meg, her sisters, Tommy, Chris, and Joe Ledford with a bottle of gin. "Things change," he said softly. "Isn't that what you said once? You were right. It's for the best."

"How?" she demanded, her eyebrows drawing together. "I'm offering you a life of comfort, purpose. You'd rather be landlord of a *hovel*?"

"I'm with someone." Whether or not Meg cared for him, he

loved her, and that would have to be enough.

She stared, disbelieving. "That woman?"

He nodded. "Her name is Meg."

Rachel leapt to her feet. "You can't be serious, Jakob. She's a *kedeshah*. She's using you. Don't be taken in by her flattery and declarations of love. They lie."

Declarations of love? "What do you mean?"

"Must I explain it to you? They'll say anything to get your money or your protection. They'll tell you you're handsome. They'll do anything to win you over. Just last week she told Ruta she loved you. I don't know what good she thought that would do, Ruta doesn't speak a word of English…"

Jake held up a hand. "She told Ruta she loved me?"

Rachel sighed. "What difference does it make? She's nothing. She's beneath you."

"It makes all the difference." He frowned. Had Meg rejected him in an attempt to push him into a more comfortable life? That would certainly explain her sudden change of heart. They had been inseparable until Rachel arrived. "Do you want me, Rachel? Or is it only that you don't want Meg to have me?"

Rachel's cheeks flamed scarlet. "Jakob, don't be a fool."

He wouldn't be. Rachel said she loved him in spite of the man he had become, while Meg seemed to love him for it. Perhaps he was broken in more ways than those Rachel had pointed out, but every blow and every scar, physical and otherwise, had shaped him into the man he was today. Ugly, maybe. Respectable? Certainly not. Still, he was strong, he was capable of great love, and he was clever enough not to let a good woman get away when he found one.

"I should get back. The inn needs me." Chris would be in the next day, and the girls would need help getting things ready for Christmas. He hated to think of what would happen if Tom returned while he was gone. "Do you want your ring back?"

She crossed her arms. "Keep it. What good will it do me

now?"

He nodded cheerfully. "It was good seeing you, Rachel."

He took his leave and as he stepped into the hall, he almost knocked over Sarah.

She stood, flustered and red-cheeked with embarrassment. She had clearly been listening. "I beg your pardon, sir."

"Sarah, wait."

She looked up at him, her bottle green eyes bashful.

How did one introduce himself to his lover's child? He cleared his throat. "We're having a Christmas party at the inn tomorrow night. Your mother would love for you to come, if you can get away."

She eyed him shrewdly, and he thought he caught a hint of her mother's spark in her gaze. "Did you mean what you said? You care for my mum?"

Jake nodded. "I'm going to marry her."

Sarah's smile was small, but genuine. "Good. I'll come if I can get away."

"Do you need me to walk you there?" he offered, thinking of all the brigands she was likely to meet along the way.

"I'll be fine," she assured him. "Thank you, sir."

"Jake," he offered.

"Jake," she repeated with uncertainty. With one last curious smile, she darted back toward the kitchens.

He watched her go, something like hope flooding his chest. Meg would be thrilled to see her. He showed himself out of the front door and headed back toward Southwark with a spring in his step, thinking of other ways to make Meg smile.

Chapter 30

Jake slunk across the bridge, his hand clenched around the coins in his pocket to keep them from rattling. After a long morning of negotiating, he'd gotten fifteen guineas for the ring. With the three he'd gotten from Larry, he had eighteen altogether.

It was more money than he'd had in his life. It was enough to buy a small house, or rent one and keep a family modestly for a good few years. It was enough to get him back to Amsterdam, or any other place he fancied going, but he was limping back to Southwark once again.

If Meg really wanted him gone, he'd go, but not until he knew she and Tommy had somewhere to live. If what Rachel had said was true and Meg loved him after all, perhaps he'd get to live there with them.

Jake sighed, relieved as if a crushing weight had been lifted from his shoulders. Rachel was well and truly behind him. For all the work he'd put into the ring, it hadn't been difficult to part with it. Now if Meg said yes when he asked her, she could pick out any ring she wanted and he'd still have enough left to keep a roof over their heads. He smiled to himself, feeling better than he had in years.

Nothing could have prepared him for the chaos he met when he returned to The Rose. The smell of smoke filled the street and he could hear Davey screaming inside. Judith stood outside, rocking the crying baby while Bess spoke to a lean young man in riding boots and a highwayman's coat. She waved when she saw Jake.

"What's happened?" he asked her.

Bess shook her head. "Meg, I assume. It looks like she demolished the kitchen and set it on fire. Davey's losing his mind."

His heart hammered. "Where's Meg? Is she all right?"

"She's gone." Bess shrugged. "Tommy, too. Even Chris has run off with one of Mark's daughters and a bottle of brandy. Didn't think he had it in him." She laughed.

He cursed under his breath. "We've got to find them. Were there any guests?"

"Last one left yesterday."

"Is the fire out? How bad was it?"

"Not bad, as far as I can make out. Judith and Pea are going to stay with me and Sue until we know it's safe to go back in."

"Good thinking." At last he noticed the boy on Bess' arm wasn't a boy at all, but a rather handsome young woman with close-cropped hair. "Sue, I presume? I'm Jake, pleased to meet you."

She shook his hand. "Pleasure."

"First things first. You lot get to safety, try to find Meg and Tommy if you can. Chris is far too well-behaved to get up to mischief. Follow the brandy, and I bet you'll find Meg. I'll handle Davey."

"Oh, thank God," Judith muttered.

Bess grinned. "You going to handle Davey like you handled Tom?"

"No," Jake dismissed, then reconsidered. "Hopefully not."

Jake left the girls in the street and stepped into the inn, eyeing the beams. He'd been into enough buildings damaged by fire to know that collapse was every bit as dangerous as open flame. Inside, the smell was overwhelming. Charred wood and burned beer mingled to create a ripe grainy smell that made him think of rancid latkes. Davey stood behind the bar, looting the liquor and the few cups left.

"What happened?" Jake asked him in hopes he knew something the girls had missed.

"You!" He pointed an accusatory finger at him. "You could have stopped this! She listens to you! Now she's gone and taken my inheritance with her!"

Jake frowned. "How do you mean?"

"The inn!" Davey shouted, his eyes wild. "This ruin is barely standing, and now the kitchen is gone. Gone! Gilbert's backed out and I'll never find another buyer. I could kill that woman!"

Jake ignored him and slipped past him into the kitchen. Far from horrified, he was impressed. He'd known she was strong, but she'd thrown a solid oak table through a window.

Worry replaced his wonder. What kind of state had she been in to be able to do that?

He returned to Davey, heart heavy with dread. "What did you say to her?"

"Me?" He scoffed. "She was down here drinking because *you* left her."

They hadn't spoken since the night before. She'd been calm enough then to sleep. She wouldn't have woken up and gone on a rampage without provocation. He shook his head. "This wasn't me. What *happened*?"

"I told her to leave," Davey spat. "Gilbert wanted her gone so I told her to go. He was willing to keep the others. She should have been grateful."

Jake took a long breath. She had been thrown out of the only home and job she'd ever known, separated from her family, and seemingly abandoned by her lover. He could feel her pain so clearly, it was as if it was his own. Panic seized him. Was she all right? The sooner Davey was gone, the better.

"Ten guineas."

Davey sputtered, his eyes wild. "I beg your pardon?"

"Ten guineas," Jake repeated. "You'll get back what you paid for it. You know it's more than this place is worth."

"You were in this together!" he accused. "You and that *harpy*!"

Jake seized him by his collar, half-choking the man over the bar. "Take the money and go." He dropped him.

Davey tugged at his collar, real fear in his eyes. "I get the girls."

"*I* get the girls and their children."

"They're worth another ten, at least."

"They are people and they are not for sale," he said very slowly as he knew the man to be stupid. "You will entrust their wardship to me, or I will get it anyway when I marry Meg."

He snorted. "You wouldn't get it unless I was dead."

Jake stared at him.

Davey was gone in under ten minutes, leaving Jake ten guineas poorer and with an extra set of keys.

Chapter 31

Meg relaxed into the chair, bone-tired and covered in God-only-knows. As awful as she felt, Jane must have had it worse. She glanced over at her. Although she had narrowly survived a traumatic birth, Jane was once again ethereally beautiful, surrounded by a half-dozen perfect children as she fed her new baby with an angelic smile on her face. Meg laughed to herself and took a drink.

"You'll finally have another boy to play with, Hugo," Jane said to the little boy sitting at her feet. Harry Townsend's son. Meg regarded him with something like pain. He looked a bit like Harry, but his hair was dark where Harry's had been fair. Harry had been transported to the colonies years before. She wondered if he was still alive. Did he know he had a son?

"Have you had any word from Harry?" Meg asked her.

"Not yet." Jane looked up at her and shook her head sadly. "Have you heard from Alice?"

Meg rolled her eyes. "She's in The Hague with your apprentice. I'm told they have a boy of their own now."

Jane grinned. "Achilles. They named him after a friend they met in Versailles. A marquis."

Meg waved a hand. "No stranger than Judith naming hers Peasblossom." She laughed. "Does Jack know the one you named after him is a girl?"

Jane blushed slightly. She really was back to being herself. "We haven't told him. He assumed the twins were boys, of course."

"Only Mark would call his daughters Jack and Harry." Meg shook her head. "What do you reckon you'll call this one?"

"Henry, I suppose. For Mark's father."

Meg nodded. "That's a lot of Harrys running around."

Jane shrugged. "At least our Harry's a Harriette. Harry and Henry?" She wrinkled her nose. "Perhaps that will get confusing. What names do you like?"

"I haven't given it much thought." She felt a twinge of jealousy as her gaze settled on the infant at Jane's breast. She would have had a dozen of her own if she could. "I have a Michael and a Tommy. I don't like Jeffreys, Lukes, Davids, Charlies, or Peters."

"You like Jakes," Jane suggested.

Meg nodded. "Yes, I do." The one at least. Much good it had done her. She'd wanted more than anything to hold onto him, but she couldn't even do that.

"He's kind," Jane said quietly. "Handsome, too."

"Hands off," she kidded pleasantly, though she was deadly serious. "We always did have the same taste in men."

Jane sighed. "I do so love a good nose. Breaks add character, don't you think?"

Meg laughed under her breath. "Just as well. Mark gets hit in the face a lot."

"Meg," Jane started, searching for words. "I'm sorry for everything that happened between us. I was so in love, it didn't occur to me that you were, too."

She squirmed in her seat, unsure how to respond to an apology from the woman who'd been her rival for years. "I'm…sorry. I behaved badly. It wasn't easy, seeing him leave. But I'm glad he did. He's better with you."

Jane's smile was a ray of pure sunlight. "I hope you can be happy, too."

Meg took a swig of the brandy. "I wouldn't hold your breath."

"I can't thank you enough for helping me today." Her voice was so calm, so damnably earnest. She was everything Meg had never gotten to be.

She didn't blame Mark for choosing Jane. More than that, it didn't hurt anymore.

"Think nothing of it. You're all right. Besides, Mark needs you to look after his sorry arse, don't he? Lord knows I don't need him hanging around my inn at all hours." Her voice cracked. Not hers any longer. She was in no hurry to leave Jane's in part because she had nowhere else to go.

"You're all right, too." Jane smiled. "Can we be friends?"

"I've been up to my elbows in you, I don't know what else you'd call that." Meg chuckled. To her surprise, Jane joined her.

"Jane!"

They looked up to see the blur that was Mark Virtue shoot through the house to join his wife at the fire. He gathered her in his arms, baby and all, and kissed her face like she'd come back from the dead. His brother, Nick, followed with his physician's bag, his face white as chalk.

"What happened?" Nick asked.

"The baby was backwards," Jane explained. "Meg saved us."

"Oh, you beauty!" Mark left Jane's side only long enough to pull Meg into a grateful embrace. It was the first time he'd really touched her in perhaps seven years, and she was surprised to find he didn't feel the way he used to. "Thank you, Meg. Thank you."

He was smaller than she remembered. Only about as tall as she was, and wiry as all get out. He had a little gray in his hair now, and he still smelled like tobacco and saw dust. She used to find it comforting, but now it just made her want to sneeze. "You're welcome, Mark."

As he returned to Jane and his new son, Nick eyed her with a puzzled frown. "You delivered a breech baby on your own with no training...and you're drunk."

She wasn't sure what he was getting at. She offered him the bottle. "Want some?"

He took it, but didn't drink. Yet. "Have you ever thought of being a midwife?"

"Honestly never crossed my mind." In Meg's experience, midwives were little better than butchers. One delivery was more than enough for her, she'd never be able to do it every day. She just wanted to look after her own children. Beyond Nick's shoulder, she saw Tommy pass the front window in the street. Where was he going?

Nick surprised her by taking her hand. "You've done a remarkable thing for my family today. If there is ever anything I can ever do to repay you, you must tell me."

A hundred things rushed into her head, beginning with murdering her cousin and making Jake love her. Nick was an earl, he wasn't God. "Thank you," she said, meaning it. "I'll hold you to that. I'd like to have a favor from an earl up my sleeve." She'd likely need it soon.

Feeling like she was intruding on the family's happy moment, Meg took the opportunity to sneak out.

Tommy was outside the house and Lily was pelting him with snowballs. "Higher," he encouraged her. "Let go earlier."

A snowball hit him in the face. "Good! Do it again."

Meg frowned. He wasn't retaliating at all, just encouraging her to hit him. "Tommy, what are you doing?"

He grinned up at her. "I'm teaching Lily to throw." A snowball hit his face and he cringed. "That one got in my ear!"

Lily giggled and packed another between her hands.

Her heart sank as she thought of the inn. They'd have to go back for Tommy's things, and Meg would count herself lucky if Davey didn't have her arrested on the spot. Perhaps she'd have to use Nick's favor today. "Sweetheart, we need to talk before we go back home."

Tommy frowned. "Can we talk later, Mum? Jake's looking for you now, you should tell him you're safe."

"What do you mean?"

Tommy shrugged. "I saw him from Nick's carriage. He was walking down Bridge Street asking for you. He doesn't go very fast."

Meg's blood raced. He came back? What if Tommy was wrong? What if it was just someone who looked like him from a distance?

"When did you see him?" she demanded.

"Just now. I waved to him from the carriage, he'll likely be here soon." He caught a snowball in the nose as he turned back to Lily.

Meg rushed to the crossroads and down Bridge Street toward the inn. There were more people about now and the carts were coming out to sell the workers their supper. Another dark carriage rolled away for the fields beyond, a rare sight south of the river. She didn't see Jake anywhere.

"Meg!"

She turned toward the voice and saw him coming from the bridge. He sped up as he saw her, almost running through the snow.

He came back.

She didn't wonder what that meant, didn't assume he was back for good. She didn't think much of anything at all except that she wanted to see him again.

She sprinted to him, the distance between them disappearing one long stride at a time. There were certain advantages to her height, and that was one of them. She launched herself at him when she was close enough and he caught her, crushing her to his chest.

God, he felt good. He always did, but after the day she'd just had, he was even better. She buried her face in his neck and inhaled the scent of cloves on his skin, relaxing as she was enveloped by his warmth.

He kissed the top of her head. "Are you well? I saw the kitchen and I feared the worst."

She cringed. "I've had quite a day."

"You and me both." She could hear the smile in his voice. "I just saw Chris. He said you saved Jane and her baby."

"I'm covered in blood." She spread her arms. "I'm probably getting it on you."

"Think nothing of it. Let's go back to the inn, I'll make you some coffee."

She pulled away, looking up at him with shame. "The hearth is...erm...not in service."

"I'll make it in the bar," he offered. "You left all the food, at least."

"I'm not stupid enough to waste good food with a family the size of mine." She looked toward the inn reluctantly. "What about Davey?"

"Davey's gone," he said, taking her hand. "Let's go home."

Chapter 32

Meg didn't say a word as Jake made coffee over the hearth in the bar. He'd scavenged enough from the wreckage of the kitchen to be able to do it. All the food for Christmas was still stashed in Judith's room at the top of the stairs, but now there was no kitchen to prepare it in. Thanks to Davey's looting, there was very little to eat it off of as well.

He didn't boil the coffee for an hour as the receipt book advised, but poured her a cup as soon as it looked black enough. Perhaps it was just that she was sobering up, but it tasted better than usual to her, lighter, smoother, and easier to drink.

Perhaps it was just that Jake had made it.

"I never thought I'd see you again," she confessed.

"I didn't take anything with me." He refilled her empty cup. "I was always coming back, I just didn't think you wanted me to."

She cringed as she remembered the night before. "I was awful to you."

He nodded. "It hurt, but I think I figured out why you did it."

She looked up at him askance. She was glad someone knew.

"You're in love with me."

Meg smirked. "You're very sure of yourself."

"I'm right."

He was. "And if you're wrong?"

He shrugged. "I'll stay anyway. I'll stay as long as you let me."

She frowned. "Why?"

"Because I'm in love with you."

Her body responded to his words before they really sunk in. Her toes tingled until they were numb, her breath caught and her cheeks warmed. In thirty-five years and God alone knew how many lovers, no one had ever said those words to her before. Better, she believed him. She wanted to hear him say it again. "Are you?"

"I think you know I am."

She climbed into his lap in the big chair in front of the fire and kissed him. It was not so much a kiss of passion or seduction as it was a kind of coming home. She needed it, wanted some contact to prove to her she wasn't having a lovely dream while passed out in a gutter somewhere.

He kissed her back, his fingertips stretching into her hair. He was very real, and he was *hers*.

"You're right," she sighed against his lips. "I love you."

He smiled. "Good. Now we have that cleared up, how would you feel about getting married?"

She sat up with a start. "You what, now?"

"I very much doubt it could be in a church or a synagogue. How does common law work?"

She blinked. Had he lost his mind? "You'd marry me?"

He shrugged. "Obviously. If you'd have me, of course."

She had wanted him for so long and now that he was here and apparently ready to marry her, she had no idea what to say. "Obviously. You have to ask?"

Jake brightened. "Brilliant. What do we need to do? What makes it legal?"

"We tell people we're married. We're already sleeping together and live in the same house. That's it."

Jake raised his eyebrows. "That's nothing. Consider it done.

Where would you like to live?"

Meg laughed. "You're being ridiculous. How many choices do you suppose we have? Davey's kicked me out of here and we can't have much between us."

"Listen, Meg," his tone changed into something altogether more serious. "It's very important to me to be able to provide shelter for my family. I wouldn't have asked you if I didn't know I could. When I saw Rachel, she gave me something that used to belong to me. I sold it and I bought the inn."

Shock hit her like a punch to the gut. "You bought the inn?"

He nodded. "I put it in your name. I wanted you to have it, even if you'd said no. I wanted you and Tommy to have somewhere to live no matter what happened between us."

She could no more stop the tears from coming than she could stop the rain. She wrapped her arms around his neck and sobbed, more relieved than she'd been in her life.

She felt him frown. "I know you hate this place a little, so if you want to leave, I understand. I have enough left over we could rent a small house if you prefer. We can keep the inn, burn it down, or gut it and build something new. We'll do anything you want with it. It's yours."

Meg wiped at her tears with her sleeve.

"Are you upset?" he asked, clearly worried.

She shook her head. "I've never been so happy."

He grinned and she felt herself melting into him. Everything was perfect, and yet—

"What are we going to do about Christmas?" She blurted.

Jake shrugged. "We can still have it, but we might need some help."

♥

Christmas Eve at The Rose and Crown was a success by anyone's standards. The bar was full of Meg's friends and neighbors eating beef roasted on a spit outside with bread and latkes from Ruta's bakery. The Virtues had loaned their small kitchen to them for the night for the rest, and their children were kept busy running back and forth between the two great houses with pies and dishes of vegetables.

The clove-studded oranges and mulled wine went some way to disguise the smell of burned beer, and everyone was happy enough to keep out of the kitchen for the night. Blankets were nailed over the broken windows to keep the heat inside and the inn was filled with the sound of string instruments being tortured.

Meg and Jake had used some of the money left over from the sale of the ring to replace the dishes and broken glasses, and had restocked the bar to make up for what Davey had looted on his way out. Behind the bar, where one might hang the king's likeness, was Jake's Christmas gift to Meg: the portrait Harry Townsend had painted of her years before. Her image smirked over the proceedings like a queen, her legendary beauty preserved forever in oil paint.

Jake paused to kiss her temple on his way to refresh Ruta's wine. Ruta sat in a place of honor beside the fire across from Joe Ledford. Neither could understand a word the other said, but they appeared to be having a pleasant enough conversation through facial expressions and creative hand gestures.

Between them, Tommy and Chris peeled oranges on the floor and tossed the discarded cloves into the fire. She might have been more irritated at the waste, but they gave off the most delicious scent as they burned and it made her think of Jake's soap. She'd get to smell that every night now, and she doubted she'd ever get sick of it.

"Missus Cohen, is it?" Mark smiled at her from across the bar.

"It is," she confirmed. "I'm a married woman now, so you and the rest can piss off."

"There she is." He chuckled. "It's good to have you back."

"How's Jane?"

"Alive and well, thanks to you." His gratitude was real and a rare thing to earn. "Listen, Meg, I can't thank you enough for what you've done for me. I'll never be able to repay you, but I'd like to try if I can."

She rested her hand on her hip, unsure of what to do with a sincere Mark Virtue. "What do you have in mind?"

"I want to fix your kitchen."

Her eyebrows shot into her hairline. "Have you seen it?"

He shook his head. "Mind if I take a peek?"

She waved him through. "Be my guest."

Mark cursed as he crossed into the other room. "How would you like to deliver the next one as well?"

She elbowed him in the ribs and he laughed.

"I'll do it," he promised. "I'll come by in the week and you can tell me what you want."

He really meant it. She didn't know how to respond to him when he wasn't being a cheeky sod. "Thank you," she tried.

"I'm happy for you, Meg."

She nodded. "Me, too. Happy for you, that is. Jane's all right."

Mark grinned. "Isn't she just?"

The door opened and Meg's heart almost stopped. In the doorway stood her daughter, Sarah, looking lost with a small trunk.

Meg left Mark at the bar and wrapped Sarah in a hug before she could object. "I'm so glad you could come. They gave you the night off?"

Sarah smiled sheepishly. "I quit, actually. Please don't be upset. It was a good position, but my mistress was becoming…difficult to work for. May I stay here with you until I find another one?"

Meg was delighted with the idea. "Of course! Stay as long as you like. We're doing some work on the inn so there are some free rooms. No guests for the time being."

Jake came over as soon as he spotted them talking by the door. "Sarah, I'm so pleased you could make it."

Meg looked from her husband to her daughter. "You've met?"

Sarah nodded, unsure of what to say. "Yeah, he knows my old mistress."

Jake raised his eyebrows. "Rachel," he explained quietly. "I saw Sarah and told her she ought to come by. You must be freezing. Come in, I'll get you some wine."

As Meg joined them at the bar, she was overcome by a tremendous sense of peace. Bess and Sue sat at a table with Judith, the three of them fussing over the baby. Tommy and Chris played beside the fire between Ruta and Joe, as Sarah put her trunk away and Jake kept the bar. Even Mark was here somewhere with his four oldest children, wrapping up some latkes to take home to Jane.

Surrounded by her family and friends, Meg realized she had everything she ever wanted. A home, such as it was. A job. Two of her children were with her and well-fed, and she had a husband she was mad about who somehow loved her in return.

A tear rolled down her cheek and into the bodice of her dress. "It happened," she said to herself.

"What's that, love?" Jake asked, passing her a glass of wine with a kiss.

She blinked, seeing the best kind of eternity in his eyes. "I'm happy."

Tyburn

The Southwark Saga, Book 1

Sally Green is about to die.

She sees Death in the streets. She can taste it in her gin. She can feel it in the very walls of the ramshackle brothel where she is kept to satisfy the perversions of the wealthy. She had come to London as a runaway in search of her Cavalier father. Instead, she found Wrath, a sadistic nobleman determined to use her to fulfill a sinister ambition. As the last of her friends are murdered one by one, survival hinges on escape.

Nick Virtue is a tutor with a secret. By night he operates as a highwayman, relieving nobles of their riches to further his brother's criminal enterprise. It's a difficult balance at the best of times, and any day that doesn't end in a noose is a good one. Saving Sally means risking his reputation, and may end up costing him his life.

As a brutal attack throws them together, Sally finds she has been given a second chance. She is torn between the tutor and the highwayman, but she knows she can have neither. Love is an unwanted complication while Wrath haunts the streets. Nick holds the key to Wrath's identity, and Sally will risk everything to bring him to justice.

Unless the gallows take her first.

Virtue's Lady

The Southwark Saga, Book 2

Lady Jane Ramsey is young, beautiful, and ruined.

After being rescued from her kidnapping by a handsome highwayman, she returns home only to find her marriage prospects drastically reduced. Her father expects her to marry the repulsive Lord Lewes, but Jane has other plans. All she can think about is her highwayman, and she is determined to find him again.

Mark Virtue is trying to go straight. After years of robbing coaches and surviving on his wits, he knows it's time to hang up his pistol and become the carpenter he was trained to be. He busies himself with finding work for his neighbors and improving his corner of Southwark as he tries to forget the girl who haunts his dreams. As a carpenter struggling to stay in work in the aftermath of The Fire, he knows Jane is unfathomably far beyond his reach, and there's no use wishing for the impossible.

When Jane turns up in Southwark, Mark is furious. She has no way of understanding just how much danger she has put them in by running away. In spite of his growing feelings for her, he knows that Southwark is no place for a lady. Jane must set aside her lessons to learn a new set of rules if she is to make a life for herself in the crime-ridden slum. She will fight for her freedom and her life if that's what it takes to prove to Mark—and to herself—that there's more to her than meets the eye.

The Long Way Home

The Southwark Saga, Book 3

After saving the life of the glamorous Marquise de Harfleur, painfully shy barmaid Alice Henshawe is employed as the lady's companion and whisked away to Versailles. There, she catches King Louis' eye and quickly becomes a court favorite as the muse for Charles Perrault's Cinderella. The palace appears to be heaven itself, but there is danger hidden beneath the façade and Alice soon finds herself thrust into a world of intrigue, murder, and Satanism at the heart of the French court.

Having left his apprenticeship to serve King Charles as a spy, Jack Sharpe is given a mission that may just kill him. In the midst of the Franco-Dutch war, he is to investigate rumors of a poison plot by posing as a courtier, but he has a mission of his own. His childhood friend Alice Henshawe is missing and he will stop at nothing to see her safe. When he finds her in the company of the very people he is meant to be investigating, Jack begins to wonder if the sweet girl he grew up with has a dark side.

When a careless lie finds them accidentally married, Alice and Jack must rely on one another to survive the intrigues of the court. As old affection gives way to new passion, suspicion lingers. Can they trust each other, or is the real danger closer than they suspect?

Jessica Cale is a historical romance author and journalist based in North Carolina. Originally from Minnesota, she lived in Wales for several years where she earned a BA in History and an MFA in Creative Writing while climbing castles and photographing mines for history magazines. She kidnapped ("married") her very own British prince (close enough) and is enjoying her happily ever after with him in a place where no one understands his accent. She is the editor of Dirty, Sexy History at www.dirtysexyhistory.com. You can visit her at www.authorjessicacale.com.

70309588R00178

Made in the USA
Columbia, SC
04 May 2017